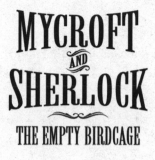

# MYCROFT
## AND
# SHERLOCK

### THE EMPTY BIRDCAGE

Also by Kareem Abdul-Jabbar and Anna Waterhouse,
and available from Titan Books

*Mycroft Holmes*
*Mycroft and Sherlock*

# KAREEM ABDUL~JABBAR

and ANNA WATERHOUSE

A NOVEL

# MYCROFT
and
# SHERLOCK

## THE EMPTY BIRDCAGE

**Titan** BOOKS

Mycroft and Sherlock: The Empty Birdcage
Hardback edition ISBN: 9781785659300
E-book edition ISBN: 9781785659317

Published by Titan Books
A division of Titan Publishing Group Ltd
144 Southwark Street, London SE1 0UP

First edition: September 2019
1 3 5 7 9 10 8 6 4 2

This is a work of fiction. Names, characters, places, and incidents either
are the product of the author's imagination or are used fictitiously,
and any resemblance to actual persons, living or dead, business
establishments, events, or locales is entirely coincidental.

The publisher does not have any control over and does not assume any
responsibility for author or third-party websites or their content.

Kareem Abdul-Jabbar and Anna Waterhouse assert the moral
right to be identified as the authors of this work.

A CIP catalogue record for this title is available from the British Library.

Printed and bound in the United States.

*It has been both an honor and a privilege to have the opportunity to create an addition to the canon of an author like Arthur Conan Doyle. The positive response to my efforts has been a highlight in my life. I would like to thank my friends at Titan Books and my manager Deborah Morales for their constant assistance and encouragement. Most of all my co-author Anna Waterhouse has been superb. Thank you, one and all!*

KAJ

*For my mother Carmen who nurtured me.*
*For Nadine and Isabel, who mentored me.*
*For Donna, Sestina and Luisa, who walked the ancient paths with me.*

AW

# MYCROFT AND SHERLOCK

## THE EMPTY BIRDCAGE

# PROLOGUE

*Three Crosses in Gower, Swansea, Wales*
*Tuesday, 1 April 1873, 9 a.m.*

HE COULD FEEL HIS HEART BEAT HARD AND STRONG against his chest. In terms of its physiological functioning, it was alive and well. But when it came to human emotions, that font of endless sonnets to love was irreparably damaged, he was sure of it. How else could he have so little regard for such an exquisite day? Or snuff out a life with nary a qualm?

He had pursued her for several days running, keeping well back so she would not notice him, observing until he was assured of her patterns: where she walked and, more importantly, where she lingered. He had plotted her death for so long, down to the smallest particular, that it felt as if he were merely following a well-trod path.

At long last, this was his moment. If anything went awry, he would be forced to end it, and it would be his corpse, not hers, that some passerby stumbled upon. But if he succeeded, there would be more. Many more.

She lived alone in a rundown shack in Three Crosses, an inland village that housed the workers of the local collieries. At eight each morning, when the fog was still wrapping itself about the limestone ridges and hillocks like ghostly ribbons, and other women of her age and station were cobbling together breakfast for their families, she would latch her front door behind her and leave, without looking back.

And why not? She was still early in her years: twenty-four or -five, he assumed. She no longer had a husband or a child to tend, having buried her only son a scant eleven months before she had buried her man. Just another miner delivered to his doorstep in a coarse brown sack that bore a perfunctory stamp: REMAINS, PROPERTY OF SOUTH WALES COAL.

Passing the cemetery where man and boy lay side by side, she would mouth a little prayer and remain a moment with head bowed and hands folded. Then she would all but fly to Three Crosses Bay, arriving in time to see the fog lift off the water like the twirling of petticoats.

He had heard the townspeople say of her: "*Mae hi'n wallgof!*" "She is daft!"

*Sick with grief, more like*, he thought.

Regardless, her problems and sorrows were none of his affair. If anything, her agony encouraged him. A quick, all but painless death was the gift he could bestow upon her.

Though tall and slender like her father, she walked with the heavy gait of her mother's peasant forebears. Still, it was gratifying to observe her from above, to watch as she removed her shoes, kneading her square naked feet in the moist seagrass like a cat. From there, she would amble closer to the rocky shoreline, always on the hunt for her precious objects, as he—her unseen, unknown nemesis—hunted her.

After loading up her treasures in the pockets of her sooty black skirt, she would drop to her knees upon the soft wet beach, her back to the cliff, her face towards the water. She would remove her black mourning bonnet, lay it beside her, and place a rock upon one of the ribbons, so that it would not fly away. That done, she would pull out her treasures one by one, blowing off the silt and dirt.

He was always careful not to make any noise as he watched, careful to shift slightly so that the light would not cast his shadow beside her but would remain behind her, where it belonged. The sun's rays bent and warped his image until his elongated head appeared to be nestling against the nape of her neck.

It was lovely, that neck: not coarse and reddish like the rest of her skin but soft, and white as alabaster against her dark blouse. Her thick hair, twisted into a knot at the top of her head, was the color of burnt umber. As she studied one of her finds, a tendril worked itself loose, swinging to and fro, to and fro…

He glanced to the sky. The sun was already high upon the horizon. Soon, even this desolate spit of sand and rock would draw a sojourner or two. He dared not tarry.

He looked down at her again. She had pulled the rocks and sticks from her pocket. Soon she would begin to construct the most peculiar little bridges: arched pathways that commenced in one spot and ended in another, all of them leading nowhere, and close enough to the water that at night the creeping waves would wash them away, as if they had never been.

He had nothing against the girl. She would die, of course. As would others. In that, he fancied that he mimicked death itself: it was not personal. Sooner or later, it was everybody's turn.

# 1

*London, England*
*Tuesday, 1 April 1873, 9 a.m.*

MYCROFT HOLMES WAS WAGING A VALIANT BATTLE against the narcotic that was coursing through his veins. Though it came as friend, not foe, he despised it. It made his keen mental faculties seem suddenly unreliable; placing him if not at the mercy of his emotions, then at least in thrall to them.

In truth, he was also hallucinating, another hideous corollary to the drug. Though thankfully spared winged horses and the like, he seemed to be staring through a tunnel at a small puddle of water. Floating therein was a medical journal yellowed by a hundred years of time. He recognized it straight away; he saw himself reach for it, clutching it in his hand. He could see his fingers carefully separating one sopping page from the other, then pausing at an article he well recalled, about the physician William Hunter.

In 1775, Hunter had declared that 'Anatomy is the basis of Surgery. It informs the head, guides the hand, and familiarizes the heart to a kind of Necessary Inhumanity.'

For years, that phrase—'Necessary Inhumanity'—had clung

to him as a useful concept, for it shut off the spigot of emotion so as to accomplish the greater good. He and his dear friend Cyrus Douglas had once debated it at length, in the back room of Regent Tobaccos, the two of them sunk into those padded red leather chairs by the fire, Armagnac at their elbows, while a winter storm moaned outside.

Douglas—who had never been fond of ends justifying means—had made clear his disapproval.

"There is no such thing," he had declared. "Either a thing is humane, or it is not."

"It all depends," Mycroft had posited—rather cavalierly, it seemed to him now.

"Upon what?"

"Upon the mindset of the one who makes the rules. For example, I aspire to live by Mozi's dictum: 'It is the business of the benevolent man to seek to promote what is beneficial to the world and eliminate what is harmful. That which benefits, he will carry out; that which does not benefit, he will leave alone.' Surely even you can find no fault with that!"

"It all depends," Douglas had parried. "Will this 'benevolent man' be benevolent to *me* in particular? Let us assume, for the sake of argument, that he is as well intentioned as he believes himself to be: he could nevertheless think me less capable than he of forging my own path. What if to him I am a brute and a savage who needs his tutelage and protection? And even if I were precisely as he supposes, both brute and savage, does that give him the moral imperative to decide my fate?"

Mycroft could still taste the smoky flavor of the Armagnac as it warmed his mouth, could see Douglas smile and lean forward in his chair as he spoke, his umber skin glowing in the firelight, his expression open but challenging.

At the time, Mycroft had had no reply at the ready. He had even less at the moment, lying as he was on an unyielding marble slab.

He began to shiver. And, just as quickly as they came, the images of Douglas, the fireplace, and Regent Tobaccos crumbled into dust, and he was left with nothing but the cold.

Barely twenty-seven years of age, Mycroft had felt for a while as ancient as Methuselah. And though the procedure he was to undergo was so rare that he could not even glean its odds of success, his rapid deterioration had made it worth the risk. He would proceed on the shred of hope that his life would continue better, once and if he opened his eyes again.

*Buck up, old man!* he adjured himself. *Count the blessings of the present circumstance!*—for in fact, there were several.

Given the agony that physicians were forced to inflict upon patients in Hunter's time, 'Necessary Inhumanity' had been an essential component to surgery. Whereas he himself would undergo little physical torment, for modern physicians used chloroform. Even the Queen had made use of it for two of her confinements. Besides, much progress had been made in the understanding of the heart's functions and therefore humankind's ability to repair it. And although his heart *per se* could not be operated upon, the goal was to aid the pericardium: the sac that lubricated it, that limited its erratic motion, that prevented excessive dilation, and insulated it from infection. Patching it up could restore his stamina and breath.

To say nothing of his reputation. His long attempt to mask his failing health had turned him into a curmudgeonly recluse, a final indignity: for 'curmudgeonly recluse' was surely a more fitting description of his younger brother, Sherlock, than he!

High time to reacquaint his small portion of the world with his more gregarious, good-natured self.

"Hands clean…?" he muttered aloud.

He heard Dr. Joseph Bell's soft Scottish brogue as if from an adjoining room: "Aye, Mr. Holmes. We have scrubbed hands and arms to the elbow, as you requested."

"With soap?"

"Aye," Bell replied in a stentorian tone that Mycroft did not care for. "And done you one better: added five percent carbolic to the mix and so now are as clean as a clergyman's knickers."

He felt a needle pierce his skin. More morphine, he ventured; for, like a feral cat in a sack, he had been refusing to capitulate.

*Why spar with the very operators who are attempting to better your life,* he asked himself, *however lengthy or brief it turns out to be…?*

A damp kerchief was pressed down upon his nose and mouth. Chloroform, a tricky proposition. Too little, and one awakened screaming in the midst of the cut; too much, and the lungs collapsed, causing the patient to sleep forever in the arms of Morpheus. He fought a fleeting sense of panic before sinking deeper and deeper until the rational part of himself seemed to him a shadowy figure standing upon the platform of a train station, waving goodbye.

"I mention hands solely because Pasteur," Mycroft mumbled, "is of the mind that washing eliminates s…"

The word he sought was 'sepsis.' But all he could manage was the longest 's' sound in the world, like a tire going flat, before darkness overcame him.

# 2

*Cambridge, England*
*Thursday, 8 May 1873, 10 a.m.*

MOST OF DOWNING COLLEGE, WITH THE EXCEPTION OF the East Lodge, was built of an oolitic limestone known as Ketton stone. On bright days it would glimmer in shades of yellow, from pale daffodil to butterscotch. Students and faculty alike would remark upon its beauty, taking especial pride in its sparkle, as if it were an earthly corner of the New Jerusalem.

Sherlock Holmes assumed that he was alone in finding it insufferable.

A cigarette dangled from his lips, its smoke forcing his eyes into a squint as he walked. His long fingers grazed the newspaper columns that he had carefully cut out, rolled into a bundle, bound with twine, and stuck into his jacket pocket. He'd reached for that little bundle a half-dozen times since leaving his rooms, for lately he had been feeling all nerves, and knowing it was there, close at hand, helped him to concentrate upon his case.

And what a case it was. Eight murders across Great Britain. Though geographically disparate, and though none of the victims had anything in common, they had surely been felled by the same killer, who had commenced his killing the first day of April and had continued with macabre but admirable regularity since then, at the rate of approximately one every four to six days, with one notable week's hiatus.

The victims thus far included, in order of demise: a young widow; a small-town banker; two boys, aged seven and fourteen, killed separately; a chaplain of middle years; a retired barrister of eighty-four; the proprietor of a horse stable; and a ten-year-old girl. None had enemies to speak of. None had died with any mark of violence upon them. All, in fact, would have been decreed to have succumbed to 'natural causes'—a catch-all phrase used by law and medicine when no clear reason made itself apparent—were it not for one thing.

The note.

At each murder site, a note had been left in the proximity of the body, almost always at the moment of death, though twice it had appeared upon the spot several days after the fact, as if to ensure that credit would be given where credit was due.

The message was always the same, four little words:

*The Fire Four Eleven!*

In terms of clues, those four little words were all but useless, in that they contained too many possibilities, which was to say none at all. Not to mention that newspapers carried a mere *illustration* of the note in question, so that one could discern neither paper stock, nor the finer details of the original handwriting. Nevertheless, Sherlock had gleaned a few facts, ones that he now mulled over as he walked along.

The artist's rendering revealed that the killer's handwriting had a looped ligature. Clearly, he had been steeped in classic copperplate, the proper penmanship of the proper English schoolboy, each letter meticulously formed, tops and bottoms obsessively uniform. But he had taken it one step further: even the spacing between the words was uniform, none exceeding the width of the letter 'm.'

It was a 'right fair hand,' composed by a person who was proud of his skill. Sherlock further posited that the man had had no academic training to speak of, beyond the first few years of school. Someone so punctilious would never have abandoned his penmanship altogether. But, had he been allowed to continue his studies, neither would he have held onto it as a capstone of scholastic achievement.

If Sherlock could but have a look at the originals, if he could calibrate fluidity, combined with pressure exerted upon each letter, he could begin to gauge the author's level of anxiety, his sense of righteous judgment, perhaps a specific reading of his age and nationality. But even without the originals, it was absurd to assume that a man so punctilious would choose his victims at random, as the newspaper accounts were conjecturing.

That the author was male was indisputable, for there were absolutely no deviations: the copperplate was roundhand from start to finish. Women by and large had a finer touch; their handwriting tended to be more individualistic and less static than a man's, either due to a lack of proper schooling, or as a nod to socially approved 'rebellion'; or simply the feminine inclination to be more choleric and melancholic than a man.

To say nothing of the fact that women did not ordinarily commit multiple murders, though nearly every country in Europe had been caught flatfooted by those who did: Hélène Jegado of France and Gesche Gottfried of Germany had both favored arsenic; Darya Saltykova of Russia had tortured and killed some hundred forty serfs, mostly women and children; and Englishwoman Mary Ann Cotton had poisoned as many as twenty-one people, including three of her four husbands and eleven of her thirteen children. Though all these women were competent and remorseless killers, they were also anomalies. It was men who seemed to fancy murder in multiples.

Sherlock's conclusions at this juncture were few and hard-won. The killer was unique in that thus far he had struck only in the daylight hours, rather than under the more typical cloak of darkness. He was a right-handed Englishman with a primary school education and a great deal of free time, which one would need in order to travel and to visit multiple locations more than once. He also had an uncanny ability to justify what he had done.

This last, Sherlock deduced from the repetition of the message: as if each time, the killer were raising a flag of victory, emphasized by the exclamation point at the end. And, given that the penmanship was neither labored nor shaky, Sherlock assumed the killer to be between thirty and fifty-five years of age.

In other words, nothing to hang one's hat upon. A male right-handed disciple of the roundhand script of between thirty and fifty-five might not be as common as dirt, but he was surely as common as clerks, of which England had a passel. And although few clerks had the economic wherewithal to travel so bountifully, this particular man had a well-honed gift for plotting and waiting, possibly fueled by a heightened sense of self-righteous revenge. He may've scrimped and saved for years to execute his plan: such a thing could not be discounted.

But against whom had he plotted so assiduously? For no seven-year-old had ever destroyed a man's life or livelihood!

What Sherlock would not give to travel hither and yon, to examine the original notes, to spy out whatever useful tidbit the law had ignored or, worse yet, mangled, to follow the various and sundry trails like a hound on the scent.

But that was nigh on impossible. He had a month left of his degree, and no resources to speak of. Might he ask Mycroft for an advance? Money seemed to attach to his brother like leeches to tender skin. But how in the world would he justify it?

He could not.

Simply put, the Fire Four Eleven Murders, as the papers had been quick to label them, were giving him sleepless nights and even a bit of indigestion—and there was little he could do about it.

Sherlock strode across the college green, past his former friends, identical twins Eli and Asa Quince. They were sparring with short staffs upon the lawn, their sand-colored hair wet with the effort, their shoe-button eyes void of anything but each other. Exertion notwithstanding, their skin remained the color of bleached flour, as if nothing could coax blood through those staid Norman veins.

Their movements, as always, were fluid and assured, but something had altered. Eli was no longer a hair's breadth quicker than his brother. In execution, as in everything else, they were now evenly matched.

*Nothing quite so dull as a rivalry between equal opponents*, thought Sherlock.

He said not a word as he passed but hunched forward, as if fighting a particularly vexing headwind. Every day of the previous term, he had beaten both boys handily at the short staff. And though he had filled many happy afternoons (and a journal and a half) gauging reaction times between Asa, whom he had labeled 'the Addict' and Eli, whom he'd dubbed 'the Teetotaler,' his long experiment had at last come to naught, for Asa had finally forsaken his substantial morphine addiction in favor of *mens sana in corpore sano*. Once this 'healthy mind in a healthy body' had been permitted to take root, all had been lost. Sherlock found he had nothing more to learn from either of them.

The twins, for their part, had likely sensed his disillusionment with their association, for they did not pursue him—the convenient consequence of befriending people with no discernible personality.

Sherlock continued on towards The Eagle, a watering hole that he favored. For his perennially gray England seemed to him to be growing more colorful with each passing year; pubs lining their floors with tiles and their walls with looking-glasses, so that the discord of human noise was free to ricochet unabated from table to table. Everywhere was the disconcerting image of oneself staring back from out some enameled mirror.

Conversely, at The Eagle he would find both quiet and blessed darkness, along with the disinterest of habitual drinkers towards a lanky nineteen-year-old mucking about with newspaper columns.

Sherlock turned down Trumpington Street past the Fitzwilliam Museum. As he waited on the corner for the traffic to pass by, a weathered mendicant sidled up to him, her face obscured by rags, her filthy hand outstretched. Sherlock dug into his pocket and pressed a coin into her hand, heedless of denomination and more to be done with her than from any sense of charity.

"Yer see, don' ye?" the crone announced through broken teeth, her eye winking conspiratorially. "Yer sees wut uvvers cannot!"

She did not wait for reply but hobbled on, clutching the coin in her spider-like fist.

Sherlock was perturbed. Though not given to pondering the prognostications of some old beggar, it left him wanting. He *did* see what others could not. He cast off the butt of his cigarette and felt about for his shag and papers. Pity that he could not yet bring himself to return to smoking a briar pipe—much more convenient. But it reminded him of failure, and of the worst kind. If he wished to succeed at his endeavors, he would have to guard against the sway of emotion, and to do so mercilessly, rather than simply assume that he was immune. As he rolled the tobacco between thumb and forefingers, he thought of his current predicament. He was very nearly done with the term. He could take books on his journeys, could he not? He would need little in the way of funds: a minimal amount for victuals, a pittance for train fare, naught but spare coins for shag. Even Mycroft could not begrudge him such a paltry sum, whatever it was! For a moment, he felt the burgeoning excitement of possibility. Then he remembered that his brother was not in London at the moment, that he had gone somewhere, for something or other.

*Bother, where was it again?*

*Ah yes, Vienna. But why?* For the life of him, Sherlock could recall no further detail of the journey, save one.

He would be residing at the Hotel Imperial. That name had stood out solely because it had sounded like rich fare for his parsimonious brother. Mycroft despised paying dearly for anything he could not thoroughly enjoy: "Hotels should deduct for the time one sleeps!" he would proclaim less than half in jest.

Sherlock knew perfectly well that the superior lodgings held, for his brother, an ulterior motive. But any stratagem of Mycroft's doubtless had to do with the political or the economic field, or some other deadly dull pursuit. He was not in the least curious.

Still, the name of the hotel came in handy, for he could send a telegram to communicate but one message: "send money."

He licked his well-packed rolling paper, lit his cigarette, and glanced about. Cambridge was not London, with telegraphs in every post office. But he did recall telegraph boys with their dispatch boxes exiting a building not so far from The Eagle.

He would plead his case to Mycroft on the chance, however slight, that he would see the merit in the thing.

After all, what did he have to lose? For all the darkened pubs in the world could not provide him the one thing he needed to solve this particular crime:

*Proximity.*

He turned to go, only to be confronted with the old mumblecrust again. He could see from her milky eyes and dim-witted smile that she remembered him not at all but thought him a brand-new mark.

"Yer see, don' ye?" she began before he cut her off.

"Yes, yes, I see what others cannot," he told her. "By the sheer luck of the draw, it so happens that you are correct. And I aim to get started this very moment. What do you think of *that*?" he added, pressing another coin into her ancient hand before hastening off.

"*Áhd mór!*" she called out behind him. "May good luck rise to ye, laddy!"

# 3

*Vienna, Austria*
*Thursday, 8 May 1873, 11 a.m.*

MYCROFT DREW A BREATH, GRATEFUL THAT HE COULD do so without wincing. He savored the myriad scents of the balmy spring morning, the alpine swifts like two-toned arrows winging across the azure sky, the rock doves cooing and pecking at scraps of bread in the cracks of the cobblestones.

Odd that something so ordinary could bring such a catch to his throat.

More than five weeks had passed since his surgery. So as to ensure the strictest confidence, he had first resigned his post at the War Office, causing untold trauma to his former employer, Edward Cardwell. He had sent Huan, his bodyguard and driver, off to Trinidad for an extended visit with his family, for Huan was a good and faithful soul who would worry about him excessively, and blather unconscionably. And although the operation had not occurred in a hovel under cover of night, it may as well have, for all the skullduggery required so that three intelligent, inquisitive people—Queen Victoria, Douglas, and of course his brother Sherlock—would remain blissfully unaware of the goings-on. Sewing up the pericardium could not extend his life: the heart was still broken, after all, and would give out whenever it chose. But there was no denying that he could breathe more easily, and was no longer as pale as chalk.

"'Designed by architect Karl von Hasenauer in a herringbone pattern and completed in record time by fifteen thousand workmen…'" Cyrus Douglas's voice read aloud.

He and Douglas had spent the past week traveling throughout Germany: Mycroft to investigate the Teutonic banking system and Douglas its tobaccos. Now here they were in Austria, purportedly to explore the Fifth International World Exhibition, exquisitely laid out in Vienna's six-hundred-acre park, the Prater—which made it larger than all of the previous World Exhibition areas combined. It boasted several hundred pavilions featuring exhibitors from thirty-one countries, each a dizzying paean to cultural and technical milestones. There were Japanese gardens and walkways, and outdoor cafés featuring the finest cuisines that the world had to offer.

So why did the whole endeavor feel so desultory?

Mycroft craned his neck to take in the Rotunda before them, the exhibition's crowning glory, as Douglas continued to quote from the map that he held in his hands.

"'The Rotunda is, at eighty-five meters high, the world's largest domed structure, the dome three times the size of Saint Paul's Cathedral in Rome.'"

"Does remind one of a greengrocer's list," Mycroft offered. "Onions, check; cabbage, check; world's largest domed behemoth, check…"

"Come, it is not as halfhearted as all that," Douglas protested.

"Mark my word, Douglas. If this folderol recoups even half

of the nineteen million gulden Austria spent for its completion, the Emperor Franz Josef should consider himself lucky."

"If you are enjoying this so little, perhaps we should go elsewhere…"

"No, no, we are here. We may as well make a day of it," Mycroft said. "For, surely, there is no censuring Vienna's desire to be transformed into a modern metropolis like Paris or London. At any other time, it might have succeeded, but not now. Not when a cloud of melancholy hangs over all this striving, majestic beauty… Smirk if you will," he added, "but all of your good-natured optimism cannot escape it."

"I have never smirked in my life," Douglas protested.

"It is in the wind," Mycroft prophesied. "People may not know that we are plunging headlong towards a crisis, but they feel it in their bones. *This! This* is what I wished for us to experience," he added, gesticulating about him. "The visceral impact, the crest of the wave, as it were, of what is about to burst onto our British shores as well…"

"Ah. And I was under the impression that we were here to see electric lighting powered by a steam-driven dynamo," Douglas muttered.

"This shallow turnout confirms my worst fears," Mycroft replied. "An economic collapse is now imminent."

"You have been predicting it for some time," Douglas reminded him. "Perhaps it is your understanding of the word 'imminent' that is at fault."

"Would you not call tomorrow morning 'imminent'?" Mycroft asked.

"Tomorrow morning?" Douglas raised the collar of his coat against a sudden onslaught of wind and looked at Mycroft dismayed.

"I am merely stating facts. You need not gape as if I have *caused* the catastrophe."

"What of Nickolus House?" Douglas asked apprehensively, referring to the boys' school that he owned and ran.

"Well, as you will not allow me to bankroll it outright—"

"No, for that would severely tax our friendship—"

"I cannot fathom why—"

"Because you do not take kindly to enterprises that do not turn a profit, and Nickolus House does not and never shall turn a profit," Douglas said.

"As I was saying, since you will not allow my bankrolling it," Mycroft replied, "I did the next best thing: in the past six months I have made sound investments for us both. Raw wool, cotton, wheat, tea, meat, beer, and tobacco should continue to see us through the decade. No harm shall come to Nickolus House!"

"Thank heaven for that!" Douglas exclaimed.

"Thank *me*, you mean," Mycroft corrected with a smile.

"As for poor, beleaguered Vienna," Douglas added with a cursory look, "perhaps the lack of visitors has less to do with 'imminent economic collapse' and more with the terrible bout of cholera that they have endured. What you and I are sensing in the air might simply be the paranoia of contagion."

They had just reached the Machine Hall, where a large knot of people was clustered. *It is now or never*, Mycroft thought. He halted, as if offended, forcing Douglas to do the same.

"Do you doubt me, Douglas?"

"What? No! I am saying that even if the Austrian economy is in crisis, you have wide-ranging influence. Could you not use it to warn their banks, at the least?"

"Banks? Banks are the problem! What do you think has caused this economic boom, this... this *Gründerzeit*? Bad speculation. Railroad bonds of undetermined value. Devil-may-care loans for real estate to fill up buildings that should never have been built in the first place!"

Douglas glanced about nervously, but Mycroft continued.

"And the banks' funds to protect investments exist solely on paper! Tomorrow, the stock exchange will plummet, there will be a panicked sale on shares, and no one will come to anyone's rescue!"

Predictably, the park's attendees began to turn their way. Douglas lowered his voice until he was nearly whispering: "But surely their National Bank has reserves?"

"The reserves do not *exist*!" Mycroft insisted, as he went on gesticulating and expounding. "They will hand out note payables, as worthless as a pauper's I.O.U. As for the Great Unwashed, they shall suffer a half-dozen years of the worst toil and drudgery imaginable!"

"Mycroft, calm yourself..." Douglas urged.

But it was too late. Two well-dressed Austrian gentlemen of middle years left the large group of visitors and walked towards them. The stouter of the two raised a monocle and peered at Douglas, his fist tightening around the ivory horsehead handle of his cane. His smaller friend, round, colored spectacles perched on the bridge of his upturned nose, stopped beside him.

Mycroft glanced at the cane.

"What do you suppose that is?" he whispered to Douglas as they drew ever closer.

"Pneumatic gun," Douglas replied, "air tank in the handle and upper portion, ramrod in the barrel, muzzle velocity some thousand feet per second. They are all the thing in Belgium."

"I struggle to recall a sillier weapon," Mycroft muttered.

"Regardless. We cannot do battle," Douglas warned. "Not here, not now."

"*Ist alles in Ordnung?*" the stouter fellow asked Mycroft, never taking his monocled eye off Douglas, while the smaller used the thumb and index fingers of his free hand to massage a few errant blond mustaches.

"*Ja, danke,*" Mycroft quickly replied. "*Mein Butler weiss nichts von der Geschichte. Ich versuche ihn aufzuklären.*"

The two stared at Douglas as if to assess Mycroft's declaration that he was simply schooling his man on some small point of history. Douglas for his part kept his focus on a patch of ground at the edge of his toes, playing to perfection the abashed servant who'd been put in his place by his younger, wiser employer.

Mycroft smiled and patted Douglas on the back, eliciting a look of disapproval from the smaller of the two.

"*Das ist Zeitverschwendung. Neger können nicht lernen,*" the little man declared.

With that, the two returned to the huddle of visitors, the smaller one casting a final warning glance over his shoulder to the tall Negro whom he had just declared incapable of learning.

"No further need to pat me; they are off," Douglas muttered, eyeing the men warily as they went.

"What possessed you?" Douglas hissed as he and Mycroft quickly made their way towards an enormous fountain with a pagoda at its center. "It was as if... as if you *intended* to create a scene."

"Really, Douglas, why would I...?"

"I cannot say. But I do know there was purpose behind it. You disappoint me, Mycroft."

They stood beside the fountain, awkwardly watching the white swans gliding by.

"Your survival depends on my being circumspect. Forgive me," Mycroft murmured at last.

Douglas did not respond directly. But as they began walking again he said, in a much lighter tone of voice: "Speaking of survival, you will never guess who asked about you."

"When?" Mycroft asked.

"I believe the more usual response is 'who.' A fortnight ago."

"Then I can guess. First, if we omit those dozen people we have in common whom I would in no way be surprised about, along with another dozen so distant that their contacting you would not have been brought up so casually, plus another handful who had no means of doing so two weeks ago, I am left with but three candidates."

Douglas shook his head. "Mycroft, you must learn to recognize a turn of phrase when you hear one…"

"And, since you prefaced your statement with 'speaking of survival,' and two of those three acquaintances have nothing whatever to tie them to that word, that leaves but *one* mutual acquaintance whose survival we ensured. Albeit one who is neither intimate enough, nor in dire straits enough, for an urgent report the moment you and I saw each other again. And that would be Deshi Hai Lin," Mycroft concluded, naming the Chinese businessman whose life they had saved some six months previously.

"Remarkable," Douglas replied.

"Not at all. Process of elimination. You told Mr. Lin you had no notion where I was?"

"Yes, as indeed I had no notion."

"And how long before he wrote back with an entreaty that, should you locate me, he would dearly love to make contact, or some such turn of phrase?"

"It was precisely that turn of phrase, and the following day. However, as it did not sound urgent, I only now recalled it."

*So I put my friend's life in peril to attract a shark, and captured a minnow*, Mycroft thought bitterly. *One who brings news that I have been dreading for months…*

As if on cue, they heard a voice behind them, calling out in a light Asian accent, its tone tremulous and slightly out of breath: "Mr. Holmes! I have found you at last!"

# 4

THE DIFFICULTY OF HAVING BUT ONE LARGE TELEGRAPH office in the whole of Cambridge was that the queues proved ever so long, the room in desperate need of air, and the petitioners sour and possessive of their seniority. As for the telegraph girls working the clanking machines, Sherlock allowed that they were skilled at their telegraphic literature, but he found them querulous. Not obliged to the public for their wages, they did not submit to ill treatment as a matter of course.

Sherlock swept a lock of unruly black hair from his eyes and was at long last approaching the counter when the blasted machine ceased its labors altogether, gears grinding to a halt like an errant locomotive. It took a half hour until the thing was in working order.

By the time Sherlock had dictated his telegram to Mycroft and was back on Bene't Street, the afternoon crowd was staggering out of The Eagle in twos and threes, their discussions and quarrels all but spent, their last coarse jokes hanging in the air, and Sherlock well resenting the entire endeavor. Why should he be forced to beg for money from his brother, of all people? How very tedious.

He opened the door of the pub, to an interior neither charming nor intimate. Instead, it was large and plain, all brick and wood, its colors inoffensive, and not a looking glass in sight. Since it was just past the lunch hour, only a handful of stragglers was left: one man of middle years noisily slurping his fish soup, and two soused Irishmen struggling mightily to remain upon their feet and conclude their game of darts.

Passing the bar, Sherlock ordered a pint of bitter, then sat at the end of a long bench before a wooden table, as distant from the other three patrons as he could manage without drawing undue attention to himself.

With the barman's eyes on him, Sherlock took the smallest sip of beer that he could, for he had precious few coins left, and he wished to remain unmolested for some time. Then he wiped his lips with the back of his hand and set to work.

He pulled the bundle of columns from his pocket, unbound them and laid them flat. He had collected fifteen columns in all: *The Times*, the *Illustrated London News*, and the *Police Gazette*, to be sure; but also the *Courier*, the *Scotsman*, the *Manchester Guardian*, the *Daily Telegraph*, the *Western Mail*, and a handful that were local to the areas where the murders had occurred. He had omitted only those that had clearly copied the details from their betters, or those whose speculations were so unsound that nothing of what they said thereafter could be trusted.

Below the columns, he laid out a small, hand-colored map of Great Britain, courtesy of Gray's, for he wished to follow the killings first in chronological and then in geographical order.

All the dead had lived in the quiet periphery of larger towns. Their domiciles were, if not in bona fide isolation, then in areas lightly populated; with few neighbors or family members who could chance upon a would-be killer in the act.

The first murder had been in Wales, near Swansea. Sherlock had already scoured newspapers to see if anything of import had taken place on or around that date but had come up short.

From Wales, the killer had traveled nearly two hundred miles to Manchester; then an additional hundred and fifty miles further north to Newcastle upon Tyne, then to Glasgow, then south again to Plymouth. After a week's-long quiet spell in mid-April, he'd resumed his butchery: first Blackpool, then Avoncliff (another two hundred miles and change), only to turn around and head northeast another two hundred and thirty-eight miles, to Kingston upon Hull.

And at present was another lull, this one interminable, as the last killing had occurred on the 29th of April, and today was the 8th of May. Had it ceased for good? Logic said yes. But his instincts said the opposite. And although he did not wish for more deaths, he dearly hoped that he would be allowed to inspect at least one victim who had not already been interred, or cut to ribbons by some overly zealous small-town doctor.

Sherlock looked over the map again, tracing a finger from one murder to the other, as if on a pilgrimage. But, unlike ordinary pilgrims, the divinity he was pursuing was his own genius: a sort of prescience, combined with obsessive attention to detail, which seemed to reveal itself only if he focused with enough intensity and single-mindedness.

The killer could not have been on foot: the timing of the murders did not allow it, nor did the extreme distances. So, on horseback? By rail? Each of the locations had access to trains, though some travelers would have to rely on more infrequent timetables and longer walks. Local transports tended to carry the same passengers over and over. Had someone noticed a stranger in their midst? *Was* he a stranger in their midst?

The advantage of killing in unpopulated areas was certainly a lack of eyewitnesses. The disadvantage was that an unfamiliar figure on horseback or taking a stroll was sure to draw notice.

A few locales were coal towns, such as Swansea, but most were not. Sherlock sought a pattern. Perhaps the killer's trajectory had drawn a letter, number or symbol upon the map, but he found nothing so obvious as that.

He scanned the victims' Christian names, their surnames, their middle names (if given), searching for acronyms and other 'coded' messages, for he had found that he had a knack for those. Again, no pattern that he could see.

None of the bodies had been mishandled. None had been found with so much as an untoward blemish upon them.

Sherlock swallowed another small sip of bitter. His stomach grumbled low in return, but he ignored the complaint. Hunger was a daily affair, as were many of the body's baser needs. Fasting sharpened his senses, and besides, he was not about to allow his gut to dictate terms of engagement. *What else?*

The victims had all died if not alone, then with no one in sight—with the exception of number eight, Abigail Sykes. The ten-year-old girl from Kingston upon Hull had succumbed in the kitchen, less than fifteen feet from where her mother stood at the stove, preparing supper for the two of them and Abigail's father, a local clerk whom they expected home within the hour.

In the newspaper account, Mrs. Sykes recalled that Abigail had been standing at the kitchen table shelling a bowl of peas, that they had been singing 'When the Corn is Waving, Annie Dear,' for Mr. Sykes had recently purchased a broadside ballad from a traveling salesman and Abigail had been keen to memorize the ditty.

"She crumpled like a stone, she did!" Mrs. Sykes had announced in tears.

But in fact, she hadn't—and not merely because stones do not crumple. Instead, she had stared at her mother with wide, terrorized eyes. Then she had turned in the direction of the window behind her and collapsed. Her back had hit the table's edge so hard that the wood had cracked upon impact. From there, she had slid to the ground. Investigators had found tiny splinters protruding from the skin of her neck.

Sherlock stood up and turned so that his back was to the table. He squatted to the approximate height of a ten-year-old female. Then he turned again, and in slow motion hit the edge of the table. Could the weight of her little body have been enough to crack it?

Perhaps a cheap wooden table, given age and rot, might have split in the manner described. And was her hair pulled off her neck, or did it hang loose? If hanging loose, would splinters have been able to pierce the skin as her neck brushed against the edge? So much that he did not know!

"Confound it!" he blurted out.

The man with the fish soup did not flinch, but the sudden noise prompted the older Irishman to make a wild throw of his dart. He let out a curse, and then glared at Sherlock with malicious little eyes.

"Buggery!" he snarled. "Think yer the biggest toad in the puddle, do ye? I've gutted yer betters for less!"

He stumbled forward, wielding the dart in his hand like a dagger.

It was not often, in Sherlock's brief life, that being young and reedy proved the advantage; for age, experience, and sturdiness surely had their merits. But not when those attributes were diluted by four drams of cheap rum and an equivalent number of beers.

Sherlock stepped gingerly out of the old souse's way, and the man went hurtling past him and into the wall.

"*There's* a rantallion!" his younger friend declared, staring at the scene with the dull, eager eyes of a born follower. "We'll take him together, eh, Michael?"

"You do," Sherlock muttered, "and I'll take out that bum right knee with one kick."

The younger man was instantly sidelined, but the older one became more enraged.

"Why, you plague-sore whoreson, I'll teach you what's what!" he cried with a wild toss of his dart, which sank into a crack in the wall not two inches from Sherlock's right eye.

"An able wrist!" Sherlock called out to the older man. "But your last three fingers are rheumatic, as are all five of your left. And your left ear ails you. One good smack would set it ringing for a week."

The old rummy, fresh dart in hand, cocked his head like a puzzled dog, thereby proving Sherlock's hunch about his ailing ear.

"As for you," Sherlock declared, turning to the younger man, "just you try to go home one more night with the makings of a brawl on you, and your missus will lock the front door for good."

The younger man stared at Sherlock, amazed. "Boy's a witch!" he announced in a hissing whisper.

"Not in the least. But we would all be better served if I returned to my pursuits and allowed you to return to yours."

The rummy lurched another half step forward and was just taking aim in the general direction of Sherlock's other eye when the barman called out: "Enough, you old muckspout."

His inflection was equitable and slightly bored, as if he would serve the man a drink or smack him out the door; it was all the same to him. "Ye've had yer fun, now behave or be gone," he added in his resonant baritone.

The old man's mood was still bitter, but the younger man grabbed his friend's wrist. "Leave it be, Michael," he murmured, no doubt spooked by the combination of Sherlock's prophesying and the barman's bulging muscles.

The two went back to their game more jittery than when they'd begun, muttering their grievances but keeping it between themselves. Sherlock returned to his crime columns, no worse for wear, frequently checking his watch to see how long before he could head back to the telegraph office for Mycroft's response.

# 5

MYCROFT SAT MUTE AND NUMB AT A LITTLE TURKISH café located outside the Ottoman–Turkish exhibition halls, dutifully sipping lukewarm coffee mixed with cardamom and sugar. Above his head, the swifts had vanished. The pretty May morning with its soft, hopeful sun had dissipated, leaving in its wake creeping clouds and a pettifogging chill that penetrated the bones.

Across the round wrought-iron table, Douglas appraised him with quiet concern, his own cup untouched.

Sometime before, Han businessman Deshi Hai Lin, impeccable in a traditional silk *tángzhuāng* the color of brick, had bowed before them, face creased with anxiety. "Mr. Douglas, Mr. Holmes," he had said in greeting. "I am well aware that already I owe you my life, but I did not know where else to turn…"

His slight Mandarin accent had thickened a bit, most likely from nerves, and his voice quavered. Looming behind him were the two good-natured dullards who had once guarded his beautiful daughter Ai Lin.

The moment that Mycroft saw them, he knew that his hunch had been correct. "Are your son and daughter well?" he'd inquired as a courtesy.

Though he had steadied himself against the reply, he could not quell his profound sense of loss when Lin replied, "Thank you, yes. My dearest daughter Ai Lin is engaged to be married…"

"Mycroft? Rain appears imminent."

Douglas was leaning across the table in a bid to gain his attention. Snapping back to reality, Mycroft met Douglas's eye.

"Rain," Douglas repeated for lack of better, with a glance skyward to prove it was indeed a prospective drenching and not his friend's mood that troubled him. "I can forego a tour of the Japanese gardens. Perhaps we would be better to be indoors, exploring the Palace of Fine Arts…"

"Nonsense," Mycroft replied as genially as he could. "No need to be chased off by a few clouds. It shall not rain, and I shall be good as new in a moment. Drink your cocoa."

"It is not cocoa, it is coffee, and I drank it."

"When?"

"A half hour ago, while it was still hot."

Douglas tilted the cup so that Mycroft could view the inside.

"Have we been here so long as that?" Mycroft marveled as he stared into Douglas's empty cup.

"Give or take a sigh or two," Douglas replied as Mycroft, to his consternation, let out another.

"And there you have it!" Mycroft declared, rising. "I have become a cliché. The jilted suitor, with the possible exception that I was never jilted, nor was I ever her suitor, which makes me twice the buffoon."

"You are hardly a buffoon for falling in love," Douglas countered, rising as well, and pulling out Mycroft's chair quickly enough so that any prying eyes would see the tall black man performing *some* task or other for his keep.

"Nor are you a buffoon because you have chosen not to pursue her," he continued, snatching Mycroft's black leather gloves from the table and handing them to him with servant-like efficiency. "For a match like that would surely cause heartache."

Mycroft had predicted Deshi Hai Lin's enquiry from the moment he had guessed his name. That too was a matter of elimination. Lin would not seek him out to remedy a setback with his business, for Mycroft's knowledge of the shipping trade, in which Lin was a principal, was scant. And neither would he wish to consult Mycroft regarding his health. No, the only reason a proud man like Lin would lower himself to ask for aid—especially so close on the heels of their *other* affair—was that one of his children had fallen into some sort of a predicament. But Lin's son studied with Sherlock at Cambridge, and Mycroft had heard nothing untoward, which meant that it was his daughter Ai Lin who concerned him. But if it were she who was imperiled, her father's request to Douglas would have been much more desperate.

Ai Lin, at twenty-two, was of marrying age. And since her father would not need Mycroft to go over the financial constructs of a match, much less some issue of customs and mores, Mycroft had assumed it was some *diplomatic* entanglement that grieved him. As had indeed proved to be the case.

"The question is," Douglas continued, "will you help to locate her fiancé, as her father pleaded, and bring him back to her?"

Mycroft slipped on his gloves and looked about. "Forgive me, Douglas, I seem to have lost my yen for sightseeing. If you wish to remain, I could meet you back at the hotel…"

"No, I am glad to accompany you," Douglas replied.

Mycroft nodded his thanks, and the two left the café.

"You are certain that it will not rain?" Douglas asked doubtfully, squinting up as if already expecting a drizzle. "I can fetch us a cab."

"I've a mind to walk, if that suits you," Mycroft replied. "Do not misunderstand me, Douglas," he added, reprising the former subject. "I do not mourn merely for myself, but for her. I think it abominable that such a brilliant creature will be relegated to a life that is little better than servitude."

Douglas lifted an eyebrow. His expression was serious, but Mycroft was rankled to note the play of a smile upon his lips. "Surely you do not think it the exclusive purview of the Asian continent?" he said. "Surely you know that it is the status of women everywhere?"

"Yes, but I was not referring strictly to domestic duties," Mycroft countered—sounding, even to himself, a tad dense— "but to, well, to… to possessiveness! And the concomitant 'woman-handling,' if you will, that occurs within the Chinese community at large, should a woman prove to be less than submissive to whatever her husband demands."

"'Woman-handling'?" Douglas repeated, his eyebrow arching even more. "Foreigners are no more or less likely to abuse their wives than are Englishmen. If you cannot fathom that a modern *British* man might be vicious towards his spouse, I challenge you to visit the London Hospital on any Saturday night."

"I have no need to visit any hospital, thank you; I well know the viciousness of which you speak."

"So then, all this talk of her woeful status is simply a philosophical detour," Douglas declared, "designed to keep your emotions at arm's length. I grant you, emotions are tricky things. But do try to remember that, unlike me, you are still young: twenty-seven, just turned—"

"Whereas you are a bedraggled wreck of forty-three—"

"And the point, which I have been struggling to make, is that you have fallen in love only twice. It shall transpire again, you know. And not only because there is divinity, to say nothing of good luck, in odd numbers, but because your ultimate happiness will be to have a family of your own."

"My ultimate happiness…?" Mycroft repeated numbly.

He could not so much as whisper more than that. To do so would be to reveal the precarious state of his health, and what a wicked thing it would be to condemn any woman to suffer it, least of all one whom he claimed to love.

"The question remains," Douglas reprised when no response was forthcoming. "Are you able to do what Deshi Hai Lin has requested?"

Lin had explained that his daughter Ai Lin had been promised in marriage to one Bingwen Shi, a thirty-year-old land investor whom she had met but once. It appeared that, on his way to a routine appointment with a client in London, Shi had disappeared. After searching for him for several days to no avail, his family and the Lins had assumed foul play.

"Even if he is dead, his family wishes his body returned to them," Deshi Hai Lin had told them. "But if he is not, might you arrange to bring him home so that my daughter Ai Lin can fulfill her destiny and become his wife? I would pay you prodigiously for your trouble."

Mycroft had made it clear to the anxious father that he did not need recompense. That, if he chose to take on the task, it would be as a favor to the Lin family, but that he would have to give it some thought.

"Mr. Holmes. I cannot tell you how dear Bingwen Shi is to me. From the first, he treated me like a father. And I too thought that he could be like a son to me; for, unlike my boy now at university, he was keen to learn my business. And he has already been missing one month…" Lin had pleaded.

"Then I am sorry to say, Mr. Lin, that the worst may have already transpired," Mycroft had replied. "For surely by now a note of ransom or news of some sort would have materialized. As nothing has, I cannot believe that another few days will make much difference."

Though Lin was barely fifty years old, he had walked away from them a much older man. Mycroft had almost called to him then and there, to say he would assist. Only Douglas's arm on his shoulder had restrained him.

"It was *you* who prevented me from giving him an immediate answer," Mycroft said as they proceeded through the large and ornate archway that led out of the World's Fair. "Why?"

"You already resent the circumstances," Douglas explained. "I would rather you not resent your decision as well. Your first impulse—to think on it—was sound, for it is a favor he asks of you, not an obligation."

Mycroft nodded, disconsolate. "I do admit," he added, "that one aspect of this mystery intrigues me. When I asked Lin if his prospective son-in-law had any enemies, he said no, but he added that he had had some business dealings with Vizily Zaharoff, who in fact was the 'client' he was going to meet when he was abducted."

"Yes, I recall his mentioning it," Douglas said. "But who is this Zaharoff?"

"A notorious dealer in weaponry, with offices in a half-dozen European capitals."

"Notorious? In what way?"

"He might have the unfortunate habit of decapitating people with whom he is displeased. That is the rumor, in any event. If

I do decide to take it on, might you join me in my quest? Your familiarity with Chinese culture cannot but help."

"Tangling, however obliquely, with a man with a penchant for beheading his enemies? How could I refuse?"

When Mycroft said nothing but continued to look glum, Douglas reiterated that he need not take this on at all; that Ai Lin might not even be aware that her father was asking such a favor of him.

"Whether she knows or does not is immaterial," Mycroft replied. "I 'take this on' because a person that I care for is suffering, and it is in my power to alleviate it."

Douglas nodded. "Then if I agree to go along, we must do as we did in years past, with no secrets between us. For I function poorly under subterfuge. The motives for action must be obvious to me."

"Of course," Mycroft said.

"And though I would never violate your privacy by asking where you sequestered yourself the last several weeks, and why you began a row in the middle of the Prater—"

"Yes, that was thoughtless of me," Mycroft interrupted, hoping that he sounded sincere, for in truth, the secrets that he was keeping from Douglas were beginning to weigh heavily on him.

*Nothing to be done*, he thought bitterly.

For a man like Douglas would never reconcile himself to the Necessary Inhumanity that seemed each day more essential to Mycroft's own dealings.

# 6

SHERLOCK HAD SAT BACK DOWN TO HIS AGONY COLUMNS and was engrossed therein when a shadow fell over his only source of light. He glanced up at the hulking form of the barman, leaning over his table.

"That one's a fair fighter when he don't have a brick in his hat!" he said, indicating the younger Irishman. "You know his missus, do you?"

Sherlock shook his head. "I know neither him nor his… missus."

"So, how'd you guess?" the barman insisted.

Sherlock sighed. No use alienating the man. "He wore a cheap tin ring," he said. "His shirt is old, but clean and well mended, though the stitch is not nearly so good as to be professional. He is not the sort of a man who would pay the least bit attention to his grooming, were not a woman at home to suggest he do better. Beyond which, though he wished to fight he seemed reluctant to take the lead, as if he had been warned to cause no trouble. And the crescent-shaped scar on his temple can be made only by a copper pot, and men rarely wield cookware as weapons. If his wife had not laid down the law, I'd likely be digging a dart out of my pupil."

The barman laughed. "You got a good head on you," he declared. "You are welcome here."

Just then, the front door opened, letting in a shaft of dim afternoon light, along with one of The Eagle's regulars, for the barman called out "Smithy!" and moved to the taps. Indeed, the man seemed to be still black from the forge. Though he had attempted to clean himself, the color of his profession had become imbedded in his skin.

Just before he sat, he turned to the barman, waved his newspaper in the air and barked: "Oi William! You cannot believe this! Another four-eleven!"

At this, Sherlock all but leapt from his seat and hovered over man and print like a ravenous bird. The startled smithy looked up.

"Here, boy, what you up to?"

"Can you read?" Sherlock asked excitedly.

"How's it your business if I can or I cannot?" the smithy replied, offended. "But if you must know, I have an acquaintance what does my reading and I don't need another."

"But I shall do it free of charge!" Sherlock declared, sitting beside him on the bench.

"What makes you think I pay a body to read for me?" the smithy demanded.

"Because William is drawing up two half 'n halfs," Sherlock said, indicating the barman, "and unless you mean to drink them both at once…"

"For free, you say?" Smithy asked dubiously.

Sherlock nodded. "And I can read *or* summarize."

"No need for your bag and baggage, boy, just summize!" the smithy replied sourly.

"Fine. So, to… 'summize,'" Sherlock began. "On the

outskirts of Chichester, at approximately eight-thirty this morning, a spinster by the name of Penny Montgomery was found askance—"

"Askance? Wot's that?" William the barman asked, for he had returned, the two pints of stout and ale hovering precariously over the printed page.

"I'll be needin' but one today," Smithy declared, a hint of menace in his voice.

"They've already got the stout in 'em," William said. "I cannot extract it again, someone's got to pay."

Smithy laid his large, stained hand over the type. "It'll not be I," he growled.

"It'll be I," Sherlock offered with a sigh as he put his last coin on the table for a drink he would never touch, and pushed Smithy's hand off the print.

"Askance," he stated, "is not the proper word, but the paper used it, not I. As she had been pulling weeds in her garden when she was found, I am assuming it means that she fell sideways—though whether to the left or the right, it does not say."

As the dart-playing rummies stumbled closer to hear, Sherlock continued: "Like most of the other victims, she was alone. No footprints leading away from her, and the only prints leading to her were her own."

Smithy drew a shivering breath like a child being told a ghost story, but Michael, the older Irishman who had tried to blind Sherlock, was not enthralled.

"No footprints? Nah, you read it wrong, boy, that h'ain't possible!" Michael proclaimed, which caused Smithy to protest that it was *his* paper, and who was anyone to say what was and was not possible?

"Killer's a phantasm," the barman said, agreeing with Smithy, and that seemed to settle it.

"This Penny Montgomery was a recluse, so the neighbors said," Sherlock went on. "Went out only to work in her garden."

"How was she found, then?" challenged the older rummy.

"The vegetable plot was visible from the street," Sherlock said.

"What of the note?" Smithy asked gleefully. "Was it there?"

Sherlock nodded again. "Near her body."

"And no footprints at all? Outside? In a garden? How can that be?" William wondered.

"Hah! You see?" Smithy offered, seemingly impressed with the murderer's boldness, while the others nodded agreement.

The front door opened. Another ray of light was followed by a blast of air. From the expressions on his fellows' faces, Sherlock knew this was Smithy's reader, come to barter his few years of schooling for an *arf-an-arf*. Sherlock rose, walked past the newcomer and through the door before anyone had so much as a say-so about it.

Outdoors again, and fresh out of shag, he considered a tobacconist when he realized that he was also penniless, for he'd spent the last of it on the beer he had not drunk.

He turned towards the telegraph office to await Mycroft's reply but thought better of it. Wiser to go back to Downing to pack the essentials, leave a brief message for his tutors, and use the last of his allowance—if he could recall where he had tucked it away—to purchase a ticket to London. For not even Mycroft could expect him to finish out his term at university, not with a murderer of this caliber on the loose!

# 7

BY THE TIME MYCROFT AND DOUGLAS RETURNED TO THE Hotel Imperial, an imposing palace with an Italian Neo-Renaissance façade overlooking Ring Boulevard, the weather had turned malevolent. The clouds were black, and the wind howled through every archway and crevice in the wide street, kicking up dust and an eerie sense of desolation in equal measures.

The Hotel Imperial had originally served as a palace for German prince Philipp, Duke of Württemberg, and his consort, Archduchess Maria-Thèrése of Austria. And because it had been conceived as a private home, however large, and not a hotel, to Douglas it seemed off kilter. The gargantuan front entrance, for example, had been designed to allow for a two-horse carriage, a convenience that tended to dwarf the mere mortals who dared to venture inside on foot, as he and Mycroft were doing at present.

"Majestic," Douglas exclaimed as he stared straight up at the man-sized French chandeliers attached to a scrolled and ornate stucco ceiling. "And yet, it stirs in one a sense of—"

"Personal insignificance?" Mycroft filled in amiably.

Douglas smiled at the accuracy of the phrase.

From his years of friendship with Mycroft, he had learned a

thing or two: he was not easily impressed, was not profligate with his money, and rarely did anything for show. No, they two were at this particular hotel for a reason, though he did not yet know what that might be. It vexed him that, after weeks of absolute silence, and promises to the contrary, another secret was being kept from him. He would need to clear the air at some point; and he hoped he could do so without rancor.

He and Mycroft climbed the large, ceremonial stairway between marbled walls that led to the *belle étage*, where a splendidly attired concierge met them with their room keys and a telegram, which he handed to Douglas with a mean little nod of his head. Douglas repressed a sigh and passed the telegram two inches to his left, for it was clearly addressed to 'Mycroft Holmes.' And he knew, from the expression on Mycroft's face when he opened it, who the sender was.

"Sherlock?" Douglas ventured as the concierge pocketed Mycroft's tip, clicked his heels, and walked away.

"He needs money," Mycroft muttered. "He wrote '*Dira necessitas*' twice. But what 'dire necessity' can he possibly have when everything is provided for him?"

"He must be desperate if he is quoting Horace," Douglas teased, though inwardly his thought was: *That torturous boy!* For his first instinct was to be protective of Mycroft. On the other hand, Mycroft did himself no favors by alternately neglecting and spoiling his brother, not to mention having few conversations with him that did not involve lecturing, hectoring, recriminations, or that sort of one-upmanship peculiar to male siblings.

"He has absolutely no notion of the value of money," Mycroft despaired as he reread the text.

"He is very nearly done with his term, is he not?" Douglas queried mildly.

"One month to go," Mycroft replied. "What in the world am I to do with him then, Douglas?"

"Please do not ask if he can volunteer at Nickolus House…!"

"I am not so big a fool as all of that. Once was enough for a lifetime. But he cannot remain at Cambridge for the summer, and I promised that I would never again force him to return to our mother and father in the country. Which means that he shall have to reside with *me*. Perhaps I can find him lodgings," he added hopefully.

"Yes, I am certain that will go a long way towards teaching him the value of money," Douglas said wryly.

"I do not intend a pied-a-terre. But a modest furnished room somewhere, though he will protest that my home has plenty of furnished rooms from which to choose."

"Not to mention servants at his beck and call," Douglas added just as a valet walking in the opposite direction sneered at him.

Mycroft did not always notice those sorts of slights, but this day he most certainly did.

"Why, how dare he?" he exclaimed. "I just might go and give him a piece of my mind!"

"No need," Douglas said under his breath. "*We* are the ones who perpetrate the ruse that I am your valet. Your insistence on separate quarters rather than adjoining rooms has no doubt set the staff's tongues to wagging about such pampered and spoiled help as I."

"It has nothing to do with the color of your skin, then?"

"None whatsoever," Douglas confirmed. "Now, as to Sherlock. For what does he require funds? He does passably well with the allowance you provide."

"Oh, he is being insufferably vague," Mycroft replied as they continued down the long corridor to their rooms, their footsteps muffled by a thick Persian carpet. "Some wild goose chase that has sprung from one of his agony columns, is my estimate. What has been in the local news, of late?"

"You mean you are not aware of the traveling murderer who has paralyzed all of England?"

"No, I… do not believe I have heard of it," Mycroft replied.

Considering that Mycroft knew quite a bit about a great many subjects, this lack of awareness struck Douglas as odd, once again bringing to the fore his friend's unexplained absence. Could Mycroft have been out of the country and only just returned? Even so, a murder of this caliber would surely have been reported abroad.

"It seems that this one kills without rhyme or reason," Douglas explained. "And with some frequency, and in various locales. And, he has not been good enough to leave a trace."

"I see. And so Sherlock seeks funds to traipse throughout the isles, hoping to hunt down this enigmatic murderer…? Ah, well. Perhaps I should allow it. At the least, it would keep him busy for a time."

"And at the most, he could become the next victim!" Douglas parried. "I hope you are in jest."

"Yes," Mycroft admitted with a sigh, "though it is awfully tempting. The most galling part is that he truly has no sense that his *schooling* would be of importance to me, or to society at large. 'My books are portable,' says he… as if rifling through pages on a train while his mind is thoroughly engaged elsewhere carries the same weight as a lecture, or research in a proper library. No. I shall not give in to his every whim!" Mycroft concluded, flicking the telegram absentmindedly with his finger, perhaps hoping it would disappear from out his hand like a card trick.

"I would be glad to accompany you downstairs," Douglas said. "Play the servant, send Sherlock a telegram with your answer."

"Not just now."

"But is he not at the telegraph office?" Douglas asked.

"Highly doubtful. I know how my brother's mind works: he has inconvenienced himself to make the petition. I must now inconvenience myself to respond in a manner that will reach him immediately, if not sooner, wherever he might be. Ah, but I am no longer a half-daft terrier, ready to spring at his command! From here on, he shall wait until I am good and ready!"

Douglas looked at him doubtfully, and Mycroft raked a hand through his hair.

"Now. The Imperial Hotel wishes to become famous for their torte," he said, "a brilliant chocolate and marzipan confection. What say we freshen up and go off for a decent lunch? My treat."

"Someone is suddenly feeling better," Douglas exclaimed.

"I told you a brisk walk would do me good."

"It was that telegram from Sherlock, more like," Douglas said. "As much of a dust storm as he kicks up, he needs you. And that pleases you."

"My Whirling Dervish of a brother needs my wallet, that is all," Mycroft complained.

"Well, that is a need, of sorts. And, given the situation at home, you are the closest thing to a father that he has."

"Yes, poor lad," Mycroft said quietly.

Mycroft's words were not said to elicit either comfort or flattery, and Douglas offered neither. He had come to understand a fair amount about the Holmes progenitors in the last five years—the strangely passive father, the brilliant but needy and hysterical mother with a penchant for morphine—yet he felt he did not know the half of it.

"The Holmes family is an odd parcel," Mycroft said as if pulling the thought out of Douglas's head and then replying to his musings. "Sherlock and I have attempted, our entire lives, to make heads or tails of its contorted alliances and skewed sensibilities. I swear to you it is not worth the bother. Do not give it another thought," he added as the two reached Douglas's quarters.

Mycroft was walking off to his own suite when Douglas called out: "That is not your decision to make!"

"Pardon?" Mycroft asked, turning. "To what are you referring?"

"I can think anything I choose!" Douglas declared.

"Of course you can!"

"You do not have access to my thoughts."

"Of course I do!" Mycroft replied with a martyr's sigh, all the while staring at Douglas as if he were not altogether sound of mind. "In any event," he went on, "it is not as if I shall find Sherlock on the doorstep when I return. I have an entire month to ponder what to do with my albatross of a brother. There is some small comfort in that."

With a wave of his hand, he turned and walked on, blithely whistling a little tune as he went.

Douglas recognized the aria, for he knew it well. It was from one of Mycroft's favorite operas, Rossini's *The Barber of Seville*.

> *Pronto prontissimo son come il fulmine:*
> *sono il factotum della città...!*
> *Bravo! Bravissimo!*

As Douglas placed the key in the lock, he translated the words of 'Largo al factotum' in his head.

The lead character, Figaro, was singing his own praises as the only man who could bring order to a chaotic and jumbled world. It was an interesting correlation. Like the Barber of Seville with his scissors, Mycroft imagined himself forever ready, night or day, for any crisis that happened to entangle England, his beloved isle, or touch the handful of people whom he cherished. Mycroft's fondest hope was that he could make Britain even more powerful and his loved ones' lives ever easier and more fulfilling… and he would not be contrary, whenever he succeeded, if they were to cry out *Bravo! Bravissimo!* in his wake.

For Mycroft Holmes acted out of honor, yes; but he was not above a bit of glory.

*You are not the only one who can read minds, Mycroft Holmes,* Douglas thought with a hint of satisfaction as he turned the key in the lock.

# 8

FROM THE MOMENT MYCROFT ENTERED HIS SUITE—
which he had been careful to leave unlocked—he could tell
that someone had been there, rifling through his things. The
evidence of intrusion was clear. The disturbance of dust served
as a roadmap. After the hotel staff were done tidying up in the
morning, Mycroft had requested that they leave the windows
ajar. The subtle deposit of soot and grime that wafted up from
the street throughout the day would quickly reveal prying fingers.
All Mycroft had to do was to follow the trail.

On the fireplace mantel, a pair of expensive pearl and gold
cufflinks had been picked up, examined no doubt the way a
crow might pore over a shiny found thing, then put down again,
but not precisely where they had been. At his writing desk, the
straight pin he had placed between the ball bearing and the
frame of the second drawer had fallen to the floor, unnoticed:
another sign that someone had been ferreting within. Near the
straight pin, he also spotted a lone white hair, which he picked
up, examined, and then discarded.

But when he opened the drawer, there was his personal
financial ledger, precisely where he had left it: the ledger that
contained his monetary deposits to the Credit-Anstalt, the

preeminent bank in Austria and Hungary, each one clearly marked and dated.

He moved on to the too-large, too-soft bed. What a ghastly thing it was, with its snow-white headboard and footboard carved with a hundred impuberal angels, their little faces creased with concern! Were the Good Book to be proved myth from Genesis to Revelation, those pudgy *putti* with their moth-sized wings still had naught in common with the towering avengers described in the Testaments—though he allowed that most people would not think a sword-wielding, fire-eyed seraph terribly conducive to restful slumber.

On the other hand, that vomitus of baby angels with their watchful eyes did hold one distinct advantage. For though the bed was soft, and though its silk cover held no pattern to speak of, the feather bed *underneath* it most certainly did: a slight blue stripe, barely visible, but there all the same. Once the chambermaid had finished with her duties, all Mycroft had to do was mark where those lines lay in relation to the cherubs' faces—a duty he had undertaken that morning before departing with Douglas. The moment someone disturbed bedcover or mattress, those telltale blue stripes would shift out of position. And someone had most assuredly disturbed them, for the cherubs were no longer looking upon the same stripes as earlier.

He felt between the mattress and the bed board for the note from the Queen that he had squirreled away. Like the ledger, it too was precisely where he had left it.

Mycroft pulled out the note, sat on the lounge chair with a contented sigh, and read it over again.

Brilliant.

He had chosen this particular hotel and these particular rooms so that he might be near the large and luxurious corner suite adjoining his. He was already relishing the thought of its occupant awakening on the morrow (from what Mycroft could only assume would be a fitful night's sleep) into what was certain to become a living nightmare. Douglas, of course, did not hold grudges and would doubtless be horrified to realize for how long and how assiduously Mycroft had held onto this one.

But he had despised the Queen's first cousin, Count Wolfgang Hohenlohe-Langenburg, from the moment he'd laid eyes on him. That dull-eyed, hefty, arrogant creature wielded his large frame about like a cannonball, all but daring others to step out of his way or else be knocked aside. Mycroft had spent the last three years following the trail of his financial misdealings, and the horrid way he used and abused those people unlucky enough to enter his sphere.

He could not threaten the blackguard with prison. He had no authority to do so, and the Queen would take a dim view. She was painfully aware that, with Gladstone in power, her popularity had waned of late. Were a relative's royal peccadillos to come to light, they would do naught but reflect badly upon her.

Now at last, and without laying so much as a finger on him, Mycroft was rather relishing the *ping* of one more nail in his enemy's coffin.

Mycroft had made no secret of his visit to Vienna, nor of his plan to take in the World's Fair. He had all but bellowed it from the rooftops of every financial institution he had visited in Germany, which was why Deshi Hai Lin had so easily located him. And of course Douglas was always bound to draw attention.

After his surgery, he had dearly wished to reconcile with his friend, and he was pleased that Douglas could join him in the outing. But there was no denying the obvious: walking about with a genteel, handsome Negro of impressive height and bearing was every bit as effective as waving a banner. As was a rather boisterous quarrel between a black man and a white man at a popular locale in the broad daylight of a staunchly conservative city—a quarrel loud enough to attract notice, yet not so loud that those nearby could overhear a word. Whatever twinge of guilt he felt for making use of the friendship was quickly snuffed out by pragmatism. He was, after all, one who kept England from falling into disrepair, the watchman on the wall. Why should he not utilize every weapon at his disposal?

Like others of means, the count had heard rumblings of possible financial collapse and was prowling the city to ascertain whether or not the rumors were true. Since he was *persona non grata* with the Queen, he could not ask her directly or even discreetly for advice, for she would give him none. Thus, the advantage of having someone next door whom the Queen *would* advise— especially were he (or his minions) to happen upon a note tucked away under Mycroft's mattress, in the Queen's handwriting. For why would Mycroft take such a note with him to this center of commerce, if not to assure investors that Her Royal Majesty was at peace with the current economic situation?

Beyond that, Mycroft's bank ledger showed no hasty withdrawals; naught but diligent monthly deposits into the Credit-Anstalt, to the tune of three million pounds. What more proof would anyone need that the economy of Europe was flourishing, and that the count's money, and that of his investors, would remain safe and sound?

And so it would. For the next fourteen hours or so.

Mycroft had no illusions that this would mark the thorough and definitive end to Count Wolfgang. Once financially dependent upon the Queen, the blackguard had managed to ingratiate himself to other powerful entities that were even now keeping him afloat. He would not be completely undone even by the substantial economic loss he would suffer when dawn broke. Even so, a setback of this magnitude should hobble him long enough that he could do less mischief.

Mycroft's stomach grumbled. It was a welcome noise, for he had not been terribly peckish of late. A pleasant repast with his friend Douglas, a rich dessert, and then afterwards, caution to the wind, perhaps even a fine cigar!

After all, he had nothing left to do now but enjoy the last night of prosperity that Europe was likely to see in quite some time.

At five minutes before six a.m., the world outside Mycroft's rococo suite was still muffled in darkness. Inside, Mycroft had allowed himself a sole lit candle whose flame he kept well back from the large windows overlooking the boulevard. The night had been cold and unpleasant. No one of consequence was yet walking about; or if they were, they'd probably not chance to look up; or if they did, they'd see nothing much beyond black.

By the time the streets of the city filled with panicked messengers bearing terrible news, it would be to Mycroft's distinct advantage to feign that, like the rest of Vienna, he'd been awakened by knocks upon doors, swiftly followed by a cacophony of broken hearts and broken wallets.

He took his key winder out of the breast pocket of his waistcoat, patiently wound his watch, and waited.

At one minute before six, Mycroft began to hear scattered footsteps up and down the halls as equerries made their way to their royal charges, and aides and assistants to their employers. He could sense the controlled hysteria as their knocks became a pounding, and hushed voices gave way to indignant exclamations, which then rose into full-blown rage and disbelief. Though he had been expecting it, it was nevertheless a startling cacophony of human agony, and he could not help but be moved with sorrow for the many poor unfortunates whose lives had been destroyed in the proverbial blink of an eye.

But then he heard another sound that helped to mitigate his sense of compassion: the tap-tapping at Count Wolfgang's suite, the squeak of his door as it opened.

Mycroft threw on a robe and slipped out into the corridor, anticipating the fear-filled eyes of his enemy. Instead, he saw a corpulent, white-haired figure in street clothes dart inside and close the door behind him.

Mycroft thought he recognized him but could not be certain; in any event, there was no time to ponder, for suddenly everywhere he looked, up and down the hall, all he could see was bedlam. Men in their nightshirts were flying out of their suites as though on fire, or hurtling towards the stairwells as if urgency alone would stop the imminent collapse of Europe's economy. Soon they would be moving through the streets in their nightshirts like a rookery of pigeons, madly pecking at the doors of financial institutions, demanding funds that had never existed, or that had vanished in the night. And this was merely the beginning, Mycroft knew; within a day or two, other great money houses of Europe would fall.

As the hallway cleared, he saw Douglas hurry towards him. He'd most likely just been awakened by the tumult, for his street clothes were askew. Unlike others, Douglas could not spring from his bed in nightshirt and robe, regardless of the emergency. Even after dressing, he seemed to have waited until he was least likely to attract notice. He drew closer, his eyes as wide as Mycroft had ever seen them.

Just then, the count's door creaked open, and a more familiar figure emerged.

Count Wolfgang Hohenlohe-Langenburg, aged fifty or so, had lost neither his fulsome beard nor his girth—and, in spite of recent setbacks, still appeared as arrogant as ever.

"Mycroft Holmes," he said in his German-inflected English. "It appears that I might be in need of your assistance."

"With what?" Mycroft asked, surprised.

The count shrugged noncommittally. "I could not prevent him. He is on the ledge."

Mycroft and Douglas pushed past him and through the open door into the suite.

# 9

THE MASSIVE WINDOW WAS OPEN, THE HEAVY WINE-RED crewelwork curtains drawn to the side, allowing the wind to blow the beige sheers inward, as if beckoning. And outside on the ledge, his back pressed to the wall, stood Nestor Ellensberg, an accountant whom Mycroft had met in Trinidad, and who had helped Count Wolfgang to hide his ill-gotten gains. Ellensberg's eyes were bloodshot. His naturally pinkish complexion was flushed crimson with drink and lack of sleep. He did not appear in the least surprised to see Mycroft, thus confirming to whom the errant white hair belonged.

Mycroft poked his head out of the window. "Cease this foolishness at once!" he commanded. "For you shall not die. At most, the force shall snap your collarbone, your left arm at the elbow as it cushions your left hip, and possibly your—"

"Mycroft!" This last was Douglas, whispering rather fiercely his disapproval as he balanced along the ledge towards the accountant.

"Come no closer!" Ellensberg warbled to Douglas as he lifted one shaky foot off the precipice and dangled it into the void.

But perhaps he did not wish to die at that juncture, or perhaps he did not imagine that he would. In any event, he hesitated—

for he was unacquainted with how quickly Douglas could move.

Douglas slung one strong arm across Ellensberg's chest and pushed him back to the wall. Keeping him thus pinned in place, his other hand reached towards Mycroft, who grabbed a hold of it. Ellensberg attempted to slip out from under Douglas's restraining arm, but to no avail. Douglas prodded him sideways, step by halting step, back inside of the suite.

Count Wolfgang for his part looked peevish, as if the whole event had been manufactured to annoy him. Crisis over, he deposited himself on a small padded Chinese bench whose thin wooden legs creaked and groaned under his weight. Ellensberg went and stood behind the bench, his legs trembling like a jelly *macédoine*.

"Sit," Douglas commanded, indicating a nearby divan.

Ellensberg complied as decorously as he could, given the circumstances, and met Douglas's dark gaze like a man trying his level best not to act as guilty as he felt.

"Well, Mr. Holmes. If you expect thanks, I shall save you the trouble of waiting. For, when one considers that you all but ruined *my* life some three years back, I owe you no gratitude for saving *his* now," the count sniffed, indicating Ellensberg with his thumb.

"We are more than happy to depart, so long as your accountant is of sound mind—" Mycroft began.

"Nestor? Are you sound of mind?" the count demanded.

Nestor Ellensberg croaked out a "Yes."

"There you have it! As Nestor is no longer in danger of doing himself an injury, and as this is a wretched day and we have both lost money, a goodly amount I wager, I should like some privacy to lick my proverbial wounds, and I imagine you wish to do the same. So, while I applaud your Negro's dexterity in my accountant's regard, for that is, after all, what they are known for, is it not? Speed and agility? I request that you both vacate my chambers at once."

"Of course," Mycroft said. "Douglas? Shall we?" he added, indicating the door and ignoring Douglas's furrowed brow. Mycroft reached the door and turned the handle. "I suppose I should mention," he said, pausing, "that our fortunes are not at all the same. For although you are correct that we have both suffered loss, I am not in the remotest danger of being tortured, nor of my head being severed from my body."

Count Wolfgang startled at that, the bench beneath him squealing in indignation. Mr. Ellensberg let out a whimper.

"Mr. Ellensberg," Mycroft said, "why attempt a leap? Do you fear that the count will blame *you* for his bountiful losses?"

Ellensberg stared at Mycroft in horror. "Mr. Holmes," he bleated. "I am naught but a humble accountant!"

"Oh, shut up, Nestor!" Count Wolfgang grumbled as he rose shakily to his feet. "Whether I do or do not, that is none of your affair!" he bellowed to Mycroft.

"So much money you were lent," Mycroft said, shaking his head in mock sorrow. "And now, however will you repay it? Oh, and I must add that I am gratified that your fortunes have not improved since we last met. As a firm believer in divine justice, I thank you for being the living embodiment thereof. But, you are correct, of course, you have your actuary to blame, and besides, it is none of my affair. Douglas, if you please?" Mycroft said to his friend as he finally twisted the handle and held the door open for him.

In the corridor once more, Douglas gave Mycroft a sour look.

"I am petty, I will admit it," Mycroft replied.

"At least it explains this absurdly dear and rather impractical hotel," Douglas muttered. "And the feeling all along that I have been had."

"Whatever do you mean?" Mycroft asked innocently.

"You were stalking the count! That is something I deserved to know, do you not agree?"

"Yes, and I do apologize. Profusely, Douglas. But, had I shared this plan with you, you would have done your best to talk me out of it."

"Hm. I suppose now you will want to go and witness the final collapse of the banking institutions," Douglas added.

"Heavens, no. Why should I?" Mycroft said as they walked back towards his suite. "For it is nothing but grief and travail. No, what I require is a spot of tea, some Apfelstrudel, and a train heading in a westerly direction towards home.

"So, unless you wish to remain in Vienna and listen to the incessant yowling of all these injured wolves of commerce, shall we meet downstairs in, say, ten minutes?"

Just then, they heard a roar of rage coming from the count's suite. They hurried back inside to find that Nestor Ellensberg had bolted from the divan, clambered onto the windowsill, and hurled himself off of the ledge.

As Mycroft had predicted, Ellensberg did not die but would be incapacitated for a good long while, for he had indeed broken his left elbow and his collarbone, along with his right kneecap. As a gray drizzle set upon the city like a mourning cloak, Ellensberg's broken body was trundled off to hospital, as were those of many others, though some, sadly, were beyond mortal aid.

Mycroft and Douglas, meanwhile, took a carriage to the train station, where they found their respective sleeping compartments and went down to read and rest.

They met up again in the restaurant car, which they had wholly to themselves, for Austria was in shock; there was no one traveling about. And although their tea was lukewarm and their Apfelstrudel stale, Douglas watched Mycroft gulp it down without minding at all.

His friend was twenty-seven now: five years older than when they had first met, at the docks. Douglas had been unloading a crate of Mycroft's then-favorite cigar, the elusive Cuban, the *Principe de Galles*. Mycroft had been arm-in-arm with a beautiful blonde girl, his fiancée, Georgiana. He had seemed to Douglas at the time like a bonny prince whose world was opening up to him with all the fanfare and fireworks that his youth and breeding expected as his due.

But then it had all gone so horribly wrong.

*He is still a handsome man*, Douglas thought, *but the joie de vivre has left him…*

Worse, his former lack of guile seemed to have been replaced by a hardness of countenance, as if a natural willfulness and self-assurance was beginning to congeal into intractability. What saved him was some humor about himself, a healthy dollop of compassion, and of course a yen for justice, rather than for personal gain…

"Unfortunately for the count," Mycroft was saying, "the Queen had not been remarking on the state of financial affairs in Britain at all."

"You are referring to her message?" Douglas replied, wondering for how long his mind had been otherwise occupied.

"Well certainly, for it was a large factor in the game. Here, read it for yourself," Mycroft declared, pulling it out from his jacket pocket.

Douglas took it, squinting at the words then holding it at arm's length—which he did with depressing regularity these days. It read:

*We shall not suffer such losses as we feared. All in all, we shall come out unscathed. All is well. A tragedy has been averted. None of our quarters shall be subjected to an economic beating at the moment.*

"It appears as if she were remarking on Britain's economy does it not? But in fact, that message refers to the most recent tragedy at sea," Mycroft explained, grinning.

"The RMS *Atlantic* in Nova Scotia? Then what in the world can she mean by 'all is well'? Five hundred souls perished!"

"Yes, Douglas, but few were British, which means there will be no recriminations against the ship's Liverpool-based owners, no levies and fines on trade, nor any other penalties."

"Ghastly priorities," Douglas pointed out with a shake of his head. "But do go on," he added, handing back the message and grimacing through a mouthful of tea.

"As for the bank ledger that Ellensberg discovered in my desk drawer," Mycroft continued, "it is a fabrication, start to finish. In truth, I have no funds at all in Austria. I simply procured a book and then wrote in a series of deposits. The simple act of hiding it gave it legitimacy and value, for people are most easily fooled when they are seeing signposts that match their desires. Like many of his fellows living the high life, Count Wolfgang did not wish to believe that the prosperity he witnessed all around him would come to a hasty and an abrupt end, and so he was ready to cling to any sign to the contrary. My sole mission was to keep him from panicking and withdrawing all of his funds before the collapse—"

"Was a casual stroll through the World's Fair meant to convey the same message?" Douglas asked. "Do not bother to reply, for I know the answer. What about Vizily Zaharoff? How were you made aware that Count Wolfgang owed him money?"

"I have been keeping tabs—as the Americans say—on the count. Though he has dealings with several scurrilous individuals, none are powerful enough to do him the sort of damage that Zaharoff can do. I noticed, on his bureau, information on Çanakkale Province…"

"Çanakkale? The site of Trojan ruins?" Douglas asked.

"Yes. I had heard in the wind that Zaharoff is interested, some say obsessed, with the treasures of ancient Troy, and the digs of one particular archaeologist named Heinrich Schliemann. My guess is that the count had borrowed from Zaharoff at substantial interest to invest in the diggings, and now cannot pay him back. Wolfgang, being a man without honor, will surely blame his accountant for the loss of funds. Which is why Ellensberg attempted suicide."

"You think that the rumors are true, then? That Zaharoff beheads his enemies?"

"In fact, I thought those stories balderdash," Mycroft replied. "But I am today much closer to thinking them true. And now I am even more intrigued by this tie between Deshi Hai Lin's future son-in-law and Zaharoff. What interest would Zaharoff have in a Chinese land developer?"

"Well, this is no ordinary Chinese land developer," Douglas replied, "but one who is marrying into a well-established shipping business."

"Precisely. The moment we return to London, I shall inform him that we are in. If you are still willing."

Douglas truly wished he could say no. But, as much as a part of him longed for a quiet life, a larger part wanted no such thing.

If he were completely honest with himself, he cared deeply for Nickolus House and the services that it provided; but his presence there created a ripple that was unpleasant and could be deleterious to its proper workings. Those who knew that Douglas paid the bills were hamstrung by the fact that they could show him no deference. And those who did *not* know assumed that he was a spy for the ever-ailing Mr. Smythe; that his sole occupation was to notice something untoward that he could then report back to his employer.

The truth was that Nickolus House ran perfectly well—and perhaps better—without him.

But he had another reason for wanting, nay, requiring, the excitement that Mycroft's proposition offered. After all, he had been born in turmoil, had lived most of his life on the churning sea, alternating between tedium and peril, so that it felt more like home than did any sort of situation that he could manufacture.

*God's teeth, Douglas, just say yes!* he thought to himself.

"Yes," he said aloud, and the thing was done.

"What matters now is that we breathe not a word to Sherlock," Mycroft said. "I have a month's reprieve before I have to decide what to do with him, and I aim to enjoy every moment!"

# 10

SHERLOCK HOLMES DID NOT BELIEVE IN 'RAILWAY madmen,' the theory that the jarring movement of a train, combined with the nerve-shattering squeal of brakes and the occasional burst of a horn, caused the brain of susceptible people to become temporarily unhinged. Yet, it was obvious that the closer they drew to their destination at King's Cross, the more the large man of middle years sitting across from him was becoming agitated.

Although the third-class compartment was unpleasantly chilly, with the wooden seats doing nothing to relieve the general discomfort, the man was perspiring. As the carriage jostled about, the lights flickered on and off; and each time, like a Kinematoscope, he would be sweating more profusely. He had undone his shirtsleeves and was dabbing at the perspiration on his arms with a handkerchief.

A fresh tattoo on the back of his right wrist read 'PII 21:23–25.'

It was all Sherlock could do to concentrate on his columns and the case before him, a case that he was now completely committed to.

He had left his studies rather abruptly and with decisiveness; so much so that neither his tutors nor the college would likely wish him back anytime soon. His departing with some animus had been on purpose, for he could not hazard that his brother would simply pay his way back into the administration's good graces. And, since Mycroft had sworn that he would never ship Sherlock back to the parental domicile, but neither would he be at all keen to have him underfoot, Sherlock was betting that he would see the benefits of the adventure.

As the lights flickered on again, Sherlock kept his eyes on his work. There was something in the killer's handwriting that he had not noticed before. One of the artists had rendered the dot over the 'i' in the word 'fire' as more of a miniscule slash. If this artist had seen what others hadn't, it seemed odd that the killer should take such pains to make his writing letter perfect, only to break form in this particular detail. He wondered which note the artist had copied, for the story had been a regurgitation of all the murders thus far.

Sherlock was so enthralled by this discovery that as the train began to slow in its approach to King's Cross station, he did not even chance to look up.

A moment later the perspiring and agitated passenger was hovering over him.

*Short torso, long legs,* Sherlock noticed, glancing up. For the man, when he stood, was even more imposing than he had appeared sitting down.

"Keen on the Fire Four Eleven?" he blurted out, eyeing Sherlock's columns.

"Indeed," Sherlock replied. "I aim to solve it."

"Solve it?" the man scoffed. "You will be lucky you do not end up dead."

"Why? What do you know of it?" Sherlock asked, suddenly at high alert.

"Cease your compunction to meddle if you know what's good for you."

With that, he strode out of the compartment and into the corridor.

Sherlock glanced at his retreating form. He wondered who he was, and why he had thought to warn him off the case.

But if Sherlock hoped to glean anything from this first subject, he would have to allow him a small head start and then track him. Based on what he'd learned of him in the half hour since he'd boarded, he could not blatantly trail this rather volatile stranger. He would need the element of surprise.

Besides, he had always considered himself, first and foremost, a sleuth. Now was the time to put it to a crucial test. As the train came to a full stop, Sherlock remained in his seat and counted the minutes until he could go on the hunt.

It was an abysmal day for stalking. With the weather chilly and dry and the streets around King's Cross clear of all but horse dung, Sherlock's ten-minute lag time may as well have been a year. He sprinted away from Regent's Canal as quickly as he could, for the stench of refuse and paint manufacture made it nigh on impossible to pick out any other odors—though all of King's Cross was heady with smells, not just refuse and paint, but grain and coal, brought here and allowed to fester until they were disbursed throughout the rest of Great Britain.

As for his quarry, Sherlock had precious little to go on. He guessed the man's age to be fifty, and he knew the smoke he favored, for the moment the imposing stranger had stepped out of the railroad car, an errant burst of air had blown the stingy, bitter aroma of Sweet Threes tobacco back inside the car.

But recognizing the blend of Turkish and Virginia weeds that made up his chosen brand did Sherlock little good. He could spot no detritus on the street that matched the man's preference; there was not so much as an extinguished stub on the ground to prove pathways trodden. This made it doubly vexing, for Sherlock had gleaned, from the potency of the whiff he'd taken, that his prey was no casual smoker but a type who used the vice to quiet his nerves, and so would certainly be partaking as he walked.

With a dearth of material clues, Sherlock relied on his memory of the stranger's appearance. The man was of modest, even penurious means, given his clothing and grooming, yet he attempted to keep himself in passable shape, indicated by the brand-new shine of his ancient shoes, his trimmed hair and beard, and the nicks of the razor on his cheeks and neck, no doubt caused by dimming eyesight and a slight tremor in his right hand, which Sherlock had witnessed the first time the big man had nervously wiped his sweaty palms on the lapels of his coat. Such time spent on grooming meant that he still had to put on a public face. He was no common employee but a businessman.

Beyond that, he carried himself with the upright dignity of a former military man. More specifically the arc of the leg, and the slight rolling gait when he walked, pegged him as a veteran cavalryman.

Sherlock had been searching a good long while, finding nothing. He had zig-zagged through one neighborhood after the other, from Agar Town to St. Pancras, past row after row of new but badly constructed dwellings, none with any purpose whatsoever beyond a utilitarian sameness.

Was he really so off the mark in his tracking? He let out a frustrated sigh. He hardly knew King's Cross. In fact, as he pushed through streets and alleyways, he was chagrinned by how little attention he had paid to this section of the city, and he added it to the growing list of quarters he would need to know intimately. He would make it his business to do so.

Finally, in the near distance, on a corner, he spied what he had been searching for all along.

It was a store that sold buttons, along with assorted odds and ends for the household dressmaker, with a small sign that read:

WELLHAM BUTTON EMPORIUM

SINCE 1825

Above the emporium were small lodgings.

It was there that the man resided, Sherlock was certain of it, for his ancient but well-mended waistcoat had sported new and rather costly buttons, of the sort one would wear only if one wished to advertise a business and an occupation. The buttons had been sewn on by an expert hand, and quite securely.

Sherlock noticed that the window on the upper floor had been opened a crack, but that the lit candle on a table by the window was not yet guttered, which meant that the window had not been ajar for long.

He calculated the length of time it would have taken the button man to walk directly home from the station, and then he gauged it against the newly melted wax.

Possible.

The door to the button shop was locked. A dangling sign in the window displayed the weekday hours, but a hastily written addendum said, "closed to-day."

Sherlock looked towards the upper window. He saw a shadow and knew by then that he had been spotted, but that the man who resided there, however put out he might be, would not emerge without some industrious coaxing.

Rather than shy at the challenge, Sherlock felt a sudden rush of exhilaration, along with a burst of rather addictive fearlessness that seemed part and parcel of the hunt. He backtracked to the middle of the street, cupped his hands around his lips and cried out: "Into the jaws of Death! Into the mouth of Hell—Rode the six hundred!"

Then, he listened.

Nothing.

Strangely, it did not matter a whit, for he felt certain that this tactic would work. He had, at long last, found an appropriate use for a tedious bit of literature, and he was not about to be undone by the recalcitrance of his subject.

He redoubled his volume and his efforts:

> *"Cannon to right of them,*
> *Cannon to left of them,*
> *Cannon in front of them,*
> *Volley'd & thunder'd;*
> *Storm'd at with shot and shell,*
> *Boldly they rode and well,*
> *Into the jaws of Death,*
> *Into the mouth of Hell*
> *Rode the six hundred!"*

By the time he was finished, there was no need to strain to listen. Footsteps barreled down the stairs, the front door burst open, and the man hurtled towards him, snarling: "Who *told* you? I will kill them all, kill them where they stand!"

His eyes were bloodshot, his breath rancid from nerves and

bile as he pressed his face two inches from Sherlock's.

"*Who told you?*" he insisted in a hoarse whisper.

"No one!" Sherlock assured him.

"*Then how did you know?*"

Sherlock was unnerved by the intensity he saw in the man's gaze. Clearly, he was a warrior with a bottomless repository of hatred and rage.

Sherlock opened his mouth, but nothing was forthcoming.

"*Who told you?*" the man repeated, grabbing hold of Sherlock's lapel with one large, gnarled, and powerfully strong hand.

"You… were with the 11th Hussars!" Sherlock gasped. "Their badge is in the breast pocket of your waistcoat! I can make out its outline, for it has worn away the fabric where it sits…"

"Liar!" the man declared. "You brayed about the Hussars in the street, before you could see anything at all!"

"No, you are wrong!" Sherlock insisted. "I noticed it aboard the train. You fought at the Battle of Balaclava and you suffer from nerves," he continued. "But you are inured to most sounds, for when the horn blared, or the brakes squealed, you did not flinch. Yet the tenor of your body betrays you, for it is constantly on alert. I thereby assume it is only gunpowder and the flash of steel that disquiet you. I know too that you are a widower—"

Sherlock had barely got that out of his mouth when the man came at him in a blind rage, propelled him to the other side of the street, and pinned him to the wall by his throat.

"Know the details of my life, eh? Track me down like a dog, eh? Give me one good reason I should not kill you where you stand!" he declared as foam began to form at the edges of his lips.

Sherlock tried to speak but could draw no shred of air. Finally, he managed to point and whisper: "The tattoo!"

"What of it!" the man cried. "You are dead, do you hear me? Dead!"

"I… did nothing… to merit it!"

The man's face was so close that Sherlock could see the broken capillaries in his nostrils and cheeks. He squeezed Sherlock's neck as if by instinct, tighter and tighter.

"I did… nothing… to merit… death!" Sherlock croaked.

As if breaking out from a trance, the man let him go.

## 11

SHERLOCK AND THE MAN SAT ON THE STEP OUTSIDE THE
button shop, both of them struggling to remain composed:
Sherlock, because he had been nearly choked into oblivion; the
man, because his life had just been laid bare before him, or so
Sherlock supposed.

"My name is Sherlock Holmes," he said, holding out his
hand.

"Noah Oldacre," the other replied reluctantly, taking it.
"Might I steal a smoke? I have done without since morning—"

"—say no more."

Sherlock removed his pouch and papers from out his pocket
and passed them over.

"You must be the very Dickens to have about," Oldacre
exclaimed as he rolled a cigarette. "What else do you know? And
beware, lest you gull me!"

"I have no reason to gull you," Sherlock replied softly. "But
will you then do me the courtesy of telling me what *you* know of
the Fire Four Eleven Murders?"

Oldacre shrugged, a gesture that in Sherlock's view meant
consent.

"I know you were a cavalryman in the Charge of the Light

Brigade," he began. "I know you saw carnage of the sort that no human should ever be forced to see. I know you keep your regimental badge close to your heart to remind you of the comrades you lost. But I also know you cannot bear the sight of it."

Oldacre sighed deeply, yet with no sense of release. "That is a fact," he said. "I saw men fall all around me. Horses too. We were led like lambs into a slaughter. *'C'est magnifique, mais ce n'est pas la guerre,'*" he quoted. "'It is magnificent, but it is not war.'"

"A certain facility with French. And a stint in the cavalry," Sherlock said. "As I suspected, you come from means. So, how do we reconcile your current circumstances with the formidable expense of a commission and a horse?"

"*You* are the Nostradamus," Oldacre said, as he exhaled smoke. "What is your conjecture?"

"Family estrangement," Sherlock said, and Oldacre nodded.

"Both horse and commission were purchased by my father," he affirmed. "And though my father did quite well in business, his roots as a small-time merchant caused him shame. When I fell in love with the woman who was to become my wife—who happened to be the *daughter* of a small-time merchant—I was disowned. I never laid eyes on my father again."

"My brother Mycroft," Sherlock told him, "was secretary to Edward Cardwell, the Secretary of State for War. It was Cardwell, at my brother's prompting, who ended the tradition of paying for commissions…"

"Bully for him, bully for your brother. Give to him my felicitations when you see him, and tell him it should have ended twenty years ago," Oldacre grumbled. "For it was Lord Cardigan, that incompetent swine, who ordered the Light Brigade to charge, and so caused needless deaths. I hear tell he paid forty thousand pounds for *his* morally bankrupt commission. May he pay it back in Hades." Oldacre placed the cigarette between his lips and wrung his hands, staring at them suspiciously, as if they were a foreign thing. "But you guessed that I am a widower…" he reminded Sherlock, returning to the other conversation. "How?"

"The meal you prepared for yourself for the train ride was put together inexpertly," Sherlock told him, "and you consumed it with little pleasure, as if you are still unused to providing for yourself. And your black cravat is the newest item you own," he continued. "That alone would tell me little, but for the fact that when she died you bought it as a sign of grief. You also removed your wedding ring. Not only can I see the faint circle it made upon your finger, but you've had a decade's-long habit of twirling it, and the thumb and middle finger of your right hand still worry it, fidgeting with nothing.

"When I saw the button shop," Sherlock added, "I assumed 'Wellham' was your surname or else her maiden name; and if the latter, that she eventually inherited the shop. She passed, oh, four or five months ago, I'd say, again judging from the age of the cravat, as well as the fading of the circle on your ring finger."

"Five," Oldacre admitted. "My Meredith was the only reason I awakened in the morning. I do so now by sheer force of habit. And because she would want me to."

"And then there is your tattoo," Sherlock went on, not wishing to be sidetracked by Oldacre's sentimentality. "'PII 21:23–25.' That is a reference to the second book of the Pentateuch, is it not? And to the three verses stipulating that punishment must above all be fair and equitable?"

Oldacre nodded. "Not an eye for an insult, or a life for a theft, but an eye for an eye, a life for a life. A much misunderstood verse…"

"Indubitably," Sherlock agreed. "For it is in fact humane; it stipulates that a punishment should fit the crime."

"I can be rather hot-headed," Oldacre admitted.

*An understatement*, thought Sherlock, *if there ever was one.*

"Meredith," Oldacre explained, "can no longer remind me that violence begets violence—"

"And so, you had it engraved upon your skin," Sherlock finished for him, since he seemed once again reluctant to go on. "For it is fresh."

Oldacre nodded. "On my wrist to stay my hand, as she once did. 'If any mischief follow, then thou shalt give life for life, eye for eye, tooth for tooth, hand for hand, foot for foot, burning for burning, wound for wound, stripe for stripe…'" he quoted. "But, as you have witnessed for yourself, it is not terribly effective. Had you not known what it meant…"

He looked away.

"But I did know," Sherlock said by way of comfort. "Which was why I insisted that I did nothing to deserve death."

"Yes, but *how* did you know?" Oldacre asked.

"I had noticed it on the train and, as I searched for you in the streets, I worked it out. Numbers like that, separated by a dash, are most usually scripture verses. The 'PII' gave me pause, until I realized it referred to the second book of the Pentateuch, and therefore Exodus. And so, you see that your reminder functioned as it was meant to."

Oldacre put out the cigarette, wrapped his arms about his knees, and then concluded with: "I do not know who the killer is. But I was acquainted with one of the victims. The second, Cantwell Squire. He had a secret. A very ugly secret. My fear is that someone who wished to destroy him and his ugly secret… is now killing others merely to point away from the truth."

"But from what I have been able to gather," Sherlock said, "Cantwell Squire was a bachelor, a small-town banker. What sorts of enemies could he possibly—"

"He was not a good man," Oldacre repeated stubbornly. He stood and brushed off the seat of his trousers. "Now I've a business to open."

"Please, might you give me just a bit more—?" Sherlock began, rising along with him.

"Ask, and I shall consider it a threat to my livelihood. But I will repeat what I said upon the train: cease your compulsion to meddle, for it will do no one any good."

*If one disregards future victims*, Sherlock thought.

Oldacre walked up the remaining three steps to the front door, then shut it behind him.

Sherlock stared at the closed door, knowing full well that, for the sake of his own health, he should turn and go. Yet, something goaded him on. He knocked upon the door politely, and was met with bulging, rage-filled eyes.

"You do not know what is good for you!" Oldacre screamed, curling his fist into a ball.

"Mr. Oldacre," Sherlock said in his best compassionate tone. "I am no threat to your livelihood, sir, and neither are these deaths!"

Oldacre stared at him.

"And I can assure you that, whatever else, no one as meticulous as this killer is foolhardy enough to take more than a half-dozen lives to cover up for one! Whatever it is that you know, you have reached the wrong conclusion."

"Leave here, boy, *this moment…*" he warned.

"Mr. Oldacre," Sherlock begged. "Your wife is deceased. She can no longer be hurt, and I shall tell no one!"

"You are a witch!"

Sherlock denied it, not for the first time. "What I do is not black magic, it is logic!" he said. "A man like you, who has lost everything that is precious to him, has nothing else to lose… save the good name of the one whom he has lost. For that is what you are protecting. Your wife's good name. On the mistaken notion that something about this case will sully it. Now, please. What do you know of Cantwell Squire?"

"Squire…" Oldacre said, as if he could not place the name.

He looked away, then at Sherlock again. Finally, he expelled all of his breath at once, as if he had been holding it for an eternity.

"My Meredith had a younger sister. Maude. Squire was once engaged to her. One day, he broke the engagement and left her abandoned in… a delicate condition. Maude died giving birth, and the girl was adopted by a family in Wales."

"The first victim was Squire's illegitimate daughter, then?" Sherlock said, making the connection.

Oldacre nodded. "Rosalie was her name. Rosalie White. You know how a thing like that goes," he said. "Now my wife's family, the Wellhams, they had nothing apart from their business. After the scandal came to light, customers ceased to buy from them. As time went on, the whiff of impropriety lessened. But they never got back to what they were. Now it threatens to come spilling out again, sullying all that it touches."

"And what of Squire? Did he suffer any ill effects?" Sherlock asked.

"Squire simply moved away as if nothing had happened. Still, though he never lifted a finger to help his daughter, I heard that he kept track of her over the years, for she was his sole relation. And Providence paid him back in kind. First, he lost a grandson that he never knew, and then, four days before his own demise, the girl. I pray he suffered every moment of it!"

"Thank you, Mr. Oldacre," Sherlock said. "I can vouchsafe that not a word of this will come out."

"You can, eh? And how do you go about doing a thing like that?"

"Because, as I say, your sorrows have nothing to do with the case at hand."

Oldacre laughed mirthlessly. "Do you not know that people can be cruel for no reason at all? 'The words of a gossip are choice morsels that go down into the inner parts.' It does not have to make sense. People will chew on a juicy morsel until others' lives are ruined."

With that, Oldacre turned, went back inside his shop, and shut the door behind him.

# 12

THREE DAYS LATER, MYCROFT AND DOUGLAS FOUND themselves back in England after a numbing journey that included train, horse, ferry, and quite a bit of shoe leather. For the first time in more than a week, they separated to their own abodes: Douglas to Nickolus House in the Devil's Acre, Mycroft to his semi-detached villa at Greville Place, St. John's Wood.

Upon arrival home, Mycroft dismissed his cab and hauled his own suitcase through the gate and to the front door, simply to prove to his brain and his constitution that he could. That accomplished, he was more than ready to lie down upon his bed and fall into a solid night's sleep.

And so he would've done, had he not been felled by the aroma.

He could smell it before his door was even unlocked, for it wafted through the keyhole directly into his nostrils, as if out of spite. By the time he stepped foot inside, he could make it out in the dim light, clinging to the rafters like a putrid cloud, this blend of tobaccos with not a one of them worth the plucking. Cheap shag. Sherlock's preferred smoke.

"Sherlock!" Mycroft bellowed as he dragged his suitcase

along while waving away the poor housemaid whose sleep he had disturbed.

"Leave it be, damnation!" he grunted as she tried to wrest the thing from out his hand, all the while apologizing that he should have let her know, *if yer please*, what hour he was due back, for she would have anticipated his arrival with a nice warm fire and so forth.

"My *brother*!" Mycroft interrupted, staring daggers at the poor woman. "Where is he? What have you done with him?"

"I have done nothing wiv 'im, sir!" the woman stuttered, offended and alarmed. "Master Sherlock is in his usual room…!"

She pointed up the stairs. "Come the night afore last, sir, Mrs. McAllister thought for certain 'e had your leave, or she would have *never*…"

*Why, that ungrateful little cluck!* Mycroft thought, taking the stairs two at a time while allowing his absurd heart to pound as much as it wished—for he was all but certain that it would pound much more avidly before the night was done.

He tried the door handle, only to find that Sherlock had locked it from the inside.

"Sherlock!" Mycroft bellowed again.

He pounded against the door, all the while acknowledging that it would surely work against his needs; for the angrier he became, the more Sherlock was wont to remain calm and rational, eyebrow arched in surprise, tone steady and diction slow, as if addressing an imbecile.

But Mycroft seemed incapable of controlling his fist; it could have belonged to someone else entirely, for the blows continued unabated.

He heard footsteps on the other side. Then the lock turned and the door opened in one great, welcoming arc.

"Brother! Home at last!" Sherlock announced, his sleepy face crinkled in a rare smile.

"What, in the name of all that is holy," Mycroft began, slamming his suitcase onto the floor, "are you *doing* here?"

Sherlock's face crumpled. His smile disappeared. "My, you appear to be perfectly unsteady upon your feet," he declared. "Perhaps it is best if we chat in the morning."

"No, it is not 'best if we chat in the morning'! What is the meaning of this? *Why are you here?*"

"Come, sit down," Sherlock said solicitously, motioning to the bedroom. "Catch your breath, for the love of heaven, for you are quite done in."

Mycroft could feel his face redden, could feel his fingers go numb as his circulation struggled to stay abreast of his rage. He walked into the bedroom, choking on the pall, moved aside Sherlock's beloved *vielle*, and sat down hard in the Thonet rocker beside the bed.

"You have two minutes to explain why you are not at Downing," he said, keeping the rocker steady as Sherlock turned up the gaslight. "After which I grant you another ten to pack your belongings, as first thing in the morning you will board the early train to Cambridge if I have to drag you there myself!"

"Well," Sherlock said, "that does pose certain logistical dilemmas but never mind; we shall get to those forthwith, for if I have but two minutes, I must use my time judiciously."

Sherlock went to the ashtray where a cigarette burned, took a long puff, let the smoke out, and then slouched against the wall.

"I cannot return to Cambridge," he said evenly. "Certainly not before next term, and possibly never. It seems that the administration was made aware, through an anonymous source, that in the *previous* term someone by the name of Holmes used a chemistry laboratory to whip up various concoctions of a dubious nature and then utilized said concoctions to experiment upon the Quince twins, Eli and Asa. You remember them—"

"*Certainly* I remember them!" Mycroft all but shouted.

"Yes, well, I would think you would—"

"And put out that infernal cigarette!"

"You have but to ask," Sherlock replied, his tone wounded.

He drew on it one final time then extinguished it.

"And I would be ever so grateful if you did not interrupt," he continued, "as you have already limited my time severely. Now as it turns out, experimenting in a chemical sense, however judiciously, upon one's fellow students, appears to be an expellable offense. Something that in my opinion they should elucidate for incoming undergraduates, as it is not a thing one would simply *assume*. The point is, I was asked, perhaps more accurately *ordered*, to leave. At that juncture, I did the noble thing: the moment I arrived in London, I considered your hard-earned money—at least, I suppose it is hard-earned—and pawned my books and what few scraps I had at market value, and now I propose to eventually earn my keep by commencing to do what I do best!"

"And what, I fear, might that be?"

"Sleuthing, brother!" Sherlock replied with a grin. "It seems I am my own iteration of an Inspector Bucket after all. Strange how I fought it for so long, do you recall? That notion of being naught but a lowly detective? When all the while it was my ticket to, if not fame or even visibility, at least *viability*. I do believe that of all the options, it is the best possible one for me.

"There! One minute forty, with twenty to spare!" he announced, checking his watch.

Mycroft's first instinct was to thrash Sherlock to within an inch of his life. But what would it serve? Best to try to have a logical discussion and see what, if anything, could be salvaged from this disaster.

"Sherlock," he began, after inhaling deeply whatever thread of oxygen was left in the room. "There are but three people who are aware of those experiments on the Quinces: you; I, who have said nothing to anyone; and a man currently in prison, for whom confession would only exacerbate his well-deserved but miserable existence."

"I do think of him periodically, you know," Sherlock interjected. "Mostly, I wonder if he can smoke his beloved briar pipe behind bars, or if convicts can partake only of the basest shag, laid out in paper so coarse that it cuts the lips; or in clay pipes yellowed and cracking with the weight of age and overuse—"

"—my point is," Mycroft cut in impatiently, "the 'anonymous source' is you. Is your education really so egregious that you would risk your own good name just to have done with it?"

"Education is beside the point, Mycroft. Neither here nor there. And it is certainly incidental to what I should be studying in order to perfect my skills."

"The sleuthing skills, I suppose," Mycroft said. "But why? I mean to say, why that? Why not, first, proper schooling?"

"Come now, that is akin to asking a fox hound why it does not care to round up sheep, why it is the sound of the bugle and not the 'baa' that entices. I do not know, I cannot say. I can declare only that this is how I am constructed, that it is my constitution. My fate, if you believe in such things. And it does no good preferring that I were this or that or the other."

"Sherlock, be sensible. Unless you propose to join the constabulary, whoever would employ you as a sleuth? And if you cannot make a go of it, a young man of your age and station has no options outside of education or the priesthood—"

"You cannot *possibly* be suggesting—"

"Don't be a ninny. The thought of you as a clergyman is laughable. My point is that you are trained for nothing. And that our particular clan has no business that could absorb you into its bosom. But neither are we of the social stature that you can live your life as a gadabout."

"But I *shall* succeed," Sherlock retorted.

"You cannot know that!" Mycroft protested. "And, even if you could, what would be your lot then, eh? An 'Inspector Bucket,' as you mentioned? That is not in line with what our people do, who we are! I do not mean to be crass, but such a 'profession' is for those of low breeding, with few means and little education."

"But there you are describing me to a T!" Sherlock protested. "Breeding aside, you yourself made it clear that I have no means, and certainly less education than what I should have. As for 'our people,' surely you could not have been speaking of our mother's drug addiction or our father's pathological passivity. For if so, which of those should I emulate?"

Mycroft, battling his own exhaustion and his deep disappointment, took another moment to think. Sherlock had shut the door on Downing, making certain that it could not be undone, at least not before the end of term. Mycroft could always cut off funds as punishment, but Sherlock would find a way to procure just enough for whatever harebrained scheme he concocted next, and he would doubtless put himself in harm's way doing so. And trying to talk him out of his plans once he'd made up his mind was, of course, impossible, for he would not be dissuaded.

"Mycroft, might you cease to rock to and fro? It is giving me nausea."

And, in fact, Mycroft had been rocking avidly enough to have moved positions. He planted his feet upon the ground and said, with renewed determination, "I know this is just your ham-fisted way of trying to follow the Fire Four Eleven Murders."

"Mycroft!" Sherlock exclaimed. "Do not tell me you have kept track of my vulgar predilections?"

"Douglas suggested that the case might interest you," Mycroft admitted. "He guessed that the telegram you sent to the Imperial Hotel was for that very purpose."

"Ah," Sherlock murmured, a shadow crossing his near-handsome face. "Interesting that he should hazard a guess about me that is closer to the mark than yours might be."

*He still remembers that it was Douglas who saved his life, and not I,* Mycroft thought with a pang of hurt and guilt. *He still resents me.*

"So, may I go?" Sherlock asked, hopeful. "Might you come to my aid? Shouldn't cost much; I am training my body to do with a minimum of sleep and sustenance. I have already made quite the remarkable discovery about murders one and two."

Mycroft rose to his feet with a groan, that abomination of a rocker fighting him every inch of the way.

"I am worn to a husk. I need rest," he declared.

"Then shall we talk in the morning?" Sherlock asked— sounding, for just a moment, like a hopeful adolescent.

"No. Quite apart from every other consideration, I cannot have you put yourself in jeopardy. But what we *shall* discuss, in the morning, is where you are to lodge over the summer, how you shall occupy your time, and how I am to insert you into university again next term. If not at Cambridge, then somewhere else. Anywhere else."

Sherlock stared at him blandly, hands folded in his lap, not even deigning to appear the least bit worried about consequences—the little beggar.

"Mycroft, sooner or later you shall have to see it my way, for I warn you in advance that I have no other plans, nor do I mean to unearth any. I am afraid it is this or nothing."

"It might have to be nothing, then," Mycroft said quietly as he closed the door behind him.

# 13

WHEN MORNING CAME, MYCROFT SENT WORD TO DESHI Hai Lin, at his residence in Pimlico, that he and Douglas would accept the charge of finding Bingwen Shi, Lin's future son-in-law. Then he had breakfast with Sherlock; or, rather, Mycroft had breakfast, while Sherlock hardly deigned to glance at the bountiful offerings, though he did appear to be greedy for cocoa. He poured cup after cup, and then asked for more.

"I have been researching chocolate," he explained when Mycroft raised an eyebrow. "Good for brain function, and for the heart, though I have no need of the latter."

"No need of a heart?" Mycroft parried.

Though he did not care for cocoa, Mycroft nonetheless ordered a cup of his own, and drank it to the dregs.

Rather than speak of Sherlock's future, as Mycroft had suggested the night before, they kept to themselves, reading the newspapers: Sherlock his crime columns, Mycroft the world news and financials. It was as if each were waiting for the other to broach the subject, which neither seemed keen to do.

While reading, Mycroft must've made a small noise in his throat, for Sherlock looked up at once.

"Yes…?"

"What? Oh. Nothing. Well, not nothing; it is, in fact, cataclysmic. The failure of the stock market in Vienna is surely a harbinger for England and the United States," he declared, indicating the article he was reading. "But of course, no one wishes to utter a peep, as if silence alone could prevent the demise of—"

He paused when Sherlock yawned.

"Never mind," Mycroft said.

"It is not the conversation," Sherlock replied.

"Isn't it?" Mycroft asked.

"Well, yes, I suppose it is, in the sense that I have nothing of import to add to matters of economy, and so it seems particularly one-sided. But surely you have not 'invested,' or whatever it is that people do, to the extent that *you* might be adversely affected by this downturn?" he added, suddenly looking concerned.

Mycroft was about to reply that, no indeed, he had not invested in any losing propositions, and that Sherlock's paltry needs were but a drop in the ocean of his bank account. But that would have entailed sharing his economic status. Sherlock was the last person to whom he wished to divulge any youthful indiscretions that may have resulted in his present fortune.

"So far, so good," he replied vaguely.

Sherlock disappeared behind his columns, and Mycroft behind his. A moment later, Sherlock's two fingers appeared at the top of Mycroft's paper, pushing it down until they were eye to eye.

"How is it possible that you have not yet noticed that the Fire Four Eleven murderer has claimed a tenth victim?" he demanded.

"Perhaps because I have not yet perused the crime columns!" Mycroft replied in his defense.

"It is on the front page! Of the very paper that you now hold in your hands! I can see it from here!"

Mycroft took a look at the front page. "A tenth victim? I gather there is more within?"

"No! That is the infuriating part. There must be a reason."

"Perhaps they do not have enough facts?"

"A reporter arrives, pad and pen in hand. *There* is the location. *There* is the body. *There* is the subject, male or female, along with an age. Then, if one does his job even passably, *there* is the position of the body; the means of disposal, if visible; the hour of demise, if noted. Surely it is not so difficult!"

"Sherlock, keep your voice down, there is nothing to shout about…"

"Details? Ha! None! Nonexistent!" Sherlock continued. "Neither location nor gender of the victim is provided, much less time of day! I know more about victim number four, Bart Swinton, aged fourteen, from Glasgow—which is *all* I know of him—than I do of this latest!"

"Swinton? Well, there you are!" Mycroft said. "The Swintons are an old line of feudal barons. No doubt many of the locals are employed by them, and are too needful of their employment to speak out of turn—"

"Well there *you* are! You are making my point!" Sherlock exclaimed.

"I am making no one's point," Mycroft protested. "And you are much too involved!"

"I am going for a walk."

With that, Sherlock excused himself from the breakfast table and marched out, paper still in hand.

Mycroft barely had a quarter hour's peace when one of the Queen's equerries arrived at the door, with a note.

*Mr. Holmes,*

*We desire a brief conference this afternoon at 2. Inform my equerry if that is amenable, and a carriage shall be sent for you at the proper hour.*

*Victoria R.*

Mycroft wondered if perhaps she wished to discuss Austria's collapse. But then why such short notice? He asked the housemaid to draw him a bath and went upstairs to his wardrobe, but he could not find what he was searching for.

"Ah, there you are, Mrs. McAllister," he said when the housekeeper replied to his ring. "Have you seen my latest purchase from New & Lingwood?"

"I have indeed, sir," she said. "It is being pressed. Shall I go and fetch it?"

"If you would… But why is it being pressed when I have only just purchased it?"

Mrs. McAllister swallowed and glanced at the floor. "I believe that Master Sherlock may've borrowed it."

"He's gone nowhere! For what?"

"When I… came upon him, he informed me that he was testing various fabrics, sir, to see what odor they emit when burned. Apparently, 'a silk warp with a weft of worsted yarn' emits a very particular odor."

"He *burned* my *shirt*?" Mycroft exclaimed.

"No, sir, no! A small singe at the hemline! Hardly noticeable, easily repaired!"

Mrs. McAllister looked so woebegone that Mycroft gave her leave to go. As she was exiting, Sherlock appeared, still holding the newspaper, and began to pace about.

"What do you mean by burning my shirts?" Mycroft demanded.

"I burned nothing. I *singed* a tiny, insignificant piece of—"

"Why does everyone seem to think that singeing shirts is insignificant?" Mycroft shot back. "You have been here but a few days, and already even the servants' standard for decent behavior has plummeted!"

"I saw the Queen's equerry drive off. Has she sent for you?" Sherlock demanded.

"Surely that is not an uncommon occurrence," Mycroft replied, baffled. "What of it?"

"This! This!" Sherlock bellowed, slapping the newspaper into the palm of his hand with equal parts elation and outrage.

"I cannot hear the litany again," Mycroft warned.

A knock upon the door, and Mrs. McAllister returned with the shirt. She handed it to Mycroft as if she'd been personally culpable of setting it on fire.

"I must get ready," Mycroft began.

"No one is stopping you," Sherlock said in a huff, clearly intending to remain precisely where he was.

Mycroft decided against the bath, discarded his robe and put on the shirt, taking care to button it before he turned around again so that Sherlock would not notice the scar upon his chest.

"Clearly, it is a conspiracy," Sherlock muttered.

"If you must continue to stand about and be a nuisance, make yourself a useful nuisance at least," Mycroft said as he handed Sherlock his cravat. Once in a while, Mycroft would experience odd symptoms, such as tingling fingers, and at the moment he was having a difficult time with his tie.

"Chin up!" Sherlock commanded as he worked. "Do you not see how I am needed?"

"Tying ties, you mean? Yes, perhaps you could become a valet, if you were not so impatient."

"I am not in the mood for your juvenile humor, Mycroft. This is a serious matter."

"How could you be needed if there is no story?"

"No story as *yet*, you mean. Even you, the eternal skeptic, must find it odd that this 'non-story' would emerge at this particular juncture!"

"What— Sherlock! Loosen it up slightly, it is a cravat, not a garrote! What particular juncture are you referring to?"

Sherlock sighed, as if the answer were obvious. "Three hours after the paper's release, the Queen asks of your availability. Sends a carriage to fetch you—"

"Yes, for that is what she stated that she would, in fact, do."

"Clearly, whoever perished must be of some import to her, so as to merit this combination of circumspection and haste! *There!*" he exclaimed with a flourish.

Mycroft eyed the cravat. His younger brother, who in the past several months had begun to grow punctilious about his own wardrobe, had tied the thing lopsided.

"Look," Mycroft said, "if there *were* some remote connection between Her Majesty and this haphazard killer, she possesses her own police force. She would not need *me*. Besides, I am neither interested in, nor am I adept at, such plebeian endeavors."

"Fine. Then might we make a small wager?" Sherlock said as Mycroft placed his watch into the pocket of his waistcoat and headed for the door. "If I am correct, and this audience has to do with the murders, you will bring me on as a consultant and pay me a living wage. If not—"

"If not, you shall never broach the subject again. Not ever. Not this mystery, nor any other cockamamie 'mystery' that might follow in this one's wake. And you shall pass the summer in suitable and safe employment, as a clerk somewhere, and when the new term begins at Downing, provided I can persuade them to take you back, you shall remain there until you are well and fully educated."

"Ah. And here I thought you were so brilliant," Sherlock said, smiling. "Then you go and make such a poor wager as this?"

With that, Sherlock stepped out and went down the hall to his own room. A moment later, Mycroft could hear him playing upon his *vielle*, a little ditty that sounded—as did everything that came out of the *vielle*—vaguely medieval. And he wished with all his heart that Sherlock were not such a strange bird. For life tended to be less kind to those who did not quite fit in.

# 14

IT TOOK NEARLY THREE HOURS TO TRAVEL BETWEEN St. John's Wood and Windsor Castle. The spring afternoon was chilly and gray, all the better to set off the myriad greens of the massive grounds, and the honey-colored Bagshot Heath stone of the palace. Though altered here and there over the years, it was still 'an exceeding profitable and commodious spot,' as William the Conqueror had once described it—and indeed it was one of Mycroft's favorite works of architecture in all of England.

He attempted to keep his focus on the architecture, rather than upon the jumbled thoughts that leapt through his mind, including, oddly enough, food.

His appetite, which had been beggarly for more than a year, had returned with a vengeance. It was all he could do to not think of eating every moment. He lay a hand on his abdomen to assure himself that he had not put on weight, and indeed he had not.

*Not yet*, he mused. *But the sedentary lifestyle does not bode well…*

Even so, he could not help but to smile a little. A few months before, he hadn't expected to have any sort of a life, never mind a lifestyle. And although it would probably not be long enough to permit him a family, the sudden concern about a growing belly seemed a peculiar blessing.

The carriage halted, and he alighted at Windsor Castle's south range, near the tower. From there, he was ushered into the Queen's private audience room, where Prince Albert himself had supervised the decor. Above his head, surrounding a chandelier so long that it reached nearly to the top of the door frame, was a high and elaborately decorated plaster ceiling cove that bore the bas-relief busts of English rulers from William the Conqueror to the Queen herself. The walls were covered in a trellis pattern, over which St. George rode majestically upon horseback. It was lovely, but also a bit dizzying; and Mycroft realized not for the first time—Bagshot stone notwithstanding—how unadorned and almost severe his own tastes tended to be.

The Queen was late, as usual, and Mycroft tried not to fret. Attempting to talk to her about the economy, however essential, was a losing proposition unless she herself brought it up. As for the rest, he'd already had a few indications that he might lose his wager with Sherlock, specifically from two display cabinets on either side of the door. Inside were miniature portraits of various royal relatives, from watercolors to enamels and plumbago drawings, but their alignment and order were altogether wrong.

Before he could explore further, the Queen made her entrance. Mycroft turned and bowed. Victoria did not extend her hand, as was her habit, but stood rather stiffly with them cupped at her waist. A slight nod of her head shooed away the secretary who'd accompanied her. Then she sat at a small sofa while indicating a lyre-shaped chair across from it.

Mycroft did as commanded, leaning slightly forward so he did not sink into the too-soft cushion.

"Mr. Holmes," she said, appraising him. "You appear less pale than the last time we spoke."

"Thank you, Your Majesty."

"Make no mistake, you have always been well put together, but for a while we did fear for your health."

"Again, Ma'am, I thank you for your concern," Mycroft replied, anxious lest she continue to pursue the topic. Thankfully, she did not. Instead, she glanced over at the cold hearth.

"Forgive the lack of fire," she said. "There are times when we cannot bear the heat, and this is one. We hope it is not too drafty for you."

"The temperature is quite pleasant, Ma'am," he said amiably, though in fact he was feeling unpleasantly warm, and it had nothing to do with the atmosphere. Simply put, his mind was elsewhere. He was strategizing a compromise with Sherlock that would not get the lad killed.

The Queen's foot rubbing slightly against the carpet brought his mind back to full focus. Queen Victoria was more adept at hiding her feelings than was the average person, male or female. Even so, there were indicators over which she had less control. Mycroft had met with her enough times to have calculated how often these involuntary movements occurred: swallowing, blinking, or drawing in air, and what they might portend. It was clear that she was unnerved.

"Now, Mr. Holmes," she said. "We have a rather delicate situation at hand. One that perhaps… well, never mind that— did you happen to read the paper this morning? Specifically, *The Globe*?"

"I did, Ma'am," Mycroft admitted, feeling like she had just thrown a spade full of sod onto his grave.

"You would think that the editor, Armstrong, being fond as he is of Mr. Disraeli, would be equally fond of *me*," she fumed. "But no. And so they have published another entry about the Fire

Four Eleven," she continued. "By the by, have you any notion to what those three words refer?"

"None at all, Ma'am."

"Knowing your brilliant mind, I can only assume that is due to a lack of interest, Mr. Holmes, which is exceedingly unfortunate in this case."

Mycroft said nothing, so she went on.

"We have been able to keep the identity of the last deceased from the newspapers, even *The Globe*, but we cannot do so indefinitely. Now, before we make our dilemma known to you, perhaps you have already an inkling as to what it might entail, for we are quite familiar with the sorts of soothsaying you perform."

"I assure you I am no soothsayer, Ma'am. I utilize pure logic. That said, I understand that speaking the name of the deceased out loud might cause you grief. I shall therefore endeavor to tell you what I have assessed from my visit thus far."

"We would be most grateful, Mr. Holmes, both to enjoy the mechanisms of your brain, and because it is far from a pleasant subject, and so it is preferable that you discuss it, rather than we."

"Yes, Ma'am. Now, of all the rooms in which you and I have met, this one is intended for friends and distant relations, rather than for government officials. I assume, therefore, that the issue before us is not a matter of state. And, because of our rather long and profitable association, as well as my loyalty to the Crown, I should think you would be able to trust me with *any* request, whether personal or political. Yet, this one created, if I may be so bold, a certain anxiety in you, Ma'am. Therefore, I can only conclude that there is something about it that you assume will not be pleasing to me. Do I have that about right, Ma'am?"

"Go on," she said, hardly looking at him.

"There is but one person in the royal family, and so related to you by blood, Ma'am," Mycroft continued, "of whom I am not fond. Count Wolfgang Hohenlohe-Langenburg. Your first cousin, Ma'am."

"I am quite aware who he is, Mr. Holmes," she responded archly.

"And, since the count has no living relatives on his father's side," Mycroft went on, "and any relative on his mother's side would also be related by blood to the Crown and would therefore not necessitate a link back to him…"

Queen Victoria cleared her throat in a manner that intimated a warning.

"Yes, Mr. Holmes. We can see that you have no need of an encyclopedia of reference and that your prodigious memory knows no bounds. We were, as you surmised, reluctant to broach this particular subject because of your animus, however deserved, for our cousin. Now, although we realize that, by our indulging in this little guessing game, we brought this upon ourselves, we suggest you tread lightly from here on."

"Thank you, Ma'am, I shall try," Mycroft replied with a slight bow of his head. "What I seek now, therefore, is a person related to the count but not, strictly speaking, to you—which leaves me but one choice. The count's stepdaughter, Elise Wickham."

The Queen suddenly lost her coloring, so much so that Mycroft very nearly offered to come to her aid before thinking the better of it. Instead, he sat perched at the edge of his chair, waiting for her to regain her breath and her composure.

"Yes, it is Elise," she admitted in a small voice. She is, or was, the daughter of the count's wife Anne and her deceased first husband, William."

Mycroft nodded. "As I waited for our appointment, I noticed that the miniatures in the curio cabinets were placed according to type: plumbagos first, then enamels, and finally watercolors. All the watercolors were neatly equidistant, except for two. I therefore surmised that one had gone missing. But surely a missing portrait, regardless of circumstance, would have quickly been replaced, or the others rearranged. Unless it had been removed from its case, and recently, by someone with full authority to do so. You yourself removed it, Ma'am. In your folded hands is a miniature watercolor of the girl, Elise," he declared, pointing.

When the Queen said not a word but stared at him with those unblinking blue eyes, he continued: "You wished to show me her likeness. Not because you thought I would refuse any request of yours, but because the girl's amiability might make me more disposed to be of service."

The Queen unfolded her fingers like petals to reveal the miniature she held inside.

It was of a girl in her late teens, with a pleasant if ordinary face, and light hair and eyes, her head at a slight angle, her eyes fixed upon the painter who was at the time immortalizing her likeness.

"Pretty," Mycroft said, not altogether meaning it, for she had a vapid look that reminded him somewhat of Sherlock's friends, the Quince boys. "Because your cousin has long been estranged from his wife, I further speculate that he does not yet know of his stepdaughter's demise, and that you, Ma'am, were hoping I might have more news to impart before he is so informed."

"Well," the Queen said with all the finality the word could conjure. "You are quite the unique character, Mr. Holmes. We are grateful to you for taking this on."

"It is my duty and my pleasure to serve, Ma'am. How long has it been since you saw the girl?"

"A long time. Her mother Anne and my cousin were together but a few years and have been separated for many more. And you? Still unmarried, Mr. Holmes?"

"Yes, Ma'am," he replied.

"Good. I do not at all consider it a misfortune when people are unmarried. For I think unmarried people are often very happy. Though I cannot say that you look happy, Mr. Holmes."

Mycroft smiled weakly and changed the subject.

"When did you first meet the girl, Ma'am?" he asked.

"The first time Elise came to visit," the Queen replied, "she must have been four, for I do not approve of smaller children traipsing about; I find them rather dreary. And the last time, she must've been six, a quiet child, well behaved. She sent that likeness just last year, to remember her by, she said."

The Queen clearly felt the emotion of it, for her small round chin quivered before she went on.

"Now, we do not wish, nor do we encourage, any contact between yourself and our cousin, the count. It seems the unexpected and unimagined collapse of the Austrian economy left him in quite a state, one from which he has not yet recovered."

*Neither unexpected nor unimagined*, Mycroft thought, *had you but listened.*

"He is at a sanatorium in Switzerland," the Queen continued, "where he shall remain until he is ready to join society again."

Mycroft assumed that the count was not suffering from weak nerves but from a weak spine. Most likely, he was hiding from his principal creditor, Vizily Zaharoff, which was the only detail of this sordid matter that held any interest for Mycroft at all.

"May I ask who found the girl, Ma'am?"

"Her mother, from what we gather. A terrible discovery for a parent to have to make. Late afternoon yesterday. And this lack of contact on your part," she added, reverting to her former train of thought, "must extend perforce to his family, in particular to his estranged wife, Anne. No one must speak to her of this, and that includes you."

"Well, Ma'am, as she is the best eyewitness to her daughter's state, and as the murder is a mystery to be solved, that makes it tricky."

"Your mind works in tricky ways, Mr. Holmes, and you have other victims' families from which to choose. You have my blessing to question them to a fare-thee-well."

Mycroft nodded, for he knew he would not win this one. "Thank you, Ma'am. And may I say how very sorry I am for your loss."

"Thank *you*, Mr. Holmes," Queen Victoria replied. "Among the astute observations you have made thus far, we were beginning to despair that you would ever get around to that particular human sentiment."

Mycroft could feel himself blush. "My zeal occasionally sidesteps my manners, Ma'am," he said.

"At the moment your zeal is more valuable than your manners, although it surely cannot hurt to possess both." She drew a long breath. "Now, can it be true what I've heard, that you are doing without a driver at present? Quite the odd time to dismiss one, just as the weather grows milder, and jaunts abroad become a pleasant diversion, but never mind. Though we are aware that you have no need of financial support, the Crown insists on paying all expenses, and that shall include a carriage and driver. I want this solved, Mr. Holmes. At the earliest. We cannot have a murderer traipsing about, thinking he can kill members of our household with impunity. And I would like him caught not just because he is bold, but because he is clearly heartless."

"Might I take on a few assistants?" Mycroft inquired. "My friend Cyrus Douglas, with whom you are acquainted—"

"You are certain that is wise?"

"In what way, Ma'am?"

"He does attract commentary, does he not?"

The Queen let her deeper meaning hang in the air between them, and Mycroft wondered not for the first time if Douglas, notable accomplishments notwithstanding, would ever be seen for much beyond the color of his skin.

"I take no issue with secrecy, Ma'am," he replied evenly. "But I find that, upon occasion, the opposite technique is just as effective; one's foes know that one is coming for them, and in their desire to get away begin to make mistakes. But, as it so happens, the second man I mean to assume is keen to pursue justice in a more clandestine manner. I refer to my brother Sherlock."

"You have a *brother*, Mr. Holmes? Good heavens. Is he anything like you?"

Mycroft sighed.

"I fear that he is, Ma'am."

Queen Victoria stared at him, almost disbelieving, after which she allowed herself the smallest hint of a smile.

# 15

SHERLOCK HAD LEARNED THAT WHEN PURSUING A LEAD, it was best to ignore voices to the contrary… even if one of those voices happened to belong to the brother in whose abode he was currently lodged. He had spent the better part of the afternoon securing his Gray's map—on which he had traced the trajectory of the murders—to the wall of the guest bedroom at Greville Place. Nearby each location, with the use of straight pins, he had attached a note with the name, age, and occupation, if any, of each of the victims.

On another note beside the first were listed time of death, and whatever details could be had from various newspapers. He'd also used balls of yarn in various hues to create possible links from this card to that. Victims under eighteen years of age, for example, were united by yellow yarn, which the label on the ball called 'munsel'; females were linked with 'blush'; males with royal blue; professionals with forest green, and so forth.

There was the newfound link between Rosalie White of Wales, and victim number two, Manchester banker Cantwell Squire. Sherlock had debated sharing the information with Mycroft, finally erring on the side of caution. Mycroft would no doubt think him foolhardy for having placed himself in harm's way, thereby lessening any chance that he would be allowed to pursue the case further.

He stepped back and admired his creation, as glorious to his eye as any work of art, all the while tracing the lines on the map for the thousandth time.

Who knows for how long the man had stalked his first victim, twenty-eight-year-old widow Rosalie White, before he murdered her? It could have been days, weeks. She had been killed sometime before ten-thirty in the morning, for it was then that an old man walking his dog had spotted her body hunched over on the sand. She had been on her knees and had fallen forward. There were no footprints leading away from her, and the only prints leading to her were her own. In a different environment, the weight of her body would have catapulted her to one side or the other. But the wet sand had formed a sort of wedge for her head, holding her corpse in the position of a Middle Eastern supplicant.

Her purported father, sixty-year-old banker Cantwell Squire of Manchester, was murdered in his own home between eight and eleven on the morning of Saturday, 5th of April. He had been found in his bed by his housekeeper, face down in his breakfast tray, the 'Fire Four Eleven!' note lying over the biscuits.

A seven-year-old boy named Will Jury had been felled in his garden while playing with his dog. The killing of a child seemed to Sherlock to be more a matter of waiting, perhaps not beyond a day or two, for the right opportunity, for—apart from walks to school and back—a child could not be counted upon to adhere to routines, and certainly not in a garden, unless compelled to do so. Jury's mother had come home to find the dog anxiously licking the boy's inert face. The note had appeared in the garden three days later, on the spot where his body had been found.

Why three days? Had the killer perhaps attempted to leave it but the dog had kept him at bay? But whether then or later, how could he deposit the note without also leaving prints? In any event, he did so and then arrived in Glasgow with time enough to kill fourteen-year-old Bart Swinton, of whom nothing was yet known… other than he came from a family who could hush up his murder.

On Monday, 14th of April, the killer struck again, his victim Phillip Rider, chaplain of middle years from Plymouth. All but impoverished, Rider had been dusting books in his rented room when he'd succumbed. The note had been left upon the desk that faced his open window. At noon, his landlady, who lived upstairs, heard a crash. It turned out to be his body colliding with the floor. No stalking required there, simply opportunity.

But the sixth victim, elderly barrister George Greyson, had been taking an early morning stroll. A man of past eighty would hardly alter his routine from day to day. Still, it could have required several days' watching until Greyson happened upon a secluded spot with no witnesses.

As for thirty-year-old Percy Butcher, the proprietor of a stable, his habits were formed by his work and could be easily discerned. He had been grooming a brood mare. The note was found inside the stall, though the newspaper account did not say where, or specify a time beyond midday, and the date, Friday, 25th of April.

The eighth occurred four days later, in Kingston upon Hull. As had been repeated *ad nauseam* in the press, ten-year-old Abigail Sykes had been at the kitchen table, learning a song. No note had been found at the time but had appeared on the 1st of May, when the servants and family were all away, attending her funeral. Then there was the ninth victim, Penny Montgomery of Chichester, killed on the 8th of May.

Those who had been murdered before noon were connected, on Sherlock's board, by yarn labeled 'sunrise,' while magenta was reserved for those victims whose notes were found later.

All but three—Will Jury, Percy Butcher and George Greyson—had fallen forward. Young Jury had been found upon his back. Butcher and Greyson had crumpled to one side: though none of the papers reported which side, as if that detail were wholly incidental. Could Penny Montgomery have also been an exception? News accounts had not been clear in that regard. None of the victims had any signs of trauma from the attack itself, though Abigail Sykes was found to have splinters on the back of her neck, purportedly from the kitchen table.

Sherlock returned to the second victim, banker Cantwell Squire. So as to make the smallest bit of headway, he had to assume certain facts. For instance, that the bed had a headboard, and that the headboard had been situated against a wall—a most typical state. Given those parameters, there was no earthly way that the impact of the blow could have originated from the back of Squire's head. Which further meant that said impact had no bearing on the trajectory of the body, for Squire had fallen forward.

It was maddening that he could not examine the headboard to see if it had sustained trauma, if Squire's head had ricocheted off of it before dropping.

He was busy pinning another piece of yarn from one spot to another when he heard a timid knock upon his bedroom door. He ignored it, but it occurred again, and then a third time.

"Enter!" he commanded.

The door opened to reveal the housekeeper, Mrs. McAllister, squinting. Sherlock realized that the room had grown dark and that he had quite neglected to put on a light. When she continued peering about like a half-blind owl, Sherlock prompted: "How can I help you, Mrs. McAllister?"

The woman squared her shoulders and declared, as if reading a proclamation: "Master Sherlock. I am here on behalf of Gladys—"

"Sorry, I am not acquainted with—"

"—the housemaid, sir. She is at sixes and sevens, for she claims you molested her skeins!"

"I did... what?"

"Molested her skeins, sir. Her balls of yarn! And pilfered her straight pins to boot. And indeed, there they are!" she added very nearly triumphantly, pointing to his creation on the wall. "Master Sherlock, we simply cannot have sewing baskets rummaged through—!"

"Mrs. McAllister, I will gladly pay for new straight pins and... and *skeins*," he interrupted, but Mrs. McAllister cried out:

"The flock!"

"Pardon?"

"The pins have ruined it!" she declared. "Do you see there? The flock is ruined!"

Sherlock sighed. "Nonsense, Mrs. McAllister. They are straight pins, not spikes. Surely the flock has survived worse catastrophes."

"But Mr. Holmes had it made especially," she explained piteously. "*Le Pais de Sérénité*... direct from Paris!"

"That is a greater condemnation of the Parisians than of the straight pins," he said. "And if there is permanent damage done to the wallpaper, I shall make restitution to my brother. Now. Is there anything else?"

It was clear to Sherlock that Mrs. McAllister had more to add, much more, but that she could not very well ride roughshod over her employer's brother. With as much dignity as she could muster, she answered, "No, sir, that is all," and then ducked back out, shutting the door behind her.

"Bother," Sherlock grumbled under his breath before resuming his work.

Mycroft had barely opened his front door when he was assailed by his housekeeper with some convoluted tale about flock and pins and skeins.

"No, Mrs. McAllister, I do not fault your reaction," he assured her, which was quickly followed by: "Yes, Mrs. McAllister, you were perfectly within your rights to come to the aid of staff."

This as he went upstairs, Mrs. McAllister in his wake, all the while wondering what new calamity Sherlock had inflicted upon the household.

Sherlock's door was ajar. His back was to the door, and he was lighting a lamp. On the far wall Mycroft noticed a hodgepodge, as if one toddler had set about to do English embroidery while another dabbled in Japanese art.

Mycroft turned and smiled at the whey-faced Mrs. McAllister behind him. "It is quite all right," he said, "I shall take it from here."

The moment she departed, Sherlock turned to Mycroft and grinned. "So? When do I start?" he said.

"That all depends," Mycroft said, "on how soon you will cease to gloat."

"Am I indeed to begin?" he asked, the grin replaced by awe.

"Yes. With certain stipulations."

"Anything. But first, come in. Come in and sit. And tell me all you know," Sherlock prompted eagerly.

Mycroft deftly avoided the rocker, making a beeline for a straight-back chair. Sherlock perched himself on the edge of the nearby desk and hovered over him like a raptor while Mycroft repeated what he had been told by the Queen.

"Bledlow?" Sherlock repeated, puzzled, when informed of the location. "I have investigated the names of all of the other towns and have come up wanting, but there is something in this name, something familiar…"

"You recall it solely because you studied it in fourth or fifth form, and—given your proclivities—it made an impression upon you," Mycroft said. "The Doomsday Book records the original name as 'Bledelai,' or 'Bloody Hill.'"

"Yes!" Sherlock cried.

"No," Mycroft countered. "Though evocative, it has to do with some musty battle between Danes and Saxons, the details of which are not important to your research. For I doubt that even your punctilious murderer could hold quite so ancient a grudge."

Sherlock bit his lower lip and nervously chewed upon his thumbnail. "Did you enquire if there was anyone who could profit from Elise's death?" he asked.

"Of course, and no," Mycroft said. "Neither her mother, nor the count, from whom her mother is estranged, nor any relatives near or far, stand to gain a sou. She died just outside of Bledlow," he continued. "Her mother's people owned a mill, they have a small ancestral home there which the mother inherited, and the girl lived with her. Eighteen years of age and just completed her education. Given family connections through her stepfather, she was expected to make a decent enough match, though there was not yet a groom upon the horizon. At the time of her death she was in the garden, on a swing, reading a book."

"Rather a prosaic ending, no?" Sherlock opined.

"Not so prosaic. When she fell forward, the swing hit her on the back of the neck with such force that the cradle cracked in two," Mycroft said.

"Truly? But that makes no sense whatsoever," Sherlock complained. "Who rides a swing so violently while reading?"

"Precisely. I assume that the killer, after attacking her in whatever manner he did, pushed the swing into her neck so as to hide something. Perhaps, unlike the others, he had left a mark on her, one that would bring us closer to understanding mode of death."

"I see. I am to assume, therefore," Sherlock said, "that, other than the blow to the back of the neck, there were no other marks on her?"

"Skinned knees from the fall," Mycroft replied with a shrug. "But no."

"What about marks on the grass? Footprints and the like?"

"How would the Queen be apprised of that, Sherlock?"

Sherlock drew a breath. "So I am really to do this?" he asked again in a small voice.

"As I said, with stipulations."

"Such as...?" Sherlock hopped off the edge of the desk and began shifting his weight from one foot to the other. "Because, if you don't mind my saying," he went on, "you appear to be altogether too sanguine about all of this. What makes you thus? Another mystery, perhaps? One that is more to your liking? Does my involvement free you from your obligation to the Queen? Oh, it is perfectly fine with me if that is the truth of it, for I am gratified that you would place such trust in me."

"I know that you are capable of this, Sherlock," Mycroft said. "The stipulations all involve your safety. I would rather not see you hurt."

"I shall not be, I can all but guarantee it!" Sherlock went to his wall chart. "You see here? There is a pattern to the killer's victims, and he is much too methodical to go half-cocked and murder someone who does not fit his parameters. For it would sully whatever point he is attempting to convey."

"Ah. And what are his parameters?" Mycroft asked. "For I cannot make them out."

Sherlock shrugged. "Nor can I," he confessed. "Not yet; but that is what I aim to find out! Brother, you will not regret this," he added, his face creasing into a grin again. "It is the start of a whole new life for me!"

# 16

THAT NIGHT, MYCROFT AND DOUGLAS SAT AT THE TABLE in the homely kitchen at Nickolus House, drinking a proper glass of brandy in proper brandy glasses. The Baccarat was a gift from Mycroft; the Cognac hailed from Douglas's shop. Mycroft had once shamed him for keeping nothing but swill in the cupboards, and Douglas was determined to have something better on hand for his friend's visits.

He poured another round of the Maison Gautier XO. Mycroft inhaled the heady aroma and continued his tale of the Queen, and her unexpected involvement in the Fire Four Eleven Murders.

"As with the others, the girl, Elisc, was found with not a mark upon her."

"I wonder," Douglas mumbled.

"Why, Douglas!" Mycroft exclaimed, smiling. "Do I detect a note of suspicion in your voice?"

"Why should my being suspicious make you giddy? I mean only that in these remote locales, neither the coroner, if there is one, nor local law enforcement has a great deal of practice with murder. Is it possible that the means of death could have been visible all along, albeit not to them?"

"Not only possible but probable," Mycroft admitted. "But

since all have been buried, no use crying over spilt milk, as it were."

Douglas lifted his brow in surprise. "Elise has not been buried, has she?"

"No, but her funeral is to be a quiet affair two days from now, and the Queen will allow nothing but the most cursory examination."

"How do you know?"

"Because I asked."

"Mycroft, really!" Douglas exclaimed.

"What social *faux pas* did I commit now?"

"Well, for mercy's sake, the girl was related to her, however obliquely," Douglas said. "The Queen cared enough about her to keep her portrait—"

"Oh, I see what you are jawing on about! What was I to do, Douglas; allow an appropriate time of mourning to elapse and then send Victoria a monogrammed note, requesting an autopsy? It is never pleasant to be asked."

"No. It is not," Douglas said quietly.

He had been required to do just that for his late wife and son, to ensure that they had indeed been killed in a riot by an angry mob, and not by some other, less dramatic means. It was a detail of his life, one of the few, of which Mycroft was not aware, for there was no reason to cause anyone else pain.

"I have mentioned, have I not, that Sherlock shall be holding the reins of this?" Mycroft asked.

"I believe you went out of your way to *not* mention it until now," Douglas said. "Why on earth would you put your only brother in such jeopardy?"

Mycroft sighed and poured himself a glass of Cognac, his third. "I did tell you that I came home to find 'my only brother' ensconced in the guest quarters," Mycroft replied. "That he cleverly found a way to get himself expelled from Downing, without my being able to remedy it. Oh, and have you *met* my only brother? Surely you know by now that he shall find a way to pursue this, whether I allow it or not! And unless you have a better notion as to what to do with him, I do not need guilt heaped upon guilt."

"A better notion as to what to *do* with him?" Douglas repeated. "No, surely I do not. Sherlock remains an enigma to me. Forgive me. You care for him; I assume you know best."

"Nonsense. I know no such thing," Mycroft grumbled. "What I *do* know is that you and I will pursue the disappearance of Bingwen Shi and allow Sherlock to do a preliminary investigation of the Fire Four Eleven Murders. I believe he needs to feel that this is *his* case, not mine, and I would rather wait to participate until such a time as our presence is needed. And, since the Queen is set on providing our carriage and expenses—"

Douglas smiled incredulously. "You mentioned that I was going along?"

"Well of course I did," Mycroft exclaimed, a touch defensively. "Why wouldn't I?"

"Oh, I can think of several reasons..."

"As I was saying," Mycroft continued, "since Her Majesty is set on providing for the two of us, I shall give Huan the assignment of driver and bodyguard to Sherlock—or shall you find fault with that idea as well?"

"Not at all. It is the wisest decision you have made yet. Huan is the best protector I can think of. So long as he does not murder Sherlock in his sleep, all should go swimmingly. I take it that he is on his way back from Port of Spain?"

"Day after tomorrow," Mycroft assented with a nod.

"Ah, he sails on the *Countess*, then," Douglas said immediately. For he was familiar with the course of every ship that hailed from the Caribbean. "Superb accommodations. That was kind of you, Mycroft."

"I have my moments," his friend said.

Douglas paused. "Will Sherlock go along with the plan? He will not be pleased to go about in a fancy carriage with Huan as his nursemaid when trains would be quicker and more convenient."

"Oh indeed, it shall prove more cumbersome, but that is the point: to tarry the entire process, while making certain that he cannot easily give Huan the slip. He also asked that I facilitate contact with the police, especially if they or the local coroner still have the body when he arrives."

"What is there to examine when there are no marks?" Douglas asked. "And surely any familiar poisons would have been revealed by now. Besides, *can* you facilitate such visits?"

"I have a passing acquaintance with *one* coroner. He works in London and environs, so if the murderer strikes close by, I might have a shot. Otherwise, to whom would I request this favor, and what would I say? 'My nineteen-year-old brother, who was expelled from Cambridge one month before the end of term, and who has no formal training in either medicine or police work, would like to examine your most publicly sensitive corpse'?"

"Surely *you* could gain access, if you tried. Did he ask?"

"Of course not. The last thing Sherlock wants is for me to get the glory, even a portion thereof. Which factors in perfectly, for I do not wish to traipse about, ogling bodies."

The two sat for a moment in the stillness that can sometimes transpire between long-time friends, but to Douglas it felt brittle, for he had a query that he could no longer hold back.

"Tell me, since you are so fond of the Queen," Douglas said in a tone that sounded a tad too icy to his ears, "how do you justify using a letter of hers to attempt to destroy her cousin, the count? Surely it would wound her to her core to know of it."

He could see that his question had caught Mycroft off guard.

"Yes, I suppose when you put it that way... Then again, you and I have different goals, Douglas," Mycroft said after a pause. "We both wish to eradicate evil, but whereas you will mete out justice when you can, I make it my vocation. And although I well know that you are not one for ends justifying means, you must trust that my motives are neither petty nor self-serving."

"No, for then you would be insufferable... and you are not that," Douglas said. "I simply wish you would not place ethics on the shelf whenever they are inconvenient to your larger goals."

"What have I to fear, when I can count on you to take them from that shelf, give them a good buffing, and place them under my nose?" Mycroft replied with a smile. "In any event, we have yet another puzzle, albeit small," he continued. "On the way here I called upon Bingwen Shi's family. A very proper family, quite courteous. But they had nothing of import to tell me. They are insular, barely speak the language. I warrant that if the future groom had anything to hide, he would do his utmost to deceive *them*, first and foremost. And so, I asked where I might find Ai Lin, for *she* is not so easily deceived—"

"Is that wise?" Douglas interrupted. "To place yourself in such a vulnerable position?"

"You wonder if I can bear to see her again," Mycroft replied. "A fair question, but since her father and Shi's family are of no help, I must speak directly to her if I mean to make headway. Besides, all I can think of at the moment is Vizily Zaharoff and what he might have to do with this case."

"Ah, and so this dealer in arms has taken on more import than a woman with whom you were in love?" Douglas asked. He realized that he sounded every bit as skeptical as he felt. He pushed away his snifter of Cognac, for he had had enough.

Mycroft leaned his arms on the table, staring at Douglas as if attempting to persuade him simply by force of will.

"Kindly note that Prussia has just decimated France in a major war. She is strong, and she is close by, with a larger population than Britain's and four times the number of troops. She needs arms—"

"Mycroft, it has been two years. You cannot continue to refer to her as 'Prussia,'" Douglas objected. "She is the German Empire."

"But I refer to all of the southeast Baltic as Prussia!" Mycroft objected.

"Nonsense. You called Austria 'Austria' the entire time that we were there."

"Britain has her flaws, Douglas… but she is our home. Within a few short months she faces financial ruin. The pound sterling may be the *lingua franca* of global currency now, but that can change in an instant. Prussia—sorry, 'Germany'—could gain preeminence, or possibly so could the United States."

"The United States are hardly a factor in the *world*. That smacks less of prescience and more of paranoia."

"I will not see this land in a war with 'the German Empire,' not in *my* lifetime," Mycroft muttered.

Douglas sighed. For a man who claimed to see the big picture, Mycroft was strangely myopic when it came to Britannia. He had tried, over the years, to persuade him to take a less martial view, but it was futile.

"Let us return," Douglas said instead, "to the small 'puzzle' you referred to, regarding Ai Lin."

"Yes. Although as a betrothed woman she is under their protection, Miss Lin does not reside with the Shi family, but in a rented room in a boarding house for young ladies in Stafford Terrace, which she uses only at night."

"What?" Douglas said.

"Unheard of, yes? Stranger still, during the day she can be found, along with her two new bodyguards, at Jennings Rents."

"But how can that be? That place is notorious."

"The family did not say, nor did I press, for it was clear it brought them pain even to mention it. But answer me this, for you know more of the inner workings of the Orient than I: would Bingwen Shi's disappearance reflect badly on his family?"

Douglas nodded. "Very badly. It might not be 'fair' to our way of looking at it, but to theirs, ill luck attaches to people for a reason. It is not random. After his disappearance, Ai Lin could have easily broken their engagement, with the excuse that she would not become a part of such an unlucky family."

Mycroft sighed. "Based on that, I surmise that she agreed to remain in this match-gone-sour because her father was keen on it; and only after they agreed to accept her own rather unconventional stipulations, including where she would live and where she would spend her days. What say you? Do we begin first thing tomorrow?"

"I would drink to it," Douglas replied, "but I am afraid I have rather had enough."

"Then I suppose a handshake must serve," Mycroft suggested with a smile.

# 17

EARLY THE FOLLOWING MORNING, MYCROFT AND
Douglas found themselves inside a commodious brougham,
courtesy of the Queen, and on their way to Kensington High
Street, site of Jennings Buildings, also known as Jennings Rents.
Just east of Kensington Square, Jennings was a rookery so
woebegone that the dreaded Seven Dials of Covent Garden,
thought to be the epitome of London's wretched refuse, would
surely be a step up. And Douglas's homely Nickolus House,
which lay 'in the consumptive heart' of Devil's Acre, as Mycroft
had once said of it, was in contrast to Jennings a veritable palace.

When the brougham began to slow, Mycroft dared have a
look outside. It was a relatively mild day, with cirrostratus clouds
that looked as if a painter had cleaned his white brush upon a
periwinkle sky. But even that lovely overhead canvas could not
mitigate the tottering wreck that lay below it.

Most of the houses in Jennings were wooden and less
structurally sound than the average matchbox. They spread
out among five courtyards like decaying teeth. The windows,
if one could call them that, were unglazed or absent altogether.
Instead of mats on which to wipe one's feet, before each door
was a dunghill composed of the previous night's waste—

monuments in offal in a place where a thousand people were said to have use of less than fifty toilets. In the center of the buildings, like a squalid town square, was an open cesspool emitting noxious gases.

"I'd heard this neighborhood referred to as 'pestiferous,'" Mycroft said in hushed tones. "Whoever described it thus is proving accurate to a fault."

"No need to lower your voice, Mycroft, for no one is listening," Douglas said. "Yet, I understand the impetus to whisper; such a place is a shock to the system. It should not exist at all." Douglas sighed. "Such is the proverbial luck of the Irish: uneducated immigrants barred even from other woebegone rookeries. You'd think that they are here because they can afford nothing better. In fact, it costs more to live in Jennings than in better quarters, but it is the only corner of the city that will have them."

"I well know how such landlords earn their money," Mycroft murmured. "As a matter of fact, I was asked to invest in a rookery of this ilk and I said no."

"Were you?" Douglas asked, surprised.

"They have no shortage of pubs," Mycroft went on, staring out. "I can count six within a stone's throw."

He was busy with other sorts of counting as well: hordes of ragged people on the street. Men, women, and children with nowhere to go, adding to those who were peering out of the windows. Their eyes, wide with surprise at the fine carriage, were quickly turning shrewd with covetousness, mingled with territorial gall.

The brougham turned around, and then around again, their driver clearly seeking a place to stop that would be dry and, above all, safe.

"Alas, these poor shall have to live out their misery elsewhere, ere long," Mycroft said as the driver performed several figure of eights.

"Why is that?" Douglas asked.

"Someone just bought Jennings Rents," Mycroft replied. "A wealthy investor, so I hear, is set to purchase the freeholds from the owners, part and parcel. He plans to give each renter two pounds per room, provided they leave of their own free will."

"None of these people has ever held more than two shillings in their hands at once," Douglas retorted. "My guess is, they will take it and will be scattered inside of a month. But why would Ai Lin be here?" he went on. "I imagine it is some sort of charity that consumes her, but even the charity workers give Jennings a wide berth, and now if it is to be destroyed, as you say..."

Mycroft took in a deep breath to calm himself. "We should send the carriage away," he said as the driver continued to turn the horses about. "For I cannot vouchsafe the Queen's property, to say nothing of the poor driver. He can return for us in an hour's time, what do you say? Are you up to it?"

"By all means," Douglas replied. "No doubt he is accustomed to more genteel environs."

Their driver was a thin, impeccably dressed and coiffed man of middle years named Carlton. Indeed, when Mycroft had first presented him with the address, Carlton seemed to have forgotten how to swallow, and beads of sweat had broken out from under his hat. Mycroft wondered how he was faring now.

Meanwhile, out of the window, he was beginning to spot the glint of knives and rocks, their brandishers looking to overpower the driver the moment he dropped off his charges. They could break down a fancy rig in the blink of an eye, and cart it off from shaft to leaf spring.

At last, Carlton found the only place to halt where wheels and men would not be instantly submerged in muck. As Mycroft and Douglas stepped out, the poor driver seemed so rattled by the whole endeavor that his mustaches quivered like the whiskers on a hare. He could hardly keep his hands still as he put up the folding step and closed the door behind them.

"Once we ascertain that we have indeed come to the right place, you need not linger," Mycroft informed him.

"Sir?" Carlton queried, puzzled.

"I said you are free to leave and then reclaim us an hour from now," Mycroft repeated.

The man looked about at the gathering rabble as if he were expecting to be struck at any moment, which was not far from the truth, and shook his head. "I cannot leave you here, sir. Defenseless." He leaned in and whispered the final word.

"I said I give you leave," Mycroft insisted.

"Sir, I cannot," Carlton repeated, his legs quaking in fear. "It wouldn't be right, sir."

Mycroft glanced at Douglas, who glanced about in turn.

"You, boy!" Douglas called out to one of some dozen scabby urchins who had begun to approach the carriage with unwholesome intent, while ragged adults lingered a bit farther afield, watching the proceedings for their opportunity.

"Yes, you!" Douglas repeated, pointing.

Some fourteen years of age, the boy whom Douglas addressed seemed the biggest and most canny of the lot.

"Wot's it you want?" the boy demanded, moving closer.

"That rock you hold in your pocket, I would like you to lob it at my head."

The boy seemed taken aback: he and the others with him.

"You want I should lob a rock at yer 'ead?" he repeated.

"If you would be so kind," Douglas said with a nod. "As hard as you can."

The boy stared suspiciously at the tall black man, as if he were being made a fool of, but too late. His mates had already begun to snicker, and to goad him on.

"Get 'im, Pete! Smack that teapot good!" they cried until the boy—Pete—had no choice but to bow to pressure.

He reached into his pocket, selected a good-sized rock, reared back his fist, and lobbed it for all he was worth.

Douglas ducked his head out of the way just as it sailed past, then lunged forward and leapt sideways until the bottom of his shoe was parallel to Pete's thorax, halting a millimeter shy of contact.

Mycroft watched this spectacle, amused. For Douglas was a master at *capoeira*, a martial art that he and Mycroft's bodyguard and driver, Huan, had learned as children in Trinidad, and which had its foundation in dance and play, rather than combat and war.

As for the spectacle at hand, it was as if the onlookers and participants had been captured in tin type: Douglas with his leg extended, the boys with their jaws dropping open, adults rearing back as if they might be next in Douglas's sights, and finally the lad Pete, staring at Douglas's foot in a combustion of admiration and dread. For it seemed all but certain that the tall Negro would complete that extremely short trajectory and end his brief life.

Instead, Douglas lowered his foot, straightened his lapels, bowed slightly to his victim as if this had been a friendly sparring all along, and strolled back to Mycroft, who turned to Carlton the driver and said, in the absolute silence that had just befallen them:

"No need for you to tarry."

This time, Carlton did not have to be told twice. He nodded and climbed back onto the brougham, his mustaches still quivering.

"You put on quite the spectacle, Douglas," Mycroft murmured as they turned their backs on their former assailants and walked on.

"I have had no one to spar with since Huan left, so I am a bit rusty," he replied. "Still, I assume we shall have fewer problems from here on out," he added with notable understatement as the denizens of Jennings parted like an unholy sea to let them pass.

He and Douglas zig-zagged to avoid various puddles of dreck until they reached the address that Bingwen Shi's family had provided. From the outside, the set of rooms appeared no less shoddy than the rest of the rookery. Douglas looked doubtful as Mycroft knocked.

"Miss Lin?" he called, then knocked again.

A moment later, it opened, and Ai Lin stood in the doorway.

She was, as Mycroft had once observed, "the sort who would look every bit as regal if covered in rags." And although far from that, she was not dressed in the sumptuous Han style that he remembered, but in modern garb, with a white blouse and a narrow, close-fitting skirt with a small train, both in lavender. The only homage to her culture was in her glorious ebony hair, combed severely away from her face, then spun into a long chignon that was held in place by two bamboo sticks.

But it was something else that nearly undid him. In the same way that a particular room or a fleeting vision could bring back one's childhood, so her familiar scent—subtle hints of lavender, chamomile and Marseille soap—returned him fully to the tiny Chinese herbalist shop where he had first laid eyes on her.

Staring at her, Mycroft inhaled sharply, a sound she thoroughly misunderstood.

"Mr. Holmes, Mr. Douglas. Please forgive my appearance, as it has been rather a trying morning."

Strangely, she did not appear to be at all surprised to see them. While Mycroft struggled to find his voice, Ai Lin once again had no trouble finding hers.

"Thank heavens you have arrived," she said, "for I am in dire need of your help."

"We are aware of that, Miss Lin," Mycroft managed to say. "Your fiancé—"

"Mr. Holmes," she interrupted, sounding slightly perturbed, "though I am grateful for any assistance you can provide the Shi family and mine in regard to Bingwen Shi's whereabouts, at the moment you and Mr. Douglas are to follow me inside, and quickly!"

*Pull yourself together, man!* Mycroft cautioned himself as he and Douglas did as instructed.

# 18

THERE WERE NO BODYGUARDS WITHIN, AS MYCROFT HAD expected. Ai Lin appeared to be quite defenseless. As his eyes adjusted to the gloom, he could see that they were in a long, tidy reception hall which had been turned into a makeshift infirmary and furnished with the barest essentials: bandages, cotton, alcohol and other unguents, along with a jar of thermometers. A pot of water burbled on coals in a hearth, with more pots beside it, all filled with water.

"As you can see, I have no one with me today," Ai Lin said, "for we were not expecting more than the usual toothache or feverish child… but look!"

She pulled aside a thick curtain that served as a door to a larger room where some thirty-odd people of varying ages lay on blankets and cots while others—those not so badly off—were seated on the bare floor, bewildered but passive. Here and there were the faint sounds of moaning and retching.

"They walked here from a nearby building, everyone in various stages of illness, and have been arriving for the last half hour or so. I sent boys out for water and have been boiling it since, for these poor people are much dehydrated, and I had barely got them settled when you arrived. Since I was informed by the Shi family that you were coming, I also took the liberty of writing up a list of symptoms: one for you, and one for you, Mr. Douglas. I assume you carry writing implements?"

Slightly cowed, both men nodded.

"Good. Please assist me in questioning them, to see how many symptoms they experience."

"Symptoms of what?" Douglas asked, for Mycroft had yet to utter a peep.

"I believe it is merely gastric distress and not cholera," she replied, "but I must be certain. We lost so many twenty years ago, as you are too well aware."

Although Mycroft did not think it cholera, his fear for her had swept all logic from his brain and every word from of his tongue. He could feel his heart tumbling like a rock downhill.

"Kindly keep the queries in order," Ai Lin was saying, "and then write down their answers most carefully. Mr. Holmes, you can start with that elderly lady in the green felt hat; you see her there? She is Mrs. Arnold. Mr. Douglas, that young woman with the twisted leg, the one who appears flushed, I believe her name is Dora. I shall begin at that corner," she went on, "and when we are done, we shall see what we have. Ready?" she added with a smile, as if she were suggesting a wade in a warm pool on a balmy spring day.

Mycroft, list in hand, approached the elderly lady in the green felt hat.

"Mrs. Arnold?" he ventured.

She looked up at him and smiled. Most of Mrs. Arnold's teeth were rotting or nonexistent, and her bare feet were filthy.

The skin on her hands let him know that she had been a washerwoman until rheumatism made such work unmanageable. He assumed that what she had attempted next, so as not to starve, was to sell her body. He surmised from the patchy hair loss, which the hat did little to hide, as well as from the ugly white pustules at the corners of her mouth, that if some gastric distress did not carry her away, she would eventually be claimed by syphilis.

"Well, aren't you the bonny golden lad!" she declared in a phlegmatic voice.

"Good morning," he began, attempting to sound professional but kind.

Then he looked down at the list in his hand and felt himself choke. Regardless of circumstances, how in heaven's name could he broach the subject of 'watery stools' or 'bits in the feces, like kernels of rice,' much less 'rectal pain' with a female more than twice his age?

Helpless, he glanced over at Douglas and was gratified to see that his friend did not appear to be faring much better with his patient, Dora; that in fact he was glancing back at Mycroft with the helpless look of a cur who'd been caught snuffling about in the rubbish.

In contrast, on the other side of the room, Ai Lin was flying through the questions, jotting down answers, chatting with those who could, all the while placing a hand on a forehead or a thermometer under an armpit with nary a pause.

Some forty minutes later, it was mercifully over. They had gathered twenty-nine completed questionnaires, had washed dozens of hands, had disposed of several buckets of bile and other bodily emissions, and had doled out every drop of water to be had. The patients were made as comfortable as could be managed and encouraged to rest.

After that, Mycroft, Douglas, and Ai Lin sipped tea at a coarse wooden table much like the one in the kitchen of Nickolus

House while Ai Lin read over the questionnaires.

"Yes, clearly a gastric complaint and not cholera. But I shall keep them a few more days, hoping that they do not become infected again."

Mycroft still had not located his vocal cords and may as well have been an empty chair for all he was contributing to the conversation.

"They did not consume the same food. Several have not eaten for days," she said. "Surely there is a contaminant somewhere in their building. It should not be so very difficult to locate the source, though I cannot imagine what can be done about it."

"Perhaps it can be repaired," Douglas ventured.

"With what money, Mr. Douglas? And, until it *is* repaired, who is able to provide clean water to fifty residents?" Ai Lin shook her head. "Ah, well. At least now we know the culprit."

"Thanks to John Snow," Douglas said.

"Yes, Mr. Douglas! I too am a huge admirer of his," Ai Lin replied enthusiastically. "The work he did in Soho was awe-inspiring, though no one believed at the time that cholera and similar diseases could be water-borne."

"What a difference twenty years can make," Douglas said.

"And I should count our blessings, I am aware," Ai Lin interjected, "but I fear there is still much prejudice to overcome. Earlier this year, the local sanitation inspector reported that the lack of lavatories here was an advantage, since it would be difficult 'to get the inhabitants to use them as ordinary persons would.' A medical man! A man whose mission it is to represent the residents, does not believe that the Irish know how, or could be taught, to use a commode!" she said angrily. "I cannot abide such craven disregard for fellow human beings. Especially from one who has taken an Hippocratic oath. Oh, and he also claimed that the filthiness of the rookery was not due to poor management, but to 'the habits of the people who inhabited them'!" she added. "How can we lift up our fellow man when faced with that sort of prejudgment and ignorance, especially among those who have been hired to assist?"

Her gaze was so intense and her indignity so complete that, although Mycroft realized she had posed a rhetorical question, he felt obliged to reply. But instead of offering some sagacious or enlightened word, as he had hoped, he blurted out: "Why are you here? And where are your bodyguards?"

Ai Lin and Douglas stared in his direction as if the empty chair had commenced not merely to speak, but to hector.

Mycroft expected Ai Lin to pronounce that it was none of his business, which indeed it was not. Instead, she said: "The bodyguards frighten some of the residents, Mr. Holmes. And those who are not frightened can become enraged. These people are not accustomed to strangers, most especially large, looming Chinese men who are better dressed and in every aspect of life more fortunate than they. Therefore, if I wish to help, I cannot have them hovering. The bodyguards bring me here, and then they return for me a half hour before I am scheduled to depart, to deposit me back at my lodgings. The Shi family has acquiesced to these peculiar orders solely because they know my time in Jennings is short-lived. In less than one month, we shall lose one precious method of understanding just how infectious disease is spread, while its former residents are elsewhere, but no better off."

"Mycroft mentioned that this rookery is to be sold," Douglas said with a nod.

Mycroft realized that Douglas was providing him an opening with which to redeem himself. But what, in the name of all that was sacred, could he say to this creature that would not have him babbling like a fool?

"Beyond that, Mr. Holmes, I am here," Ai Lin resumed in the awkward silence, "because, as I shall never be a physician, this is the next best thing. And because the death rate in Jennings is twice that in neighboring Kensington, and the average life span all of seventeen. So, where else should I be?" she finished with a gentle smile.

"I…" Mycroft looked down at the table. "I fear for your health, Miss Lin, that is all. No judgment beyond that, I promise."

"Thank you. You are kind and thoughtful, as always. By the way, how is your heart?"

Mycroft sat up. "Sorry…?" he said, though he'd heard her perfectly well.

"Your heart, Mr. Holmes. You had some disturbing symptoms some months ago—"

"Ah. Yes. Never better, Miss Lin," he said quickly. "The herbs you gave me were of tremendous value."

Out of the corner of his eye, Mycroft noticed Douglas's baffled expression.

"Excellent," she said, though Mycroft could tell from her frown that she was not quite believing it. She took a sip of her tea, then, clearly realizing that she had touched on a delicate subject, changed it. "I am also investigating hog cholera," she said, "for I wonder if there is any link to humans, and the possibility of cross-contagion, though for now there does not appear to be…"

Her voice trailed off. For a moment, she looked impossibly sad. Then she reached out and took their hands, a gesture that he assumed was unheard of in her culture, as it was barely tolerated in his. Mycroft did not dare to glance over at Douglas but allowed his hand to be held. And although he did not squeeze back, the touch of her fingers was enough.

"Mr. Holmes? Mr. Douglas?" she said, looking at each of them in turn. "You are more than acquaintances to me: you are dear and cherished friends. You saved my father and my brother, and for that alone, I owe you my life. So, let me speak plainly. The Shi are an old and noble family, and they bring that ancient nobility to the match. We Lins are neither old, nor noble—"

"And yet, you can trace your ancestry back fourteen generations!" Mycroft protested.

"Ah, you remembered!" she said, brightening. "Yes, I suppose by Western standards this would be considered unusual. But compared to the Shi, our pedigree is of little account. Therefore, my marriage to him is necessary for the good of both families. But I must confess that Bingwen Shi's disappearance, much as it wounds me for the pain it has caused, was a liberation. I now find myself betwixt and between, neither married nor single, in a country with more privileges than has my native land. And, because I am of an age where I can no longer be treated as a child, I have experienced in this interim a sense of freedom that I never fathomed."

She paused and then continued: "That said, please believe that I shall do everything in my power to help you find him. And that, if he is still among the living, I shall fulfill my duty and be a good and faithful wife to him for the rest of my days."

Mycroft found his voice. "Might you be able to shed any light on your... fiancé's disappearance? When was the last time that you saw him?"

Ai Lin let go their hands. "Climbing out of a sleeping car, Mr. Holmes."

"Sorry?" Mycroft said, assuming he had misheard.

"This is where well-bred women usually assure you that it is not what you think, and in fact it is not," she declared. "You remember the launch of the first sleeper service from London to Glasgow at the beginning of April?"

"Yes, I… recall that," Mycroft said. He had read something about it, though it had not held his interest, for the only person he knew in Glasgow was Dr. Bell, and the doctor made frequent trips to London.

"I was anxious to try it," she continued, "for Glasgow is one of the few large cities in Britain without a children's hospital, and so the need for services such as mine, services 'sans portfolio,' if you will, are great. But, for my maiden voyage, I chose to be accompanied. I could not ask my brother, and so risk both his studies and his relationship with my father. Nor could I ask the bodyguards, for I already punish them enough, as you have seen. So, I sent word to Bingwen. Would he purchase a ticket on a separate car and take me there and back? I had ulterior motives, of course; for I had met him but once at that point, and I wished to see if he had any sort of progressive bent in regard to women."

"And did he?" Mycroft asked.

"Yes and no. Though he agreed to accompany me, he made it clear that after we were married I would cease this sort of activity and dedicate myself to him, to his family and to our future. Which I promised to do. And so we spent the day in Glasgow, traipsing from one makeshift sick house to the next—"

"Forgive me, I do not understand. Was he not terribly concerned about you?" Mycroft asked. "After all, those places can be contagious."

"The Shi family needs the income that my father's ships provide, Mr. Holmes," she said evenly.

Mycroft sat back in his chair. Though she had revealed nothing that he did not already know, he felt as if he had been punched in the gut all the same.

"I have developed a reputation, which I myself have fanned, as hard-headed. I have taken full advantage of the fact that I am my father's only daughter. As the Shi have no daughter to offer to my brother, if they wish to join our family, they have no option but me. And if I were to sicken and die, the hope is that I would have the courtesy to do so *after* a child is born, and not before. Do you understand?"

"But if you are to marry, and eventually… perform the duties of a normal wife," Douglas said, "why go to Glasgow at all? Why tempt yourself towards a life you can never have?"

"Originally, the engagement was to last six months. Not long, I know, to continue on as I have. But if I can save even one life, or ease one person's suffering, or discover just one small detail that can add to medical knowledge…" Ai Lin blinked a few times and continued: "As to Bingwen's business affairs, the only light I can shed is this. He said he was a consultant to Vizily Zaharoff. Do you know of him?"

"We do," Mycroft acknowledged. "Industrialist, arms dealer—"

"—and purported merchant of death," she added ruefully.

"In what matters did he consult Zaharoff?" Mycroft asked.

"In truth, I am not certain. Bingwen was loath to speak of it; and the moment I realized he had business with that man, I made it my mission to end it. When I asked, or perhaps I should say demanded, that he sever the link, he demurred at first, but at last he consented."

She took a sip of tea, as if bracing herself.

"I last laid eyes on him the night of the 4th of April, when our train returned to London, just before midnight. Neither my father nor the Shi family are aware of our journey—"

She was interrupted by the sound of a carriage pulling up outside. Mycroft and Douglas stood as Ai Lin rose.

"I ask forgiveness for taking up so much of your time," she said with a small curtsy, "and will now rejoin my patients."

Mycroft dared to glance at her one more time before they headed out the door—and was gratified but also pained when she deigned to glance back.

"Deshi Hai Lin owns four ships, yes?" he whispered to Douglas as he closed the outer door behind them. "*Orion's Belt*, on which that contraband was discovered six months ago—"

"—and also the *Maritime*, the *Latitude*, and the *Royal Richard*," Douglas enumerated, nodding. "Quite unusual."

"In what way?"

"Very few coal-powered ships of that size are used exclusively for cargo. It is too dear."

"The price of coal versus the price of wind? I should say so," Mycroft replied as he headed up the carriage steps, with Douglas behind him.

"But wind is slower and more capricious. To have on hand four British-made ships with experienced sailors, well-marked routes, a solid history of delivery, and plenty of storage?" Douglas said. "The Shi family could do worse."

*Whereas Ai Lin could do infinitely better*, Mycroft thought sourly.

# 19

HUAN, MYCROFT'S TRINIDADIAN DRIVER AND BODYGUARD, arrived the following morning, looking hale and hearty and ready for more travel—at least, that was how he appeared to Sherlock. But Mycroft seemed of a different mind.

"He has barely set foot on dry ground, after a week's-long journey!" he scolded. "Surely you can allow him a few hours' rest!"

"A few *hours*?" Sherlock repeated, dumbfounded.

This was to be his first official day of sleuthing, and already his brother was interfering, to say nothing of the fact that it was Mycroft's whims that had made them short of time to begin with! The Wycombe Railway made a stop in Thame, a little more than six miles from Bledlow and less than five from the Wickham house. By train, it could have been a journey of slightly more than two hours end to end, rather than the four by carriage. Agreeing to the carriage at all had already been a compromise, and now Mycroft wanted more!

Sherlock turned to Huan. "Are you in need of rest?" he asked, and Huan grinned.

"I am here to serve!" he announced in his soft lilt while raising his hands to the sky.

Sherlock lifted an eyebrow towards his brother and spun upon his heel, with Huan dutifully following behind.

"Sherlock!" Mycroft commanded. "You are to wait until your admittance arrives."

"My admittance to what?" Sherlock asked.

"The funeral!"

Sherlock tried to keep his composure.

"Mycroft. Who in his right mind would attend a funeral he had no need to attend?"

"The deceased is related, however tenuously, to the Queen," Mycroft explained. "What if you journey all the way there, only to be refused entry?"

"It has been nearly a week since the last murder. Already, we are hamstrung by our mode of transport, and now this?"

"You agreed to this arrangement," Mycroft retorted calmly. "We shook on it. I now insist that you prove yourself docile in the execution, or Huan will be instructed to go home and rest, and we shall be done with it."

"And what am I to do with this… this *admittance*, once it arrives? Do not tell me that I am there to represent the monarchy or any such foolishness—"

"Why would anyone choose *you* to represent the monarchy? You are not to mention it at all! It is only to be brought out should anyone remark upon your presence there."

As always Mycroft had his way. So, while they used up half of the morning awaiting a black-ribbon admittance, Sherlock smoked and fumed in the garden and kept his distance from the study where Mycroft was holding court with a half-dozen Oriental men who had come to greet Huan and to partake in the rum that he'd brought back from Jamaica. Although Mycroft had made a perfunctory offer that Sherlock join them, nothing sounded less appealing than a long recounting of musty adventures in faraway places. As for rum, he had no interest, though a glass of Vin Mariani might hit the spot.

He rummaged through Mycroft's cache of wines in search of it, but he recognized none of the labels. And, in utilizing his admittedly limited knowledge of German, French, and Italian, not a one of them had been suffused with cocaine.

At long last, the Queen's messenger arrived with the dispensation—or admittance, or whatever it was—for the funeral, and their trip was underway.

Sherlock deposited his traveling bag and *vielle* inside the coach. Then, instead of taking a seat in the back, as expected, he climbed up beside Huan at the reins.

"What in heaven's name are you doing now?" Mycroft demanded, for he had emerged to see them off.

Although squeezing into the sprung seat was not ideal, Sherlock despised the notion of riding within, like some cosseted passenger.

"You insisted that I utilize the carriage," Sherlock grumbled. "You did not specify which part."

"There is nothing worth noting along the road, and it threatens to rain!" Mycroft declared.

"If Huan can endure, then so can I," Sherlock countered, folding his hands upon his lap and staring straight ahead. "Huan? Proceed," he commanded, and a moment later they were on their way.

Sherlock was aware that he was acting impetuously, that his own agitation and passion would need to be brought to heel before they cost him mistakes he could ill afford. But he was not about to let Mycroft know that he had guessed his state of mind. And although he was loath to admit it even to himself, sometimes Mycroft's readable doubts about his current abilities could be demoralizing.

Besides, there was something about Huan's presence that helped to steady his nerves. Huan was a humble, congenial fellow; he seemed always cheerful, energetic, and content to be of service, while at the same time capable of weathering anything.

Before long, however, Sherlock was rethinking his impulsivity. The sprung seat was brutally hard, and the Irish Cob's endless high-stepping and mane-tossing were beginning to grate on him, as did the mean little breeze that stung his cheeks and deposited dust from the road directly into his eyes, nose, and mouth.

After another hour, his body had gone quite numb. He was no longer feeling the cold, or much of anything.

To distract himself from the discomfort, he permitted his mind to freely roam over the case and to explore the very edges of possibility. From his pocket, he retrieved a map of Buckinghamshire, tracing and retracing its confines with his finger.

"What is it that you are doing?" Huan asked.

*Might do to talk it through*, Sherlock thought, even if he would be all but conversing with himself, since he supposed that Huan would understand little of it.

"As I have done with every other murder site," Sherlock began, "I am following the confines of Buckinghamshire to see what it might manifest. If perhaps this outline could be reimagined as a letter of the alphabet, say, or a number."

"Ah! And can it?"

"No, it cannot. However, if one were to anthropomorphize it, then it looks remarkably like a standing griffin, or perhaps a little dog, begging on its haunches."

"Ah, but that is lovely! Such imagination!" Huan replied.

"Yes, well, if *every* shire resembled some beast or other, then perhaps it would be useful. But as Buckinghamshire is the only one thus far, that particular conjecture is far off the mark."

"I am very sorry to hear it," Huan replied, sounding as if he truly was.

"No need. We are but at the beginning of our journey and have a way to go. Besides, it is always best to exhaust every simple explanation first, before one moves on in complexity."

"Your brother calls that the 'Occam Razor,'" Huan said, nodding.

"He does indeed," Sherlock confirmed with some surprise. "He has spoken to you about it?"

Huan shrugged. "Sometimes. Mostly, I hear things. When I cannot help it." After a pause Huan said, "Is it that maybe the ages of the victims create a code?"

Sherlock stared at him. "A code? What sort of a code?"

It was one thing to regurgitate the name of a problem-solving principle, quite another, for a man whom he knew to be functionally illiterate, to use the principles of induction on a puzzle.

"I have heard," Huan went on, clearly mistaking Sherlock's bewilderment for a lack of comprehension, "that numbers sometimes can be like letters. Yes?"

"Yes," Sherlock confirmed. "Divination, for example, uses certain numerical substitutes for letters. But it could also be more straightforward, such as 'A' equals 'one,' and so forth. And yes, I did think of it. I have tried the various ages of the victims both in sequence and in reverse. I even speculated that a code might be had from missing numbers—"

"What do you mean, missing numbers?" Huan asked.

"The children, for example. Their ages at death were seven, ten, and fourteen, or, in *order* of death: seven, fourteen, ten. The missing numbers are therefore eight, nine, eleven, twelve, and thirteen. But nothing has coalesced, you see. Unless you think 'HIKLM' might be a useful clue, it is all gibberish."

Huan shook his head and sighed. "This thing that you do, it is so very difficult."

"It is not difficult in the way that you mean it," Sherlock said. "I have seen you do battle, Huan. To land a blow perfectly, to learn complicated maneuvers, to control one's breath and heart, one's muscles and nerves, all the while avoiding being pummeled? Most would consider that difficult, if not impossible. But for you it is like taking a stroll, is it not?"

"A sometimes painful stroll, but yes," Huan admitted with a grin.

"That is how this is for me. I see this case as a very large puzzle, with many pieces still to be found. My objective, do you see, is to find and then to arrange the pieces to ascertain what might be revealed. This I must do without predetermining the final picture."

"Years of practice, they help," Huan offered.

"They do. Just as you are a cannier, more adept fighter today than you were at nineteen, I expect to be better at puzzle-solving ten years from now, or twenty. It is not the perfect analogy, I confess," Sherlock amended, laughing a little, "as physical prowess tends to accompany youth."

Huan nodded. "I am not faster. But I am smarter. Save more energy now. Get to the point more quickly."

"The simplest answer is that the victims, however unknown to each other, have a link to the killer," Sherlock said, shifting back to the problem at hand. "And although I am perfectly willing to be persuaded otherwise, thus far it fits. Unfortunately, it also does not tell us much."

"Not yet! But you are very wise, Master Sherlock, smart as your brother perhaps. You will catch him!" Huan said, his grin firmly in place.

Although Sherlock did not care overly much for the word 'perhaps,' he had to admit that it felt salubrious to be praised, however undeserved or premature the plaudits might be. In spite of the numbness and the cold—try as he might—he could not help but smile in return.

# 20

AT LONG LAST, SHERLOCK AND HUAN ARRIVED AT THE
Thame railway station, which served the towns of Thame
in Oxfordshire and Bledlow, in Buckinghamshire, a mere
five miles on foot from the Wickham residence where Elise
was murdered. Trains made frequent stops, enough so that
strangers would not be especially noteworthy. Nearby woods
provided several well-trodden and less trodden paths. The
killer could have easily disembarked, hidden himself for as
long as necessary and then, when no witnesses were about,
arrived at the Wickham residence after little more than an
hour on foot.

"So? Where to begin?" Huan wondered. "Perhaps ask people
if they have seen anyone strange?"

"The Queen's desires notwithstanding," Sherlock replied,
"by now every resident has heard the news and spread it abroad
that the Fire Four Eleven killer struck near Bledlow, and that the
murdered party had a link, however tenuous, to Victoria. Had
anyone seen anything of note, they would have already hastened
to the constable to report it, if for no other reason than to
possibly ingratiate themselves to Her Majesty."

"Perhaps you can ask in any case," Huan said.

"Yes, perhaps I could, Huan. But I am guessing that few of the locals would be amenable to my peppering them with queries about suspicious characters, considering that I am likely far and away the most suspicious character they have ever laid eyes on."

Huan's white teeth gleamed in his burnished copper face.

"You have not many illusions of yourself, Master Sherlock," he said.

"Mark me, Huan, I can well utilize my unusual looks to my advantage. But I am also aware when they are of disadvantage. To say nothing of the fact that the Queen has forbidden us from questioning the only person who might be helpful: Elise's mother, for she was the one who found her, and she is the one who might be persuaded to reveal whether the girl had any enemies."

Sherlock took one last look at the station. "No need to linger here," he added. "Let us hasten on."

Half an hour later, they reached Holy Trinity, Bledlow's parish church. It was a flint and limestone affair, lichen-tinted, and overlooking the gently rolling green hills of Aylesbury Vale. Sherlock and Huan had barely joined the knot of mourners, several dozen all in black, when the church bells began to toll, for the funerary carriage was arriving.

The white hearse bearing Elise Wickham's mortal remains was pulled by two high-stepping white horses. Through its window, Sherlock could see the flowers surrounding her coffin.

Standing next to Sherlock was an elderly lady of modest means but of upright demeanor. She had one purple-veined hand clutching her umbrella, the other at her throat, a ready clue that something was displeasing her.

"*White?*" she clucked. "Unfathomable in my day!"

Sherlock looked about but did not see anyone whom he would mark as the mother of the deceased. He wondered if perhaps she was already inside the church: close family members sometimes chose to eschew the arrival of the casket in favor of welcoming guests to the service itself—or so his brother had reminded him.

"Her family may've preferred white, Mrs.…?" Sherlock replied evenly, engaging only in the event that the old biddy knew something of note.

"Partridge," she declared, "and it's *Miss*," before adding: "Makes no difference what one *prefers*, Mr.…?"

"Holmes," he said.

"Ah. Scottish," she frowned, her tone dripping with condescension. "Now. Miss Wickham was eighteen her birthday last, about your age, I surmise. Young ladies and gentlemen have no need to go about in a child's carriage!"

*She is the former governess*, Sherlock thought.

"And let us not even speak of the fact that the girl is to lie in state until after dark, at which time she shall be buried. After dark! When no one shall be left to witness it! And where are the mutes?" she exclaimed. "Why, the last funeral I attended had *four* mutes trailing behind the coffin, two on either side! But not to be interred until evening!" she repeated. "Shocking, would you not say, Mr. Holmes?"

"Quite," Sherlock replied, though his inattentive demeanor made clear that he thought it nothing of the sort, for he was wearying of Miss Partridge. "Might her mother be inside, do you know?" he asked.

"From what I understand," the old woman sniffed, "Lady Anne has not bothered to come. And she sets the tone, for you see what a poor assembly has gathered here. Mind you, it is none of my affair, as I have not been a member of the household for nearly two years. But the countess has no living relatives. And though her second husband, the count, is of royal pedigree, there is no one here to represent his side of the family. A ghastly breach of protocol, for I was hoping to see one royal at least," she muttered, her lips pursed. "Unless you…"

"I?" Sherlock said. "No, madam, far from it!"

"Ah. And who are you?" she asked, appraising him with small, suspicious eyes.

"Assistant to the undertaker at your service, ma'am," Sherlock said with a slight bow. "I helped to prepare the body for burial. Perhaps at some future date when you might have need of our services…"

When she went pale and turned away, Sherlock whispered to Huan: "Right after the final hymn, when the rector accompanies the mourners out, you must cover for me."

"For how long?" Huan asked.

"For long enough that I might examine her."

Huan, who had been following the hearse's sad approach, was looking suddenly as mournful as if he'd been Elise's nearest relative.

"You take whatever time you need," he whispered back. "Someone must do right by that girl!"


Once sat in a pew, Sherlock looked about in case Lady Anne Hohenlohe-Langenburg had changed her mind and decided to make an appearance, but he saw no one who resembled Elise and so could have been her mother. In fact, the first row reserved for family was strangely empty, containing only two ladies of late middle years who were sniffling intermittently, though they were wholly dry-eyed. Relatives, he guessed. Aunts, most likely.

As the service droned on, Sherlock was conscious of hymnal books opening and closing, the occasional cough or sigh or rustle of petticoats, but all his attention was on that little white coffin surrounded by flowers.

The rector's final words on behalf of the deceased were the usual kind-but-bland statements that one voices when someone dies too soon to have made any particular mark. As the small congregation rose to its feet and made its quiet way outdoors again, Sherlock approached the two women who had been seated in the family pews.

"Terribly sorry for your loss," he said to the one in the lead: a short, rotund blonde.

Though they looked very much alike, with features that seemed made out of putty, the one he addressed was slightly older, her face more pleasant and her manner more open than her sister, who was nervous and pinched.

"I take it you are members of the family?" he asked her gently.

"Yes," she said. "We are, or were, her aunts. Our dear departed brother was her father. Death is a tragedy, no doubt, but especially so when one dies so young."

She made it sound not so much murder as a twist of fate.

"Elise was a remarkable young woman," she added, while the other managed to nod her agreement.

But when Sherlock asked in what ways she had been 'remarkable,' the aunt equivocated and in the end could not say. And when he asked how long it had been since they had seen their niece, the more nervous of the two looked away, seemingly embarrassed; while the mouthpiece declared that the family home was nearby Leeds, and therefore quite far for casual visits, and that neither she nor her sister had laid eyes on the girl since she was five.

*About the time that Count Wolfgang and her mother Anne separated,* Sherlock thought. *When the royal association ceased, mother and daughter were abandoned.*

Sherlock walked them to the door of the church and then waited a moment. Finally, ascertaining that no one else was about, he hurried to the casket and pried open the lid, which lifted with a groan. A second later, he found himself staring down at the remains of Miss Elise Wickham.

The small likeness of the girl that Mycroft had given him had been exceptionally well executed. He could note little difference between the girl in her coffin and the one in the portrait. Her cheeks were rosy, her forehead unmarked with care, her overall mien calm and void.

Upon closer inspection, he could see an ugly stain at her neck. Blood had coagulated under the skin of her scalp where the swing had struck her. A lace foulard, in the same shade of black as her frilly taffeta dress, had been placed over the high collar in an effort to mask the nasty bruise. Had the impact shattered bone? When the killer had hit her with the swing, what had he been attempting to hide?

And why had he not done this to everyone whom he'd killed? Why her?

Sherlock heard a sound, heard Huan's voice at the open side door, speaking to the rector. He could spy the rector's profile, framed by the door and looking uncomfortable, while Huan was loudly declaring that, "In my country, we have an open coffin! One more look for a proper goodbye, that would be good, no? Ah, and it is our custom to say of the body, 'Does he not look well!' Sometimes, over the dead we pass a young child three times to keep the spirit from causing harm…"

Sherlock slipped a hand under the girl's head.

The skin was rough to the touch, most likely the work of tweezers pulling out splinters from the swing. But then higher up, at the nape of her neck, he felt something else, a spiny protrusion that had sunk deep; for when he tugged at it, it was much longer than it had felt at first.

The only other victim with an injury to her neck, and splinters, had been little Abigail Sykes. But surely the killer had not arranged for Abigail to spin and fall and break the table!

Huan's voice, was growing in volume and beginning to sound slightly hysterical. His Trinidad patois was thickening; he was losing his audience.

"It is not a rare t'ing that we mourn forty days?"

Sherlock pinched the splinter between his fingers, pulled it out, and shut the lid only a moment before the rector excused himself and walked back in.

# 21

SHERLOCK'S BORROWED CARRIAGE PROCEEDED DOWN
the long drive lined with ploughman's-spikenard, and dotted
here and there with St. John's wort and gooseberry bushes,
towards the house where Elise Wickham had grown up and
died. The entire property was well tended and well maintained,
with chalk grasses and field pansies seeming to grow wild
but in truth situated for best effect. The residence itself was
surrounded by a low stone enclosure, which separated the
green without from the green within, and was set off by a
large, ornate wrought-iron gate with acorn-shaped finials atop
the posts on either side.

If any other houses were within eyesight, Sherlock could not
make them out.

Huan parked beside the stables just outside the walled
garden. There was no groom to greet them, or to water and
feed the poor Irish Cob that had brought them such a long way
without a whinny of complaint. There seemed, in fact, no one in
the grounds at all.

Inside the stables were two well-brushed Hackneys of
middle years and a Chapman mare, who blinked at them
without interest.

*Nicely kept but undistinguished*, Sherlock thought, eyeing the horses.

"Quiet. Not just the stables," Huan commented. "No sound anywhere."

"Indeed," Sherlock replied, glancing about.

"The servants, they were not at the funeral," Huan continued. "That seems quite unusual."

"Yes. Nor does Lady Anne appear to be receiving guests after the service, for there are no servants bustling about. I am guessing that they—six, I'd say, judging from the size of the house— all left together, along with Lady Anne."

"Why do you say that?"

"For one thing, they took the cart."

"What cart?"

"It was parked nearby that barouche to your left, you see the empty space? The wheel marks on the ground? And secondly, I would say, given the copious bales of hay stacked up and the grooming implements on the wood block, that four horses are being used."

"*Four* horses? Impossible. There are but two empty stalls!"

"Huan, you surprise me," Sherlock remonstrated. "Look at those brushes. Are not two of them meant for double coats? Do you spy any horse in the vicinity that is double-coated?"

"Perhaps the horses they took, they are double-coated!" Huan countered.

"They are. Those two brushes have seen a lot of wear; the handles are shiny with use. But it is because they are used not on two horses, but on four. Note the placement of the feeding troughs. What does that tell you?"

"Closer to the ground. Ponies?" Huan guessed.

"Four Shetland ponies," Sherlock affirmed with a nod, "which fit two per stall. Most likely, they were a wedding present from the Queen, since the entire country knows that Victoria favors them. A good Shetland can pull twice its own weight, and a cart could easily accommodate Lady Anne and her small household."

"But why would a countess use a cart?"

"Normally, she would not. But a girl Elise's age would have no such qualms. She would see it as an adventure, and she probably utilized it—and the ponies—with some frequency, perhaps with friends. Lady Anne and the servants must have gone to mourn Elise's death together, and in private—people who sincerely loved the girl, rather than busybody former governesses or long-lost aunts who grow scarce right around the time that the royal link is severed.

"And, like every other young girl since time immemorial, Elise no doubt had a favorite spot," he continued, "some place where she liked to walk and to reflect. And that is where they went," Sherlock concluded.

Huan shook his head, baffled. "These behaviors, they are… not so British, yes?" he mused.

"It *is* flouting the rules a bit. But the moment that the old biddy at the church objected to the color of the hearse, or huffed that the burial would not take place until evening, it was clear that Lady Anne is thumbing her nose at convention. Perhaps out of grief or spite, she is sending a message that she will do things her way. In either case, she and her household will visit the chapel long after the others have departed, where they will see their precious girl interred properly."

"I like this Lady Anne," Huan said.

"As do I," Sherlock agreed.

While Huan filled a water trough and purloined some hay for the Irish Cob, Sherlock made his way through the gate, walked up the little footpath, knocked upon the front door for courtesy's sake, and was not at all surprised when no one answered his call.

With no living soul to disturb him, he slipped around to the garden at the back of the house, where the swing was, and where Elise had been murdered. Here, the low walls were lined with bushes, a perfect place to hide, albeit at a fair distance from where the victim had been seated. A rose garden, closer in, grew fulsome and well tended but provided inadequate covering. A small arbor awash in trumpet vines was closer by, but it too could not compete with the bushes.

He glanced back at the house, to the windows that overlooked the garden. What were the servants doing in the late afternoon, that not a one of them had chanced to look out? Or perhaps they had, but had been unable to see the killer.

The garden was alive with the singing of jays and yellowhammers. Butterflies flitted about, unmindful of the dank, unseasonal weather, or of a stranger in their midst. It was in every way bucolic, except for one thing: the swing, split in two, and dangling by a length of chain from an ancient alder. The breeze pushed it so that it twisted and swayed, and the chain, where it linked together over the branch, rubbed and whined.

Sherlock approached cautiously. Something about it gave him pause. Dropping to his knees, he closely examined the splintered wood. Then he took the little sliver he had found embedded in Elise's neck, which he had kept pressed between thumb and forefinger of his left hand, and matched it to what he saw before him.

Though it confirmed a hunch, nevertheless it startled him so that he heard his breath catch... and then a twig break behind him.

"Wherever this is from, it is not from the swing," he said without turning around.

Huan knelt by his side, eyeing the inch-long splinter pressed against Sherlock's thumb, which Sherlock carefully passed his way.

"What do you see?" he asked Huan.

Huan held it before his eyes. "Different color," he noted, frowning.

"Yes," Sherlock replied. "It is lighter, very nearly blond, with smooth borders. And although I could break off a splinter of this length and width, it would be altogether more brittle, whereas this has flexibility."

Huan looked around with a haunted expression. "It seems impossible…" he began.

"It does," Sherlock confirmed. "I have seen drawings in nature books, though I have never seen one up close. Huan, I am loath to ask, for I fear the reply, but however outlandish, tell me what you think it might be."

"Cactus spine," Huan said at once.

Sherlock nodded solemnly. He took it back and, piercing the cotton of his shirt just above the pocket, threaded the splinter through.

"Maybe we check for cactus?" Huan suggested dubiously.

"Merely to be thorough, for we shall not find one. Look about you: have you ever seen a more quintessential English garden than this? Not a whiff of anything remotely exotic."

"But this is a very big clue!" Huan declared. "A joyful moment, no? Why are you not happy?"

Sherlock sighed. "It is a very big clue indeed, monstrously so. But, much as I attempt to be up to any task required of me, I find that with this, I am also monstrously unprepared. I could tell you of tobaccos, and prints, or tracks, or dirt! But cactus? I am not acquainted. I have done no research! Though I recall reading that there are nearly two thousand types, I could not enumerate more than a dozen, I can barely surmise where it grows. I never assumed there would be the need; how could I?" he added in his own defense. "Once again I see that assumptions based on nothing shall always be the enemy of the sleuthhound—"

"Don't know what type of cactus that is," Huan agreed, cutting short the soliloquy. "But I know it is big, like… a prickly pear. They grow well in the center of my country, in Upper Carapichaima. Could the killer have come from Trinidad?"

"Doubtful. He was educated in the English system, not the French," Sherlock said as he worried the thorn between his fingers. "What would a man like that possibly know about exotic plants and poisons? Unless he traveled abroad…"

"You are saying the cactus spine was covered with poison?" Huan asked, concerned.

"Well of course it was!" Sherlock replied, a bit testy. "Unless next you'll tell me that the spine of a prickly pear can kill a human being. But what *sort* of a poison?"

"Perhaps you should not be rubbing it into your skin," Huan suggested, frowning.

"Huan, I have had it between my fingers for the past twenty minutes. If it still carried a toxin, I surely would be dead by now. Besides, it probably needs to penetrate the skin in order to be effective."

*And if I should break out in symptoms, however mild, it might make it easier to identify*, he thought to himself.

But there was another problem. If the killer used cactus thorns, why were they not found on the other victims? They were unusual, and the killer had not gone from murder to murder, each time destroying some nearby wooden object in order to mask his mode of death!

Sherlock rose, turned away from the swing, and knelt down again.

"Hit me—" he began.

"I will not!" Huan protested.

"—with the swing," Sherlock clarified, turning to look at him. "Not hard. Just enough to trace the trajectory of Elise's body."

Huan rolled his eyes to the sky. Sherlock ignored this, turned around again, braced himself, and a second later felt first one then the other piece of wood tapping him at the base of his shoulder blades.

He glanced over his shoulder, giving Huan a sour look.

"You said not hard," Huan protested.

"Hard enough that I at least get a notion!" Sherlock countered. "She was shorter than I; it will strike me in the shoulder blades, not the neck. Surely I can withstand more of a blow than that!"

A moment later, he felt both parts of the swing hit him with enough force to push him forward.

"Apologies!" Huan called.

"No, that was perfect," Sherlock replied. "Here is where she fell, do you see? Off the swing, onto her knees. For a moment, the soft wet grass held her in place, much as the sand sustained the first victim, Rosalie White. And here, you see, are the imprints from her hands, though someone tried to obliterate them…"

"Who would do such a thing? The killer?"

Sherlock shook his head no. "The gardener. There were almost undoubtedly other marks that he did his utmost to hide."

"The gardener did this?" Huan repeated, staring at the expanse of lawn.

"Nothing nefarious. He simply did not want Lady Anne to see where her daughter fell, or possibly even the footprints of the man who murdered her child. It is obvious that the servants care for her."

"That is a good thing," Huan said, sounding as if he craved some positive news.

"Though, again, why the killer should leave marks this time and not the others..." Sherlock muttered, rubbing his chin. "As for the servants, their feelings for Lady Anne are immaterial, were it not that the detail is important to our investigation. For it means that if any of them had witnessed something untoward, they would have intervened. Which further means that not one of them saw a blessed thing. Now. Before our wandering little group returns and we are forced to make small talk with the lady of the house while abstaining from asking anything of substance, let us carefully explore the bushes and see what we can find. Stop at any indentation, any trifling displacement that gives you pause."

Sherlock walked along, trying to spy out broken branches or other sign of disturbance. As he wandered the perimeter of the garden, more questions swirled about his head.

"Master Sherlock!" Huan called out from behind a hedgerow.

Sherlock hurried over. Huan pointed to a shoeprint in the soil. The grooves on the sole were too faint to make out, beyond the fact that they were boots, though not the sort that a gardener was likely to wear. But the outline, better defined, was clearly of a man's right foot, of average size and width, and pointing towards the swing. But where was the left foot? And why were there no other prints nearby, either coming or going?

"He must have breached the wall at this juncture," Sherlock said. "Jumping over, landing here."

"Jumping over on one foot?" Huan asked.

"You see the fallen leaves on the bush to the left of the print? The tiny broken branches? What does that tell you?"

Huan looked from the wall to the bush in front of him.

"He put his left knee against the bush to steady himself," he said.

"Then he climbed over," Sherlock said with a nod. "Walked across the grass, pushed the swing into the back of her head, left the note, and was gone."

"But a bow cannot shoot so far!" Huan declared, suddenly whispering.

And in fact, though the swing was in the killer's sightline, had he aimed from the location where he'd purportedly landed and left a footprint, he would have had to shoot the dart just under one hundred yards. Although an arrow from a longbow might travel as much as four hundred, a cactus spine was no arrow.

"Huan? Have you ever seen a blowgun?"

"Yes, I have seen hunters use them in my country. But to shoot such a long way? Never."

"Just because you have not seen it does not mean it is impossible," Sherlock argued.

Huan shrugged consent. "Perhaps there are better shooters in other countries."

"Being compelled to shoot from such a distance might address why the killer strikes solely during the day. For he must see clearly to aim and to fire, or to spit, or whatever it is that one does with a blowgun."

Sherlock and Huan continued their hunt but found nothing else worth reporting: no other prints, no unusual signs of ingress or egress. When it started to drizzle, they ceased their labors, lest they leave their own tracks, and call attention to their trespass.

While Huan went to fetch the carriage, Sherlock took advantage of his absence to unlatch the kitchen window and climb inside. The thought that the note might be so close without his laying hands on it was past all bearing. Unlike the other notes, copies of which had made the papers, this one had not. In deference to the Queen, a more thorough recounting of the murder had not as yet been written. And although it could have ended up in police custody, Sherlock had a hunch that Lady Anne had kept it—a strong enough hunch that he chanced unlawful entry to find out.

He quickly discarded the notion of her boudoir as a hiding place, for it was far too intimate for such a loathsome object. The same could be said of the desk in her study, where the killer's epistle would perforce share space with family letters, and where Lady Anne would sense its presence each time she composed a missive or settled a bill.

Where else? Not the drawing room. She would never be able to read a book in peace while recalling that it was somewhere nearby, keeping her company. Placing it in the dining room, aside from it being quite the odd choice, would surely spoil any meal.

No, it had to be somewhere where she could readily lay hands on it, if she had to, but not somewhere she was likely to linger.

*The hallway*, he thought. The moment he saw the banquette by the umbrella stand, its latch adorned with a black crepe ribbon, he knew what it held. He opened it and looked inside. It had been cleaned out, save for one thing: an envelope bearing Lady Anne's initials. She had placed the note inside, and sealed it.

## 22

MOMENTS LATER, SHERLOCK CLIMBED ABOARD THE carriage, the envelope tucked in the breast pocket of his jacket. He was more than anxious to read what was inside, but he knew he would have to be patient. He did not wish Huan to see it, not yet; nor did he wish to chance it being damaged by the unseasonable weather. But the moment they reached an inn and were safely ensconced, he would pore over it—through the night, if need be.

"You are so quiet, Master Sherlock," Huan said.

Huan had one hand on the reins while the other peeled the skin off an apple with a penknife. "You are hungry, perhaps," he added.

Without waiting for a response, Huan handed him a slice, which Sherlock took merely out of politeness, for gastric juices interfered with the brain's ability to function.

"Master Sherlock," Huan said, as Sherlock nibbled. "I am your driver, it is what I do. But some things I know. You are protective of your coat. And when you climbed aboard, your breath was heavy…"

"Why, Huan!" Sherlock exclaimed. "Do I detect my brother's influence upon you? Next, you shall be telling me that my heart pounds at precisely sixty-two beats per minute!"

But Huan was refusing to be teased. "I know what I must know for the fighting," he countered. "If a man guards a pocket, I eye it for a knife or a gun. If he has no breath, I decide how weak he is, or how strong. The key to winning is to make changes as one goes, yes?"

"You mean adapt. My brother was wise to select you as my driver and bodyguard. I owe him a debt of gratitude. And to you, I owe the truth. I have in my pocket the killer's note. The original, I hasten to underscore, not an artist's rendition!"

"You went into her house?" Huan exclaimed, looking suddenly alarmed.

"Was it not you who adjured me to avenge the girl?"

Huan shook his head. "It seems I must guard each word that comes from my mouth…"

At that moment, down the green slope of a hill came a small group of travelers, doubtless Lady Anne and her servants, their cart pulled by four Shetland ponies, just as Sherlock had predicted. It had begun to drizzle, and the wagon was making haste to reach home before it fell in earnest.

"Huan. Increase your speed. *Now*, if you please."

Sherlock watched Huan appraise the situation in an instant, and note precisely trajectory and point of impact.

"Hi ya!" Huan cried, giving the horse his rein and cracking the whip high into the air. The carriage careened up the little hill directly into the path of the cart. Huan expertly halted before impact, but the driver, already panicked by the shrieks of his passengers, drove into the mudbank at the side of the road. His left front wheel sank and refused to budge.

Sherlock and Huan jumped down from the sprung seat, acting chagrinned and apologetic. Huan offered to help to pry the wheel loose as Sherlock made a beeline for Lady Anne, holding out his hand so that he might assist her down off the cart.

"All apologies," he said with a slight bow. "I beg you to step inside my carriage, where it is nice and dry, and when my driver is done assisting yours, we shall escort you home."

She turned, a bit rattled, ordered her servants home, and then did as Sherlock suggested.

As the servants dismounted and hurried away, Sherlock opened the door, and set down the stairs. He lit a lamp, for it was already dark within, and as she entered the carriage, he stole a better look at Elise Wickham's mother.

Although she eyed him apprehensively, Sherlock did not think it had to do with him. He marked her as one of those women who are apprehensive by nature, regardless of circumstances. No more than forty years of age, she was blond and rather tepid, like her daughter. That aside, she had fine hazel eyes and a compassionate face.

"Countess Hohenlohe-Langenburg," Sherlock began. "I was hoping to speak to you in private, albeit not like this."

"Do you know me?" she asked, curious.

He nodded. "I attended your dear daughter's funeral. As a humble emissary of Her Majesty the Queen," he said.

"Truly?" she said, surprised. "I was certain that we had been forgotten."

"Not at all, not at all," he replied. "Her Majesty was grieved to hear of the tragedy. In all confidence, she keeps Elise's portrait in the private audience room of Windsor Castle, alongside those of other family members."

All the while, he was racking his brain to recall where he had put the invitation. Suddenly remembering, he opened his *vielle* case and drew it out with a flourish.

"Mr. Holmes?" Lady Anne inquired, peering down at it. "An extraordinary coincidence, for I have heard of you, and of your relationship with Her Majesty. Quite circuitously: something about your helping to ensure a so-called 'zero-sum' game between England and Scotland last year?" she added as she returned the invitation to him.

"Ah, yes. Yes, of course," Sherlock said as he placed it back inside of the case.

As for the football game between Scotland and England, he knew nothing of it, nor what Mycroft might have done to achieve such a score; which meant that he had to change the subject as quickly as possible. But Lady Anne seemed of a different mind.

"I should explain," she said. "My late husband knew Charles Alcock, a player for England, from the time that Charles was a boy. When England failed to win, our daughter Elise insisted..." She paused and then continued. "Elise insisted that we send our condolences to Mr. Alcock, for although Elise does not... *did* not follow the game, she understood that if an entire country is in mourning, then it must have some import!

"Several days later, Mr. Alcock sent a reply," she went on, "wherein he mentioned, with some bitterness, that there had been 'subterfuge.' That a 'Mr. Holmes,' a friend of the Queen, had intervened to even the score. Perhaps he was mortified by the tie and wished to find an excuse. But he did not realize that my link to Her Majesty is tenuous, and was hoping that I, in turn, would spread it abroad that Her Majesty's little ruse had been found out. Payback for him, I suppose, in the wake of such a loss. Whatever the case, I cannot imagine that the Queen would have *two* confidantes by the name of Holmes!"

"No indeed!" Sherlock said with a laugh.

He had expected a bereaved mother who could barely form a sentence, who would have to be coached to reveal what she knew. But, although bathed in grief, she seemed determined to carry on, to speak of her child in a forthright manner. He had to admit that it aligned more closely with a woman who would skirt convention when it came to the funeral and burial of her only daughter, and he wondered why he had imagined her fragile.

Unfortunately, he had no time to think of a new tactic, for the driver and Huan were nearly done extracting the wheel, and he was losing precious time.

"Would you allow me to use my skills and resources to capture your daughter's killer?" he blurted out.

"I would be indebted to you for such kindness," she replied, looking slightly startled, "and to Her Majesty."

For the first time, her eyes welled up with tears.

"Yes, about that," Sherlock replied. "Her Majesty requests, nay *commands*, that no thanks be given her. She was quite firm in that regard."

"Yes. Yes, I see," Lady Anne said mildly. "So. What is it you wish to know, Mr. Holmes? And please. You may call me Lady Anne, for I am not terribly fond of my more formal title. In truth, it has brought naught but sorrow."

"Thank you, ma'am. Lady Anne. Now, I must perforce ask questions of a delicate nature, if you are willing."

"I am," she said as she crossed her dainty hands in her lap.

"As you were the first to find your daughter's body, did you notice any footprints in the garden, anything amiss?"

"Forgive me, Mr. Holmes," she said. "I saw only my child. And the horror, the utter impossibility of it…"

"I can but imagine, ma'am. However, can you recall anything else? Even something of seemingly no consequence?"

"Well, I know that there *were* footprints, for James, our gardener, obscured them. He is a dear soul who has been with us for years. He does not know police procedure; he knew only that he did not wish me to see them. Oh, and I did hear a crow moments before I came upon Elise, but I would not mark that as strange, merely unnerving, given the circumstances. It was a *sort* of crowing."

"In what way, ma'am?"

"Well, it was a… a guttural sound, a burbling, I suppose you would say. Perhaps the creature was ill."

"And have you enemies that you know of?"

"That I know of, no. And neither did Elise, although my estranged husband, the count, has several, I believe."

"He must have been aggrieved to hear of her death." Sherlock could hear the murmur of Lady Anne's driver as he calmed the Shetlands and checked their harnesses. The wheels of the cart had been freed. He could hear the clanking as they refastened the chains that linked the cart to the horses' breast bands. They would soon be back on the road.

"Oh, the count has not heard a whisper of it, from what I am told," Lady Anne replied, "for he is in Switzerland, recuperating from nervous exhaustion. But if he had, he would have no emotions to speak of. He is a rather hard and brutal man. I was a young widow, and like many of my age and station, I was enamored of his links to royalty."

Sherlock heard Huan climb back aboard. The carriage began making its way back to the house. He did not wish to be invited inside, for under no circumstances could the servants overhear him questioning Lady Anne about her daughter's death. Servants were not known for their discretion, and since Sherlock had been prohibited from having contact with her, he preferred to remain for them an anonymous gentleman whose carriage had collided with her cart.

Then, too, there was the possibility that she would bring out Alcock's letter, for it did serve as a point of contact between them. And although Alcock may have referred to Mycroft only as 'Holmes,' it was entirely possible that he had mentioned his Christian name, and that Lady Anne had simply forgotten it. Sherlock could not chance it.

The carriage ceased bouncing and was now moving smoothly up the drive.

"What of investments, ma'am?" he asked, attempting to wrest the last bits of information.

"Truly, could such details be useful in your search for my daughter's killer?" she wondered.

"Investments gone sour can sometimes produce hard feelings, Lady Anne. And hard feelings, revenge."

"I have but one investment. Set up by the count before we… went our separate ways. In that, at least, he has been faithful, or so my bankers tell me. It is the Via Esmeralda Mining Company. Oh, and it seems I have also invested in the work of a man named Heinrich Schliemann. Although we have not as yet seen a profit, I have been assured that we shall."

"What sort of work does Mr. Schliemann do?"

"I believe he digs for gold, Mr. Holmes."

The carriage halted, and as Sherlock pushed open the door, Lady Anne rose to her feet.

"Might you come in and warm yourself a while before hurrying away?" she said, her expression hopeful.

"Sadly, we must be off," Sherlock said.

As she proceeded towards her door, he noted the burden of death that she carried upon her, one that she would not discard until she herself was beneath the earth.

*You are mine*, he vowed to the murderer. *I shall find you, and I shall bring you to justice. That is my guarantee.*

# 23

LONDON WAS EXPERIENCING THE SORT OF WEATHER that made one question the calendar. Though it said spring, the low, dark clouds, bitter winds and needle-sharp rain bespoke a winter with a veritable stronghold and in no hurry to abandon it. This was particularly onerous, given that Mycroft and Douglas were sitting in the back of a chilly carriage with a newly faulty wheel, courtesy of a hole in the road, and heading to one of Mycroft's least favorite places in all of London, the St. Katharine Docks.

Even on milder days, St. Katharine, north of the Thames, was plagued with slick walkways and surrounded by large warehouses that kept the air from circulating until all one could smell was an unholy mixture of coal dust and dead fish. Those everyday unpleasantries became that much worse in foul weather and had recently been compounded by a sinister memory: not six months previous, Sherlock had very nearly forfeited his life upon those selfsame docks, with Mycroft unable to come to his aid. The thought of it still stung.

On the other hand, just that afternoon had come an intriguing telegram from Sherlock with two names. The first name, Mycroft recognized. Heinrich Schliemann was that archaeologist who had been laboring at a dig in northwest Turkey for more than two years. He based the areas of his search upon clues in Homer's *Iliad*—a passion of both arms dealer Vizily Zaharoff and, more recently, Count Wolfgang. Of the other name, a mining company called Via Esmeralda, Mycroft was not aware. And, although intriguing, it would have to wait; for Mycroft and Douglas were to meet a man who claimed to have concrete knowledge of Bingwen Shi's fate.

Kang Chen, boatswain on the cargo ship *Temptress*, had proved helpful to them in the past.

"How did Sherlock come to hear about Schliemann and the Via Esmeralda?" Douglas asked as he clung onto the door, for the damaged wheel was now causing the carriage to swerve most unmercifully on the road.

"No notion," Mycroft replied, as he too held on for dear life. "For he did not say."

"And you did not ask, for you did not wish to know."

*True*, Mycroft thought. Why verify what he feared? That, in his quest for particulars, his brother had already broken a commandment or three? The only possible punishment was to abort the case, something that appealed to neither of them, albeit for different reasons.

As the carriage steadied, Mycroft pulled aside the curtain and glanced out of the window, but he could see nothing except for rain and a veil of his own spent breath. The carriage turned a corner and careened again; the brusque movement extinguished one of the kerosene lamps.

Carlton the driver opened the trap.

"My apologies, gentlemen!" he called back before closing it again.

"And where are they now, Sherlock and Huan?" Douglas inquired as he stood to his feet. Balancing upon the unsteady floor of the carriage, he removed the chimney.

"They were first heading to Elise Wickham's funeral, as you know, which I imagine they attended, else he would have sent news to the contrary. From there, they planned a night's sojourn at an inn on the way to Avoncliff, where Percy Butcher, owner of a stable, was murdered. Then, from Avoncliff to Chichester."

"What was in Chichester again?" Douglas asked, rubbing the wick to coax oil to the top, before lighting a match.

"The ninth victim, the spinster Penny Montgomery," Mycroft replied.

"Ah, yes. She succumbed in the morning while gardening, did she not?"

"She did. I imagine that he and Huan shall pop up at Greville Place sometime in the next few evenings for a good night's sleep in a proper bed before heading north. And I of course am hoping that Huan will curb some of Sherlock's worst impulses, while protecting him from those that he cannot prevent."

"You are asking much," Douglas said. "Of Huan, I mean. As for your brother, he *will* grow up, you know. At which point, you can cease worrying."

"*Can* I," Mycroft replied, his voice dripping with doubt.

"I wonder whether your relationship with Sherlock will ever be fully above-board," Douglas mused.

"Whatever do you mean, Douglas?"

"Nothing. It is none of my affair." Douglas replaced the chimney upon the burner, and then blew out the match.

In fact, Mycroft knew precisely what he meant. The idea that Elise Wickham's funeral should require a formal admission had been a ruse, which Mycroft had been obliged to concoct. Huan's presence was required at Greville Place, for Mycroft—a *gweilo*, a ghost, a white man—would not be welcomed to gallivant through London's Asian enclaves. Even Douglas, who was not a *gweilo* and who was better acquainted with the community's inner workings, did not have the cachet to extract potentially perilous information. Whereas Huan, with his gracious nature and fast capacity to make friends, to say nothing of his part-Shanghai pedigree, had formed inroads among London's Chinese community and had gained their trust.

As community leaders arrived to greet him, Huan had been able to impart to them Mycroft's queries in a manner that they would find palatable. But the trick had been to keep Sherlock cooling his heels without his taking untoward interest in the proceedings.

Thankfully, Sherlock knew next to nothing about the protocol of funerals, nor did he care, and therefore he was not likely to probe further.

In fact, after having been handed the black-ribbon invitation, Sherlock had cast it into his *vielle* case and would not deign to look at it again. In the same way, he'd not been likely to sit and consume rum with his elder brother and members of the Chinese community, which in turn allowed them and Huan to confer in peace. And though Mycroft was not keen to keep secrets from Sherlock again, neither could he allow his younger brother to poke his aquiline nose into a different mystery altogether.

For the time being, the division of labor would have to remain.

"There are the docks!" Douglas announced, glancing outside the carriage window.

Mycroft looked out. It made no difference that they seemed as forbidding as the gallows and were encircled, like a crown of thorns, by angry brown water. To Douglas, they were as welcoming as an old friend.

The two alighted and hastened down her slick, pitted walkways. While the churning waves sloshed over their toes, they elbowed past a steady barrage of sailors and travelers moving in the opposite direction, all of them buried inside their coats or wielding umbrellas like swords so as not to give an inch of ground.

And while Douglas marched steadily onward, head held high and a slight smile upon his face, dodging errant waves and pedestrians with equal aplomb, Mycroft was Scotch-hopping this way and that while trying to protect himself against spray, irksome winds, and the menacing prongs of umbrellas.

"Ah, no. Do not consider halting to point out some ship or other!" he warned Douglas the moment the latter's pace began to slow. "Though I grant that your affection for this hellish place is at times endearing, this is not one of those times."

At long last they reached the *Temptress*.

"So!" Douglas said, his gaze softening affectionately. "Have you missed her?"

"Not for a moment," Mycroft replied. "But I am nevertheless relieved to see her, for she will at the very least be dry."

They climbed onto the bridge. The Chinese guard stationed there waved them through, and they made their sodden way to the rather homely dining hall where they were to meet Kang Chen, the long-time boatswain.

Chen was a slight man of middle years with a shaved head, a gracious demeanor, and kind eyes. He shuffled his feet along the ground as he went, for his ankles were weak from long-ago chains, and the nerves at the bottoms of his feet damaged by repeated caning. And, though mostly hidden by a jaunty cravat, on his neck he still carried a hideous scar that looked as if someone had attempted to remove his head from his body, which in fact someone had.

"Mr. Holmes, Mr. Douglas," he said, hand outstretched. "I am all in sorrow for the dismal weather."

"Mr. Chen," Mycroft said, taking his hand and smiling. "I cannot imagine that it is your doing."

Douglas shook Chen's hand in turn, and the three sat at the end of a long mess table as a galley hand brought them tea. Chen waited until the man was safely back in the kitchen and then said in a quiet voice: "Mr. Holmes. I hear in the wind that you seek information about Bingwen Shi."

"Yes. Do you know him?" Mycroft asked.

"I do not. But a man in my position, traveling back and forth, is privy to much, possibly more than he should be. I make it my business not to betray confidences that float my way, whether intentionally or inadvertently. But in this instance, and because of my great regard for you, I shall tell you what I know, heedless of the possible cost to myself or to my family."

"Thank you, Mr. Chen," Mycroft said with a slight bow. "I do hope the cost to yourself is negligible, and to your family nonexistent. That said, should you lose business because you revealed a secret to a *gweilo*, I shall endeavor to make it up to you."

Chen nodded a little and then said, "We on the docks are more tolerant of white skin than are others of our kind. My merely speaking to you should not raise hackles. That said, it is not my business affairs that are in play, Mr. Holmes, but my life. Regardless, I leave that to the vagaries of fate—"

"We wish to do nothing that puts your life in jeopardy," Douglas interrupted.

Chen regarded him earnestly. "Mr. Douglas? Six months ago, the actions of my brother Ju-long Chen very nearly cost the life of Mr. Holmes's young brother. I therefore consider it my duty and honor to help. Now, what I can tell you both is this. Your Bingwen Shi was taken. I cannot say by whom, nor where specifically, for I do not know—"

"Taken. Do you mean kidnapped?" Mycroft asked.

"That is your word, Mr. Holmes. I prefer mine," Chen said with a slight nod. "He was transported back to China and there accused of high treason against the government."

"High treason?" Mycroft inquired, surprised. "Whatever did he do?"

"It seems that he attempted to sell arms to Japan."

"We were told that he deals in land, not arms," Douglas said.

"Bingwen Shi works with Vizily Zaharoff, the arms merchant," Chen replied. "I have never heard that Zaharoff requires a broker of land. China sees the selling of arms to Japan as a betrayal of the highest order."

"But that is what Zaharoff does," Douglas protested. "He sells to competitors. It is an open secret."

"Yes, it is, Mr. Douglas. But you see, Mr. Zaharoff is a necessary evil, much too powerful to be a target, especially if a country chooses to do repeat business with him, which they all do. Bingwen Shi, on the other hand…"

Chen left the rest unsaid: Shi may have been a sacrificial lamb. It was simply the way of the world.

"Do you know where this meeting between the Japanese and Shi might have taken place?" Mycroft asked.

"Forgive me, I do not," Chen replied.

"And do you know if the sale of arms to Japan was completed or still in process?"

"I believe it was completed, Mr. Holmes, but then I heard a rumor that it was not carried out. I do not know why."

After a moment's pause, Douglas volunteered: "I only traveled to Japan once, a long time ago. And I have heard that, since the Meiji Restoration opened up the country to trade, it has undergone quite the rapid modernization, is that so?"

"It has, Mr. Douglas," Chen responded. "Under Emperor Meiji, everything has changed. Whereas our poor China was weakened by the Opium Wars. And now both countries squabble over the Ryukyu Islands, which threatens to explode into yet another war. So, for someone born on Chinese soil to sell arms to an enemy is a major offense," Chen concluded. "And I regret to say that in the past two weeks Bingwen Shi has been tried, found guilty, and sentenced to *lingchi*."

Mycroft was shaken by this news. Out of the corner of his eye he noticed that Douglas was no less shocked. When neither replied but simply stared, Chen looked at them, puzzled, and then asked: "You have heard of it?"

"Oh, yes," Douglas said, quickly reengaging. "The death by a thousand cuts."

"And you, Mr. Holmes? You have heard of it too, surely?"

"I have," Mycroft answered tentatively. "Though I cannot gauge what of *lingchi* is a Western cautionary tale and what is truth. All I know for certain is that it is meant to humiliate the victim first in life, then in death, and that the torture is painful and excruciatingly slow.

"Is it still a *thousand* cuts?" Douglas asked.

Chen shrugged. "That will depend on the Empress

Dowager, and whomever has her confidence," he said. "One can only hope, for your Bingwen Shi's sake, that the first few cuts sever arteries and he will not feel the rest, whether they be ten or ten thousand… The tea is not to your liking?" he added, concerned.

"It is perfectly adequate," Mycroft said. "I am afraid that your news was such that I forgot all about it…" he added as he lifted the cup and took a polite sip.

Later, Mycroft and Douglas walked back to the carriage in a daze. The rain had turned to drizzle, coloring the sky and water the same shade of indigo. Mycroft no longer cared where he stepped, for he was wet through and through, and the more he thought about his promise to Ai Lin's father, the unhappier he became.

"One bit of good news," Douglas said, eyeing him worriedly. "Chen seems to think that the *lingchi* has not yet been carried out."

Mycroft looked over at him helplessly. "Douglas, it is useless to put on a good face. He is 'somewhere in China.' That makes the proverbial needle in a haystack seem like a game of noughts and crosses."

"Perhaps the Queen might intervene?" Douglas suggested.

"Perhaps," Mycroft said, unconvinced. "But what does Bingwen Shi have to offer that makes him worth saving? And of course, as barbarous as *lingchi* is, if Shi was in fact treasonous to his homeland, *should* he be saved?"

"Well of course he should. It is a barbaric act!"

"Technically not barbaric, Douglas, as they are a more ancient civilization than ours—"

"You know perfectly well what I mean!"

"You are saying that it is brutal, as opposed to our tried-and-true method of breaking the neck?"

"Well, in any event, I appear to be in the unusual position of defending England's mores and honor against your onslaught," Douglas said. "And so now I hesitate to ask…"

"*No*," Mycroft replied, feeling a tad exasperated. "My fondness for Ai Lin is beside the point. I am quite in earnest when I wonder if a man who betrayed his country should be spared. That said, I promised both her and her father that I would try to save him, and so I shall. Indeed, I believe there is only one way to discover what, precisely, occurred and where he might be; and then to attempt a diplomatic solution."

"You *cannot* be thinking what you are thinking," Douglas muttered.

"I believe I am. There is one person who knows what Shi may or may not have done in terms of selling arms, and that is Vizily Zaharoff. We must spend the next several days in diligent research. You might begin by sending telegrams to your contacts at various ports with instructions to immediately telegram back such information as they are willing to share about Zaharoff or Bingwen Shi. I shall perform my due diligence at the War Office. It will doubtless cost me time in small talk with Lord Cardwell, but never mind…"

"Small talk with a former employer who is inordinately fond of you, what a hardship that must be," Douglas murmured with a smile.

"Once we have found out all we can," Mycroft went on, choosing to ignore the jibe, "we must go to Zaharoff, utilizing whatever intellectual arsenal we have at our disposal, for time has never been more of the essence. Are we agreed?"

"We are," Douglas said as they boarded the waiting carriage. "Though it does seem a shame. For I have grown inordinately fond of my head."

# 24

AVONCLIFF WAS A VERDANT, NO DOUBT APPEALING little town, but by the time Sherlock and Huan had traversed the ninety miles southwest from the chalk hills of Buckinghamshire, with an added stop to send a telegram to Mycroft, fog and night had descended and there was nothing left to see. The two travelers were road-weary and sore, with a horse that, however willing, was faring little better than they. And so they sought a room at the first inn they spotted: The Cross Guns on the canal towpath. Their visit to the stables where Percy Butcher had breathed his last would have to wait until morning.

The inn, built during the reign of Queen Elizabeth, attracted a combination of millworkers, quarrymen, and bargees, if one were to judge by the clientele within. A snug on the western extension of the inn had been added for this hard-drinking, card-playing clientele. From the looks of it, they were very well served indeed. In one corner was a blazing fire that mitigated the pervasive damp of being so nearby the water. It was the sort of place that attracted Sherlock precisely for its loud jocularity and dissolute homeliness—to say nothing of its all-but-unbreathable air, for nearly every hand that gesticulated on a point of contention, or that beckoned for another drink, did so with fingers clutching a clay pipe.

Best of all, Huan's presence raised no eyebrows. Or, if it did, all pretended to the contrary. For bargees, even if they'd never traveled further than from one local waterway to the next, considered themselves kin to the open sea, and were therefore quick to take a 'Chinaman' in stride.

Huan was affected not a whit by others' approval or lack thereof. He scouted out his resting place, back to the fire, eyes closed and mouth slightly ajar, his egg-and-sherry untouched before him. Sherlock had teased him about ordering such a frilly concoction, but Huan would not be put off, although sleep arrived before he could indulge.

Sherlock nursed his beer, finished his cigarette, and listened for a moment to the chatter all around him. Mostly, the clientele was arguing about the state of the local aqueduct, a structure whose central span had begun to sag from the moment it was built—and had suffered much patching since.

"They put in th'incorrect stone!" one man brayed. "First frost cracked it in twain!"

"Nay, but it was good local stone!" argued another.

"Bath stone is what's needed!" bellowed a third.

And on it went. Certain that no one was paying him the slightest attention, Sherlock carefully withdrew Lady Anne's envelope from his breast pocket. Then he removed the note, placed it upon the table, and stared down at it.

It was small, three-by-five. He wondered if all were of equal size, for no mention of how small they were had made the papers. Sherlock looked for a brand mark but could find none. The paper had been cut from a larger sheet, perhaps to avoid the manufacturer's name.

*Unusual,* he thought. For it was a common enough stock, milled and sold all over Great Britain. Who would go to the trouble?

*The Fire Four Eleven!* it proclaimed.

He rubbed the paper stock between his fingers, then smelled it. It was what it appeared to be: hemp. Rather thick and unpleasant to write upon, as it tended to sop up too much ink, this hemp had been treated with rosin soap to mitigate the bleeding. Hemp was also hardier than any linen-cotton mix and so better resisted the elements. He supposed that the killer had chosen it, for he could not predict for how much time his missive would have to remain, often out of doors, before it was found and read, remarked upon and copied.

As to the handwriting: the artists' renditions had been quite faithful. Elise Wickham had been the killer's latest victim, yet the writing on the note was perfectly calibrated and well spaced, the hand steady and robust… one might even say joyful. There was no variation that Sherlock could see between this and the artist's rendering of the very first note, which he knew so well that he could see it before his eyes. The multiple deaths had not affected the killer's sense of purpose, nor his resolve.

Sherlock paused.

One of the newspaper artists had rendered the mark over the "i" in the word "fire" as a tiny dash. He had been correct, for that was precisely what the killer had done.

Had the killer broken form on purpose? It was possible, though not likely, that only two of the notes contained dashes— the one in the artist's rendition, and this one. But, more likely, they all did, and the other artists missed it; for a dot was the expected mark, and therefore a dot is what they saw. But there was no ink inside of the dash. It was a mere indentation on the page, as if the man had taken a miniscule blade and nicked the paper above the "i," not deeply enough to perforate it but enough to leave an imprint.

Was the tiny incision his special signature? His brand, as it were? Or did he intend to communicate something specific?

As Sherlock was considering this, something caught his ear.

"Percy Butcher met his end while grooming a mare," the voice opined. "And his dog, an old cur whose sole job it was to warn him of intruders, made no sound!"

Sherlock looked over. The speaker was a well-dressed man of middle years, with a smooth tenor voice and a know-it-all demeanor.

"Saw it with my own eyes!" he exulted.

Sherlock put away the note, swapped his glass of beer for Huan's egg-and-sherry, and sauntered past the braggart's table.

"He collapsed right there in the horse stall!" the brash storyteller was declaring to one and all.

As Sherlock passed by, he took a sip of Huan's drink, almost choking on its sweet viscosity.

The braggart, his own egg-and-sherry in hand, looked up at Sherlock and nodded in recognition of a fellow imbiber.

Sherlock was not certain why men would bond over their drink of choice, but he was aware that many do. And so, he took advantage of the opening to declare, in the stranger's own cadence: "I hear tell he wasn't in the horse stall at all, but outside of it—"

"Then you heard wrong, lad," the man countered. "In the stall he was, and in the stall he remained, and on his side. And the dog made no sound!" he repeated to the others.

"Which side?" Sherlock queried.

"Which side? Why, his… left! Left hand, left side! Resting

on his elbow with his hand underneath his head, as if he were having a nap!" he added as the men at his table chortled.

Sherlock downed the awful concoction he had purloined from Huan and lifted up the empty glass to the man.

"Room for another?" he asked. "For I've a yen for a third myself."

"Never say nay to a free drink, lad," the man replied, laughing.

"And you never do, Daniel!" a brutish man nearby exclaimed, to the general mirth of the table. He had the large, square head of a bulldog, along with a bulldog's jowls, and a tuft of thick black hair that fell over one eye.

Sherlock held up two fingers to the innkeeper, then turned his attention back to Daniel.

"I hear tell there was no note..." Sherlock lied.

"Why, of course there were a note!" the bulldog growled. "Are you daft? Man always leaves a note."

"I saw it," Daniel said, holding up his hands and putting an end to the incipient argument. "It'd been dropped right beside him in the muck!" He turned back to his brutish companion. "Dirtiest stalls as I ever laid eyes on..."

"Come to it by inheritance is what *I* heard," a sallow-cheeked younger man in the corner interjected.

"An inheritance from whom?" Sherlock asked, and the sallow-cheeked man shrugged. Sherlock turned his attention back to Daniel. "So. How did you come to be at the stable that day?" he asked.

Daniel ran his thumbs down his lapels. "Constable's a friend of mine," he said proudly. "I happened to be in town. He knew where to find me—"

"Here, right here!" his thuggish companion announced to more laughter.

Daniel lowered his voice as if he were recounting a mystery. "There we was, half-dozen of us, all invited in to have a look. Eerie, I tell you. Percy Butcher lying there, dead before his time. Just because someone keeps a dirty stable, it don't mean he deserves to die," he added somberly, and other patrons nodded that this was so.

"The papers said that Butcher owned an old dog," Sherlock said. "But that no one heard him bark."

"Oh it was a fine watchdog, that one!" one man declared. "But it was half-blind. So if it didn't smell 'em, it didn't see 'em."

A barmaid laid down their drinks. Sherlock pulled some coins from his pocket and put them on her tray, realizing it was probably too much only when she exclaimed: "Thank *you*, sir!" and added a curtsy.

His largesse did not go unnoticed by his newfound companions, nor was it well received. They pulled into themselves like sea urchins, eyeing him diffidently. But he had no time to assuage their suspicion that he was above them. After all, he was questioning his second witness; he would not squander the opportunity!

"How large was the note?" he asked, and Daniel shrugged.

"There's an odd question, boy," the bulldog said, staring up at Sherlock through chary eyes.

*Tread lightly*, a voice inside Sherlock warned, but he found that, like a runaway locomotive, he could not.

"So big," Daniel said, forming a square of approximately three-by-five with his fingers.

"And who has the note now?" he asked. "Your constable friend?"

"Aye…" Daniel said, this time looking at him quizzically. Even so, he seemed willing to engage until he caught the bulldog's mistrustful gaze. "Why d'you ask?" he added, as if silently challenged to do so by his companion.

"Mere curiosity," Sherlock said with a shrug before continuing on. "Did you perchance see any mark upon Percy Butcher? Anything you deemed unusual?"

This time, without prompting, Daniel rose to his feet.

"Say," he declared, dragging out the word so that it was the length of four syllables. "You are the nosy sort, aren't you, with all your moneyed ways! Who are you? Why all these questions?"

"He never did strike me as an egg-and-sherry man, Dan!" the bulldog declared. "Not from the first! Boy, if you need a lesson in minding your own business, I will be glad to oblige!" he added, flexing a bicep nearly as wide as Sherlock's ribcage.

Without giving him time to respond, the bulldog came crashing over, his stool clattering behind him, and wrapped his burly arms about Sherlock's chest, pinning him in place so that he could not move.

"Tell 'im what's what, Dan!" the bulldog prompted.

Daniel did just that, his reddened face a few inches from Sherlock's.

"Who are you!" he demanded a second time. "Why are you here? Why have I not seen you before? Out with it, lad, or you shall soon have half the teeth you come in with!"

Some of the others suggested to Daniel that he "leave the queer lad alone," but it did no good. Daniel had shifted from jovial braggart to enraged drunkard in the blink of an eye.

With his body immobilized, Sherlock was preparing to mount a verbal defense, which seemed his best option under the circumstances. But when the bulldog growled to Daniel to get on with it, Daniel decided he could not wait it out. Holding Sherlock's purchased egg-and-sherry in one hand, he balled the other into a fist, drew back his arm, and aimed his bare knuckles directly at the midpoint of Sherlock's left cheekbone—when his drink suddenly flew through the air as if someone had shot it out of his hand. And the other fist, the one on its way to a reckoning with Sherlock's cheek, was routed instead to the ulnar nerve of the man who held him fast.

He released Sherlock with a roar of pain, rubbing his elbow.

"I cannot let you hurt him," a voice said, the soft lilt carrying a hint of apology.

Sherlock's two aspiring assailants stared at Huan.

"You kicked the glass from my hand!" Daniel marveled. "With your foot!"

The novelty had washed away his harsh feelings. But his ruffian friend was in no such august mood.

"You are dead," he announced with tears in his eyes.

"Jack, hush," Daniel scolded, and this time the other patrons were in agreement. He turned back to Huan. "Then you used your open hand to divert my fist, yes?"

Huan nodded and smiled.

By that time, the other men at the long table were all on their feet, eyes wide with wonder, a few clapping Huan on the back.

"Might you show us how it's done?" Daniel asked.

That was when Sherlock stepped to the fore.

"He shall indeed," he declared, "if you'll but answer another question or two…!"

## 25

THE FOLLOWING MORNING, AFTER A BEATING AVERTED and a decent night's sleep, Sherlock and Huan made their way to Percy Butcher's stables. The stables themselves had no tales to tell: Butcher's body had been buried for more than a month and the stalls had been cleaned until they shone, for the wags had it that Butcher's relations planned to sell as quickly as possible. Sherlock made inquiries but found out that none lived nearby; that no one in town had ever met them; and that Butcher had never talked about them.

The order to clean and to sell had come by way of Butcher's accountant, one Mr. Sand, whose shingle hung a few doors down from the stables. But the loyal Mr. Sand, citing a matter of confidentiality, would not say from whom he'd received his orders. When Sherlock insisted, his foot ensconced in the doorjamb, Mr. Sand threatened to fetch the constable.

"Mr. Sand," Sherlock told him in what he hoped was a more conciliatory tone, "I am perfectly willing to have my foot severed in exchange for a smidgen of information. Where do Butcher's relatives reside? If you will but tell me that, I shall go on my way and be an annoyance to them, rather than to you."

"I would like to see you *try*," the crisp little man spat out.

"For Butcher had but one uncle, and he resides abroad!"

"Does he indeed, Mr. Sand?" Sherlock said, pressing on. "And does the name Via Esmeralda mean anything to you?"

Sand pushed with all of his might until Sherlock was forced to remove his foot lest it be crushed, and slammed the door in his face.

"What is Via Esmeralda?" Huan asked, for he had witnessed the little encounter.

"A mining company," Sherlock replied. "I know nothing beyond that. But our Mr. Sand certainly seemed to."

"'Esmeralda' is 'emerald' in Spanish," Huan said.

"So, an emerald mine," Sherlock replied.

He and Huan returned to the stables. With nothing to see on the inside, Sherlock concentrated upon the outside. But there were so many shoeprints and hoofprints and carriage wheel grooves pressed into the soft earth that any marks the killer may have made a month before would have been obliterated. Besides, the newspaper accounts of the Fire Four Eleven Murders all underscored a distinct lack of prints. Some of the more salacious rags even went so far as to intimate that the supernatural was involved.

Sherlock noticed Percy Butcher's old dog lying half out of one stall, his eyes cloudy with cataracts, growling low if anyone dared to venture too close.

Some fifty feet from the stables' doors, just beyond a proper little paved avenue that led to and from town (and where even newly laid prints would hardly be legible) was an anomalous bit of green, no doubt kept for the horses to graze upon when days were too cold to wander much farther afield. In the center of the green was a downy birch of decent size. Had someone chanced by and noticed him, the killer could have looked for all the world like a dendrophile inspecting the catkins, which were just beginning to bloom at the time of Butcher's death. It was also enough in the public thoroughfare that a dog, blind or otherwise, would not have been alarmed by a foreign presence there.

While occasional passersby gawked at the stalls, commenting in somber tones upon the terrible tragedy, Sherlock inspected the square of grass from every possible angle. Percy Butcher, who'd been inside and brushing one of the horses, would have been well within the killer's sightlines. And the rain imminent the morning of Butcher's death would have obliterated any stray prints left upon the grass itself.

Having seen all they needed to see, Sherlock and Huan were climbing into the carriage again when an elderly gentleman strolled by. He carried a hand-whittled cane and sported a white beard that reached down to his breastbone.

"Strange bird," he commented, glaring at Sherlock and shaking his head.

Sherlock assumed that the elderly man was referring to him, until he pointed to the tree with his cane.

"Up there in the birch! Strange bird. Born and raised in these parts and never did see its kind." But when Sherlock and Huan dutifully looked up, he scowled. "Did you think it would loiter about, waiting for the likes of you? It flew away, didn't it!"

"What sort of bird was it?" Sherlock asked.

"How should I know what sort of bird? I am not bird mad, like some!" the old man growled as he walked on.

"Here, old fellow! Might you describe it to me?" Sherlock called out as he jumped out of the sprung seat and hurried after him.

"Describe it? It was a crow, but not a crow! Strange beak. Feathers round its neck all… buffeted about, as if it had been in a windstorm."

A crow-like bird? Lady Anne had not seen one, but she had heard one cry out.

"A rook, perhaps?" Sherlock attempted.

"Do I look the sort of man who has never laid eyes on a rook?" he spat.

"Is there anything else you recall?" Sherlock pleaded, and the old man turned, planted his feet, and raised his cane.

"I served in the Sikh War, young man, where I learned respect for my elders, along with a thing or two that I am still more than keen to demonstrate. Now you leave me be," he bellowed, "or I shall give you a good thrashing that you will not soon forget!"

Sherlock would have been ready to insist, had Huan not stepped into his path.

"Master Sherlock," he mumbled, eyeing the old man and his cane with some apprehension. "My head still smarts from yesterday's adventure. Might we let it go?"

The night before, Huan had been as good as his word to the little throng gathered at The Cross Guns. He had demonstrated various *capoeira* moves, and his rapt audience had rewarded him with drink after drink... which Huan, not wishing to insult his newfound friends, had been too polite to refuse.

The great master of Caribbean fighting arts had in the end wrapped a heavy arm about Sherlock's shoulders and, still smiling, allowed himself to be led, step by halting step, to his bed.

The old man went on his way. Before he climbed aboard the carriage again, Sherlock returned to the stables. He picked up a few sticks and threw them in the general direction of the old dog to see if he would notice or twist his head in their direction, but he did not.

As he and Huan drove off, Sherlock mentally tucked away Percy Butcher's dog and the crow-like bird, for he could not as yet formulate anything substantial. Better to retread additional facts that he had gleaned from Daniel at The Cross Guns, in exchange for Huan's performance.

Butcher had fallen on his left side, his left hand most likely rising to the back of his head as he did so. Had Butcher been left-handed? Daniel had not known, and neither had the others at the table, but Sherlock's guess was no.

"If he fell to the left, then it stands to reason that he was struck on the right," he said as the carriage made its way to Chichester, their next destination some ninety miles southeast, where Penny Montgomery had perished. "And as the door to the stable was on his right…"

Huan pulled his cap down low to protect himself against the drizzle that had just begun to fall and reminded Sherlock in a weary voice: "The hit, Master Sherlock, does not cause them to turn this way or that. You yourself said so."

Sherlock wrapped his arms about his torso, lifted his shoulders, and tucked in his head like a condor, as if any of those activities could mitigate the annoying mist.

"Indeed," he agreed. "I do not believe it causes propulsion, as such. But you know better than most that it is still human nature, when one feels so much as a pinprick, to move the body *away* from the offense while moving the hand *towards* it, as balm or defense against further injury.

"Butcher, from what we were told last night," he went on, "was a hefty, muscular fellow. If indeed it was poison that felled him, as I surmise, it would take a bit more time to have its effect… long enough for him to raise a protective hand. Whereas ten-year-old Abigail Sykes 'crumpled like a stone,' in her mother's words. The poison affected her so quickly that she simply spun and fell."

"Yes," Huan assented with a nod. "Any move that places the hand above the heart line, it takes more strength."

"Precisely. The little girl's spin was most likely involuntary," Sherlock concluded.

"But earlier today," Huan countered, "you said you believe Butcher is *right*-handed, no? If so, would he not move his stronger hand, the—how do you say—dominating hand, to protect himself?"

"That is why I believe him to be right-handed," Sherlock replied. "He moved his left hand to his head because his dominant hand, his right, held a grooming implement. Logical to the point of obvious, would you not agree? Still smarting a bit from last night, are we?" Sherlock added with a smile. "You put down enough eggs to start your own hatchery. Ghastly concoctions they are too."

"I shall never touch another," Huan declared unhappily, pressing his temple with two fingers.

Sherlock glared at the steel-colored sky. He had a hunch, in fact, more than a hunch; and he would have loved nothing better than to take out the killer's note again to examine it, but at the moment he could not. And so he sat, wrapped in his own thoughts, as the rain kept on falling.

# 26

SPINSTER PENNY MONTGOMERY FELLED WHILE PULLING weeds, the headlines had read. If not the exact wording, a version thereof had rather breathlessly announced her death in every column that Sherlock had carefully clipped and saved. And, no matter how many times he had perused the news beyond the headlines, it was hardly enlightening. Each mentioned her marital status or lack thereof as if it were of primary import, while leaving more pertinent information—such as her number of years on earth or her general constitution—unremarked upon. The politeness that omitted age or weight and yet insisted upon divulging a lack of spouse seemed to Sherlock the height of arbitrary.

"I cannot know if she was elderly and frail, or of middle years, with robust constitution and a perfectly sound mind," he complained to Huan. "All things, I assure you, of more use to me than the fact that she was with or without husband! The only possible use of such a man would have been his 'busybodying' out of the window so that he may've got a look at the villain who murdered her!"

When they finally reached Chichester, the drizzle had turned to an unseasonably cold rain that kept most people indoors.

Sherlock asked the few locals that could be found such questions as seemed to him useful, only to be looked at askance for wishing to know the weight and mental acuity of the deceased. Not a one of them responded with a shred of goodwill.

Miss Montgomery's abode was a two-story terraced house. Because it was on the end of the row, hers was the only one with a bit of land on one side, and she shared but one wall, rather than the usual two, with her neighbors. These terraced houses had been built on the ancient Roman road known as Stane Street; quite convenient for the killer, Sherlock noted, as the town was both an unromantic little backwater, and thus unlikely to attract crowds, as well as remarkably well paved, with good access in and out. And although Chichester did not yet have such amenities as a piped water supply, it was nevertheless connected by railway to Brighton and Portsmouth, allowing the murderer easy access.

The spinster—for so she had been referred to in life and would be referred to evermore in death—had been plucking stubborn weeds from her vegetable garden in that bit of earth on the corner of Stane Street that she had claimed for herself. Though large windows overlooked the thoroughfare, there were no side windows with a view of any garden except for Miss Montgomery's own. The hour was early enough that there would have been little to no foot traffic on the road; and the town large enough that strangers would attract hardly more than a cursory glance.

"After being struck, she could not have fallen forward, for then she would have hit the wall," Sherlock said aloud as he knelt on the ground, ignoring both mud and pelting rain. "And a bruise upon her forehead would surely have been commented upon," he added. "More likely, she fell to the side, though which side is still a mystery. I should take a look within…"

"Within? Do you mean to enter without permission?" Huan asked, and Sherlock shrugged.

"We have come all this way."

With Huan reluctantly standing watch, Sherlock tried the knob and found that the door was unlocked, typical for a town where all the neighbors were well acquainted. He wiped mud off the knees of his trousers, pushed open the front door and became, for the second time in as many days, a felon in the eyes of the law.

Miss Montgomery's two-story dwelling was composed of sitting room, dining room, and kitchen downstairs, along with two small bedrooms upstairs, one of which had been converted into a study. All of it was rather dark and frayed, but tidy. Sherlock moved through one room after the other, seeing nothing that piqued his interest. In her desk, he came upon a ledger of bills all paid on time; and a note to herself, dating from Gladstone's last birthday, where she remarked that she was born the same year, thus making her nearly sixty-four years of age at her death. From the writing itself to the positioning of the papers and documents, every indication was that she was right-handed; nothing unusual in that. She had no correspondence of note, beyond a pile of letters—some four dozen in all—tied with a red ribbon. The return address read simply "Harold Navarro Rogers." From the postmarks Sherlock deduced that a letter arrived on average once per month. And inside each envelope was a check made out to Miss Montgomery for ten pounds.

None had been cashed. Perhaps Miss Montgomery could abide without the extra funds. Or perhaps the checks, signed by Harold Navarro Rogers, who in each accompanying note declared himself her "loving nephew," were worth more than the money.

*You shall no longer be needing these, old girl,* Sherlock thought as he pocketed the package.

Near the window that overlooked the vegetable garden was only one other item of note: an empty bird cage.

*Odd*, he thought, recalling both the old man's puzzlement at a strange bird lurking about, and Lady Anne's mention of a crow cawing. But Chichester was more than ninety miles from Avoncliff. And Miss Montgomery's birdcage was small, much too small to hold anything resembling a crow.

Sherlock inspected the cage. There was seed in a miniscule bowl and a container with a thimbleful of water at the bottom. Three mottled gray-and-yellow feathers upon the liner suggested that the missing inhabitant was not the smallest crow in creation but a parakeet. And Miss Montgomery was much too painstaking in her housekeeping to leave seed, sitting water, and feathers lying about… to say nothing of a few drops of dried blood.

The latter, Sherlock noticed just to the right of the little door, on the inside of one of the bars. There was a possibility that it was Miss Montgomery's own blood. Had she been sewing and pricked her finger, she might have inadvertently left the stains as she reached inside the cage. But what would she have been reaching for, with blood on her fingers?

No, the most practical explanation was that it was the bird's own blood. Why the creature might have been bleeding, or why it was no longer in its cage, even though the door was closed, were two mysteries that Sherlock could not as yet solve.

He was leaving the house when he saw a most unusual sight. Standing in the rain under a massive umbrella and staring at Miss Montgomery's vegetable garden was a heavy-set woman wearing a small lavender hat, with reddish hair that fell down in rather excessive ringlets below her shoulders. Huan, unseen behind her, was in the process of executing a *capoeira* move whose sole goal was to kick that umbrella clean out of the unsuspecting woman's hand.

A second later, his foot made contact with the canopy and sent it flying.

As she stared at her fleeing umbrella, the woman cried out; only to fall into slack-jawed silence as an Oriental stranger seemingly manifested out of the raindrops, pursued her runaway umbrella, and handed it back to her with a shy smile and a bow.

This final exchange, Sherlock glimpsed out of the carriage window, where he had hurried to sequester himself. For he had gleaned Huan's intent to provide a needed distraction—lest the woman with red ringlets should observe Sherlock exiting the home of her deceased neighbor and take it upon herself to call a constable.

"Isn't your man terribly kind!" she exclaimed to Sherlock as he stepped out of the carriage. "But should he not get out of the rain? I cannot know what people do in China, of course, but here in England we seek shelter, else we catch a chill and die!"

"Madam, might we have a word?" Sherlock asked, touching the brim of his hat. "For we have come a very long way and are most eager to know more."

"From where do you hail?" she asked, in an upper-class accent that seemed thoroughly invented.

"From London, madam."

"Ah! Well now, I cannot invite you indoors, for you are strangers to me," she said, "especially given that one of you is a Chinaman. But you are welcome to step under the eaves so that we may talk. My name is Miss Boyd…"

"I am Mr. Holmes, madam, and this is Huan."

As the two men followed her to slightly dryer ground, Miss Boyd continued: "You are a detective, then, young man?"

"No, madam, I am not. I am simply fascinated by the darker deeds that humanity wreaks, one upon the other."

She smiled and tipped her head coquettishly to the side. "Oh, well put, well put. I understand *perfectly*. Although the poor unfortunate was my neighbor, it is the *humanity* of it all that intrigues me.

"Now, there were none today," she went on, "not in this miserable, spitting rain, but most days we have quite the number of gentlemen and ladies stopping by to have a look, and very nearly to a person they marvel that I am not undone by the idea of a monster lurking about! I do confess, however, that the notion has done nothing for my sleep!"

Sherlock was certain that her sleep had not suffered a whit. After all, he had caught her staring at the little vegetable garden as if hoping to frame every moment of the savagery, as she understood it. And nothing he had heard thus far failed to confirm what he'd already deduced: that she confounded meanness of opinion for honesty; and was the typical small-town busybody who feigned repulsion but was instead fascinated by evil. And, as time passed and the commotion at last moved on to fresh calamities, she would miss it like her own life's blood.

"You are Miss Montgomery's neighbor?" Sherlock stated rather obviously, as they now stood directly before the two front doors.

"Yes. That is hers. *Was* hers, I suppose, and this one here is mine."

"And you were well acquainted?"

"Hardly," Miss Boyd sniffed. "I knew little of her. She kept to herself, had for years. Oh, I know it is not kind to speak ill of the dead, but she was the snooty one, I fear to say. 'Neglectful neighbor' is how I would put it. Perhaps if she had been more generous with her time, she would not have been alone at the moment of death. For we neighbors do watch out for each other," she concluded without a shred of irony.

"What will happen to her house?" Sherlock asked.

"It will be let to someone else. Someone a bit more engaging, I should hope!" she added with a small, tinkling laugh.

"Had you heard her mention a nephew named Harold?" Sherlock asked.

"A nephew? Why, no! I knew of no relatives at all. I doubt she was in touch with anyone. I have not known her to darken the doorway of a post office, for she hardly ever left her house. I could count on this one hand the number of times she wished me so much as a good morning. I am someone who enjoys a bit of a chat now and again, but not she! She made *that* perfectly clear."

*As would I,* Sherlock thought, though what he said was: "I am curious how someone as... sturdy as Miss Montgomery could have been felled so quickly."

"However would you know it was quick?" Miss Boyd inquired, sounding displeased at the prospect.

"Because, had her killer taken his time, surely someone would have noticed his presence and been suspicious."

"Ah, I see. No, she was not sturdy in the least, my heavens, she was a frail old thing, seven stone sopping wet, I'd say."

"I was told..." Sherlock said, leaning in as if he were revealing a great truth, "... that she had a little bird. Would you happen to know what became of it?"

Miss Boyd, having leaned in for the morsel of confidence, looked at him askance.

"Her bird?" she repeated. Suddenly fidgety, she readjusted her little hat upon her head while removing a stray lock of ringlets that had, in the wet, become stuck to her cheek.

"Well, it was dead," she declared. "Dead in the cage, I mean. Good riddance, too. Squawky, noisy thing. The day after Penny's demise, when I did not hear it, I went inside and there it was. Perhaps it had starved to death. Is that possible? Can birds succumb in just one day?"

"You went into Miss Montgomery's house?" Sherlock asked.

"Yes, why not? No one around these parts locks their doors. We are not London, you know!"

"Of course. So, upon finding the bird… deceased, you took it out of the cage. And after removing it, did you shut the cage door?"

"I may have," she said, frowning. "I suppose so, yes."

"And did you then bury it?" Sherlock asked.

"Bury it? Dear me, no! I tossed it out with the rubbish. With pleasure, I might add."

"You tossed it out? Is it perchance retrievable? Might I recover it, if I wished to?"

"You would wish to retrieve a dead bird? Whatever for? And no, for the rubbish was burned three days ago."

"When you found the bird, was it bleeding?" Sherlock asked with more verve that was probably warranted for the occasion.

"Not that I saw. It was simply… dead."

"And the morning of Miss Montgomery's death, do you recall that it cried out?"

"You ask quite peculiar questions for someone who is not a detective," Miss Boyd complained.

"I might someday become one," Sherlock replied. "Was it making sounds?"

She shrugged. "No more than usual. It always chirped in the morning, or whatever budgies are wont to do," she replied in an indifferent tone. "Penny—Miss Montgomery—would open the side window, you see, place the cage there, upon the sill, then go to work in the garden. Quite proud of the fact that she was the only one among us with a bit of dirt to call her own. When she was done, she would close the window and put the cage back… well, wherever she kept it. A creature of habit, that one," she said, confirming what Sherlock had suspected. "Open the window, put the cage at the sill, work in her garden, remove the cage, close the window. For years, she did that."

"But the newspapers described her as a near-recluse. How would one be privy to her habits?"

"Well certainly one can watch what a person does at a window. Or in a vegetable garden. Surely there is no harm in observing someone while they are in the public eye! As I stated, I am a student of humanity! And in point of fact you seem more taken with the bird than you do with Miss Montgomery's demise," she added, eyeing him sourly. "Or with my welfare, for that matter, given that the murderer has not yet been caught!"

"And do you recall any days that she did not go out into the garden as usual?"

"Why, yes. Nearly all of the last week. I heard her with quite the cough. But the moment she was better, there she was, at it again."

*There is your answer to the killer's delay between killings*, Sherlock thought.

"Miss Boyd," he said. "We need no longer intrude upon your time and patience. Good day."

With that, he turned and hurried through the downpour back to the carriage.

"Well, how… remarkable!" she called out peevishly, and Sherlock smiled to Huan beside him.

"Clearly, bird queries are not salacious enough for our dear Miss Boyd's tastes," he whispered as they climbed into the sprung seat and bid a stormy *adieu* to Stane Street.

# 27

ELSEWHERE IN CHICHESTER, SHERLOCK AND HUAN FOUND shelter at The Fountainhead, a fairly modern pub that reclined, like a body upon a fainting couch, against an ancient Roman wall. It was said to be haunted by several ghosts, among them a Roman soldier, or so the young barman enthusiastically announced as he brought their meat pies and ale. He had the thick, coal-black hair and ice-blue eyes of Joe McPeel, the lad from Nickolus House whom Sherlock had befriended for a time; though he did not possess McPeel's raw intelligence. He was instead a rather bovine creature.

"Be on the lookout. You especially," the barman added, pointing to Huan, who was drying himself by the fire. "The Chinamen, they perceive things that we cannot," he explained to Sherlock with an expression of earnest wonder.

While Huan sat down at a little table and dug into his meal, Sherlock rolled a cigarette, lit it, and then pulled the pile of letters from his coat pocket.

"What is that you have there?" Huan asked, eyeing them.

"They belonged to Miss Montgomery," Sherlock confessed on the exhale.

"You *stole* them?"

"Not at all. I borrowed them."

"But… Master Sherlock, you must return them!"

"To whom? Their owner is deceased! Besides," he mumbled as he rifled through them for interesting tidbits, "there is nothing terribly relevant here."

*Beyond the fact that the nephew's affection for her seems genuine*, he thought.

From the little he could piece together, Harold had lived with his aunt for some months as a child, though he did not mention when, or why.

"Harold Navarro Rogers," he said aloud. "Clearly, either the father or the mother did not hail from these parts. And clearly, Harold did not expect a reply from his aunt, for the return address has listed only his name. My guess is, he did not wish to burden her with the need to reply, for he knew that she could not."

Her neighbor's vituperative words had brought to Sherlock's mind something that he had read. A psychiatrist in Berlin, Carl Westphal, had coined an interesting term: agoraphobia; '*agora*,' from the Greek meaning 'place of assembly,' and phobia, or fear. Westphal had used it to indicate the state of persons who, possibly through no fault of their own, were loath to leave the confines of their own abode.

"Navarro is a common enough surname in Trinidad," Huan said, looking up from his meat pie. "It too is Spanish. Like the Via Esmeralda."

"There we are again, eh? We seem to have a link, however tenuous."

"Wonderful!" Huan said with an expectant grin, as if Sherlock were about to reveal something of import.

Sherlock sat back in his seat and drew a breath. He suddenly felt inadequate to the task, as he had when he had discovered the cactus thorn in Elise Wickham's neck. Even if he were sitting not at The Fountainhead but at one of the world's finest libraries, with the most comprehensive research at his fingertips… for what would he even begin to search?

He fought off an unexpected shiver.

"Do you believe in ghosts, Master Sherlock?" Huan asked, eyeing him, as he took a sip of ale.

"No, Huan, I do not. Though I confess I am feeling rather haunted at the moment."

Sherlock stared glumly at the flames in the hearth. He took out the killer's note again. Three inches by five. Why create a note so small and symmetrical? Sherlock weighed it in his hand and inspected it for the hundredth time, especially around the edges, looking for something in particular, something he surmised but could not yet discern.

In a corner of the paper, he noticed a light creasing that he had at first attributed to it being mishandled. Now, looking at it again with a new perspective, it did not seem to be that at all. Could it have been made by a beak? Surely a trained bird could carry a three-by-five note and place it wherever the killer wished—thus explaining the lack of human footprints!

Lady Anne had heard a crow caw. The old man near the stables had seen a small crow-like bird that he swore he had never seen before. And now a parakeet had been found dead in its cage, spots of blood indicating that the death may not have been natural. Might some sort of tamed, crow-like bird have attacked the parakeet inside its cage? But if so, would it not have been a messier demise? And yet, Miss Montgomery's neighbor did not recall any traces of blood on the little avian corpse.

As for Percy Butcher's dog—it was, for all intents and purposes, blind. Sherlock had dutifully tossed a few sticks towards it to see if it might have noticed a bird flying by, but of course it had not.

Young Will Jury's dog, on the other hand, was quite active, playing with his young master in life and licking the boy's face in death. Could a barking, hysterical dog have kept the bird at bay? Is that what had caused the killer to add the note for his third victim at a later date?

As for the eighth victim, Abigail Sykes, her mother was close by the entire time. Surely a bird flying in through the window with a note in its beak would have drawn her notice. Her constant presence must have been why the killer had to return on the day of her funeral, when he—and, purportedly, his trained bird— would not be so easily spotted.

Sherlock traced the slash above the "i" with his forefinger. It suddenly seemed a spiteful little gesture to the world at large. Again, a trained bird could surely make such a mark, utilizing its beak!

"Huan? What do you know about crows?" Sherlock asked.

Huan smiled. "Master Sherlock, the islands of Trinidad and Tobago are famous for their many colored birds! Hundreds and hundreds we have, all different, and so beautiful. But no crows. I know nothing of crows."

"I know somethin' of crows!" a voice announced.

It was the black-haired barman. There were few people in the pub and, apparently bored, he had gone from one table to the next, cleaning as he went, moving closer and closer to their conversation.

"They are a portent of evil, so they say. But I do not believe it, lest he tells me different," he declared, staring at Huan with the same wide-eyed wonder.

"Do you happen to know how many types of crows there are?" Sherlock inquired, which seemed to leave the man at a loss.

He tilted his square head, rubbed the back of his thick neck with the rag that he had been using on the tabletops, and shrugged his shoulders.

"Now, I don't know as to how many types in all. But me mam found a small one, one what had felled out of its nest. She began to feed it breadcrumbs and scraps and such. They is very bright, with the gift of recall, and they learn tricks too!"

"What sorts of tricks?" Sherlock asked.

"Fetching! They can fetch, like a dog!" the barman said. "Not just big objects. Tiny ones! They'll pick out a mote of dust among many if you train 'em right!"

"Do you recall it ever utilizing tools?" Sherlock asked.

"Tools?" the man repeated. "Like a hammer and such?"

"No, more like a stick."

"Nah. Like I say, it would pick up things for me mam."

"Is the bird still around? Might we see it?" Sherlock asked, rising.

The barkeep brushed the back of his neck with the towel again.

"Nah. Our da didn't care for the cawing. Killed it two years back. Me mam couldn't bear to see it dead and had me bury it. When I saw it up close, I could tell it wan't no proper crow. It was smaller, with rough feathers. A rook!" he concluded proudly.

Sherlock thought back to the old man, and his description of a bird that had the look of a crow or a rook but was neither.

Holding up the killer's note but keeping it face down, he said: "And what of this? Do you suppose your mother's bird could have carried something of this dimension in its beak, and perhaps deposited it where she wished?"

The barman scratched his chin. "Never seen that, specific. But if you're asking could it pick up and carry, aye. I've seen it carry bigger and heavier, for they are attracted to shiny things… Be something amiss with your pie?" he asked, and it took Sherlock a moment to realize what he was referring to.

"No, no, nothing," he said, picking up his fork.

He was saved from having a bite when another patron came through the door, and the barman excused himself to take his order.

"Perhaps you should eat and not smoke only," Huan chided him.

"One keeps me awake and one puts me to sleep, Huan. Which of the two do you suppose I need more at the moment?"

"I think you can rest a little, for you have made great progress already, Master Sherlock!" Huan announced.

"Oh, undoubtedly," Sherlock replied. "Now all I need to find is some sort of traveling clerk or other bureaucrat with a murderous bent who keeps a trained crow that is not a crow but something else entirely."

"There, you see?" Huan answered, grinning. "As I say! Progress!"

# 28

MYCROFT CROSSED THE STREET TOWARDS THE OFFICES of the Secretary of State for War in time to feel the first rain of the morning. Though he knew that it would come, and that it hailed from the southwest (he could sniff out the changes in the air), he had renounced the umbrella that the driver, Carlton, had held out for him. In truth, it was preferable that he arrive upstairs slightly disheveled, as if the journey had cost him—if not dearly, then at least decidedly.

It had been six months since he had quit his employment at the Cumberland House offices. His employer, Edward Cardwell, had not yet replaced him and would probably never, for it was Cardwell's intent to retire within a year at most, which made the hiring of new personnel superfluous, and also allowed him to make Mycroft the scapegoat for the paucity of manpower.

*Whomever could I dig up to replace you, Holmes?* he would announce each time they met, in the vaguely accusatory tone of the jilted suitor, accompanied by a hangdog expression and a mournful shake of the head. Since his surgery, Mycroft would have happily done hand to hand combat rather than make a social visit to Cardwell.

Then again, he was also thoroughly aware that his association with his former employer was the quickest, most expeditious way to gain access to Vizily Zaharoff. One word from Cardwell, and Zaharoff's doors would spring open to him… if not in welcome, then at least in grudging acknowledgement of his existence. For, in spite of Zaharoff's impressive power and notoriety, no arms merchant worth his salt would wish to be on the wrong side of Britain's well-regarded Secretary of State for War.

From the relative safety of the building's overhang, Mycroft watched the rain start to fall down in sheets, accompanied by a volatile wind that blew the drops first this way and then that. He pulled out his pocket watch, almost as if to delay the inevitable, when he saw young Charles Parfitt arrive at a gallop astride his chestnut Warmblood, Abie. Parfitt, reins in one hand, umbrella in the other, tossed the reins to an awaiting groom with more practiced aplomb than Mycroft had ever beheld, unhooked a cake box from the saddle, and then hurried as quickly as he could towards the front entrance… only to skid to a stop when he noticed Mycroft loitering in the doorway.

"Ho, Parfitt! Let us go up together!" Mycroft called, at which point Parfitt smiled broadly.

"I went to fetch cakes, sir!" he called back, holding up the box as proof. "Mr. Cardwell is quite particular about his cakes—"

"Yes, and the temperature of the tea too, as I recall. Hurry out of the rain, for pity's sake. Hello there, old boy," Mycroft murmured as the groom turned Abie around and past him on their way to the mews. "And how is this one getting on?" he asked Parfitt, giving Abie a steady scratching on the bridge of his nose, a move which Mycroft knew he favored, for the gelding had once belonged to him.

"Oh, splendidly, sir! He is well cared for."

"I can see that."

Abie's ears came forward and he exhaled a breath, a signal

that he recognized and was relaxing under his former owner's touch.

"He remembers you still, Mr. Holmes!" Parfitt said, beaming.

"Yes, well…"

Mycroft pulled his hand away and motioned for the groom to walk on. He was not keen to acknowledge the regret tinged with melancholy that Abie produced in him.

"You received my note, Parfitt?" he inquired as he and Parfitt opened the outer door, removed their damp overcoats in unison, and made their way to the second-floor offices. "You were able to ferret out the information I requested?"

"Oh yes, sir. I made notes on Via Esmeralda, as well as on the German gentleman you inquired about. I have not yet been able to secure a list of investors in Via Esmeralda, as the Board of Trade has been quite intractable."

"I may have to do some smoothing of feathers," Mycroft said with a sigh.

"Yes, sir. As for your latest inquiry, it was just as you surmised: fascinating, really, though I still do not comprehend why you would point me to Somerset House, of all places."

"Lucky guess, Parfitt," Mycroft replied quickly, a lie that he could tell did not fool Parfitt in the least, while also knowing that the lad would not pursue it. If Mycroft found himself face to face with Zaharoff, as planned, it would be to Zaharoff that he would reveal the whys and the wherefores of Parfitt's latest investigation.

"I believe you will be quite pleased with my discoveries, sir, if… if I am not too bold to say so."

"Good lad, Parfitt. Good man, I should say."

"Yes, sir. Thank you, sir," Parfitt replied, his cheeks reddening at the compliment.

For Parfitt had, not so very long before, been an inexperienced boy with bad skin and a painful stammer whom Mycroft had persuaded Cardwell to hire as a favor to his former landlady, Mrs. Hudson. Bringing her nephew into the fold had, as it turned out, been a savvy favor indeed. For Parfitt, now nearing twenty years of age, was a quick learner with a keen memory and a prodigious gift for unearthing the arcane but useful tidbit.

"Do you happen to have those notes upon your person?" Mycroft asked.

"Oh yes, sir. I haven't let them out of my sight! Would you like them now, sir?" he whispered as the two crossed the outer suite and stood at the door to Cardwell's private office.

"If you don't mind," Mycroft replied with a smile, at which point Parfitt slipped them out of his inner jacket pocket, his eyes darting about as if he half expected constables with manacles to appear from behind the bookcases.


Some half an hour later, Mycroft and Cardwell were seated at the conference table by the large windows with a splendid view of Pall Mall below. That is, it would have been a splendid view, had the day not continued to be wet and dreary. Mycroft's own dampened state had gone all but unnoticed, as Cardwell had insisted upon the windows remaining wide open so as to provide a 'nice lungful of healing air'—along with the occasional gust of moistened wind, which made it feel as if they were attempting to have tea in a monsoon.

"Our reserves have at last been raised to thirty-six thousand men!" Cardwell announced with some pride.

"Well done, sir. They were a mere thirty-five hundred when you assumed the post, I believe." Mycroft wiped his cheek and forehead after the latest onslaught and repocketed his handkerchief.

For the past half hour, Mycroft had been awaiting a natural pause into which he might inject Zaharoff, but he had found none. Instead, Cardwell had recounted, in minute detail, each victory and setback during his five years in office, including the two during which Mycroft had been at his side.

Still talking, Cardwell rang a bell, and Parfitt arrived with the teapot.

"More tea, sir?" he asked Mycroft.

"Thank you, no, Parfitt," Mycroft began, but Cardwell cut him off.

"Nonsense, a second cannot but do you good," he announced, "provided that it is served at the correct temperature! You have stomach issues, do you not, Holmes?"

"No sir, I do not believe I do—"

"Ah. Well, this shall remedy whatever ails you."

Cardwell held up his cup and pointed commandingly to Mycroft's, and Parfitt dutifully poured more tea into both.

"And take a cake, man!" Cardwell thundered. "I had them bought specially. Parfitt, put one on his plate. Make it two! As I was saying," he added, "a tenfold increase in troops is nothing to sneeze at. There is even talk of raising me to the peerage. Annie is quite pleased at the prospect. Of course, the moment I am ennobled, I can no longer serve as a politician," Cardwell opined, frowning.

"Ah, well. Handy then, that you were planning on retirement."

Cardwell sighed. "Yes. I did dearly hope that a Holmes would assume my post," he muttered, assuming the hangdog expression that Mycroft so detested. "You have a younger brother, yes? Perhaps *he* might choose to go into service when he is older…"

*Sherlock as Secretary of State for War?* Mycroft thought with some amusement.

"I failed to retain you, Holmes, the regret of my career, for now I shall leave office without a general staff system, something I am all but certain you could have helped me install, for although you have no political clout, you are clever, Holmes, very clever. This government needs you, man."

"At the moment, sir, I am needed elsewhere," Mycroft said, seizing his opportunity.

"Oh?"

"Yes, sir. I happen to be in the unenviable position of needing from you an introduction to Vizily Zaharoff."

As injections went, it was hardly well executed. Cardwell reared back in his chair.

"A *terrible* man! Why should you wish to have to do with *him*?"

"As a favor to a friend, sir."

"Hm. Must be a good friend indeed. I would not go *near* that bloodthirsty Ottoman on a bet. Now, I have no qualms with arms dealers, but this one is not above selling faulty products to one country if a second, rival country greases his palm. He will also entice a country into buying the very latest weapons at a nice discount, and then terrify its enemy into buying the same for twice the amount—"

"I understand, sir, but I have made certain promises—"

"Ah. As you did to me," Cardwell complained. "That you would remain in my employ, for starters—"

"Sir?" Mycroft interrupted so as to remain on the subject. "Have you heard tell of a kidnapping some weeks back? A Chinese native named Bingwen Shi was taken from a London street and spirited away to China."

Cardwell's eyes narrowed. "How do you know about this?"

"I know his future father-in-law, Deshi Hai Lin, along with Lin's daughter, who is engaged to be m— married to Shi," he replied, detesting the way his voice frayed at the word 'married.'

Cardwell drummed his fingers upon the tabletop, then tugged at the bristly brownish-gray whiskers upon his cheek until he resembled a howler monkey readying itself for confrontation.

"Bingwen Shi was indeed kidnapped," he confirmed, dropping his voice, "while walking to Zaharoff's offices in Berkeley Square. His crime was that he, a Chinese national, was selling arms to Japan."

"But why would Zaharoff give a Chinese national such an assignment and risk losing an employee? It does not appear to be an error that he would make," Mycroft said. "Unless Shi was to be a sacrificial lamb. The question then becomes 'why?'"

"Why indeed. Don't just stand there with your mouth open, boy, pour!" Cardwell thundered to Parfitt as Mycroft's stomach twisted at the sight of the full teacup—his third, along with two cakes, at least one of which he would have to consume before leaving.

Cardwell took another sip of tea and said, "Zaharoff was not in your purview while you were here at the War Office, yes, Holmes? For you dealt with armed forces, as opposed to armaments or arms merchants."

"Yes, sir, that is correct."

"Hm. Well. You have certainly guessed it: Zaharoff not only did not make an error, it was he—from what I am told—who alerted the Chinese authorities to Bingwen Shi's perfidy."

Mycroft leaned forward. "Why would he do that?"

"I cannot say. Whatever the reason, I have no interest in the man's intramural squabbles. Only in forcing him to remain on the right side of the law whenever he is in England. But if you are hungry to find out, I shall provide a messenger with a proper introduction… on your word that you will not go there alone, or unarmed. Are we in agreement?"

"Whatever you wish," Mycroft said.

"Might you meet with him this afternoon, then?"

"If he is in town and available, do you mean?"

"Oh, he is, I assure you. I am always well aware when that man is anywhere *near* London. As for 'available,' yes, he shall be. Unless he wishes to be sent packing, he is 'available' to this office whenever *we* choose, not he!" he exclaimed, eschewing his quieter tone for his more familiar bombast.

"Sir?" Mycroft said. "Might I take an hour to peruse whatever information you have on Zaharoff?"

"Well, naturally," Cardwell said, rising. "For you can do in an hour what most could not accomplish in a week! Parfitt, put down that teapot and go fetch the Zaharoff files, and put them on Mr. Holmes's old desk.

"Your speed comes in handy," he added, turning to Mycroft again, "for I want this expedited, Holmes. Whatever your dealings with the man, strike first and strike hard. Do not give that fox enough time to strategize any moves against you. For I still consider you one of us and always will. Now eat your cakes quickly, man, and be about it!"

"Thank you, sir," Mycroft said right before pushing one of the cakes, very nearly whole, into his mouth.

# 29

OUTSIDE A FOUR-STORY BRICK TOWNHOUSE ON BERKELEY Square, a stately carriage and pair were waiting. The driver and chestnut horses, the initials 'VZ' inscribed in silver upon their liveries, had a covered space reserved for them, a rare sight indeed in the congested West End. The townhouse itself had a very fine view of the square, as it lay diagonally across from the Lansdowne fountain by Alexander Munro with its water-bearing nymph. A row of remarkable plane trees shaded "her rather woebegone labors," as Mycroft muttered to Douglas when the latter arrived at the entrance to meet him.

"Why woebegone?" Douglas asked, glancing back at the fountain as the two hurried up the steps of Zaharoff's offices.

"Her expression is filled with ennui. And, speaking of labors, I hope you will forgive me for pulling you away from yours."

"Perhaps she is woebegone because her creator was dying of consumption as he sculpted her," Douglas replied. "Speaking of which, your message seemed a bit breathless."

"Cardwell's idea," Mycroft explained as a doorman held open the door. "He desired we visit post-haste. You brought your gun?" he added, lowering his voice as they stepped inside.

Douglas patted the pocket that held his trusty firearm: a

Smith & Wesson top-break, single-action Model 3. "Were you expecting a shootout?"

"I promised Cardwell that I would not come alone or unarmed."

"Ah. So, I am to be your second. Should I wield the thing about as I enter, or simply pat my pocket meaningfully? I imagine an international arms dealer will be caught hopelessly off guard by such a show of brute force."

"Well, aren't we the jolly valet this afternoon," Mycroft replied. He passed his calling card to the attendant on duty while Douglas stared at nothing and followed Mycroft down the hall.

"Gallows humor," Douglas whispered before recanting. "In fact, things are going rather well at Nickolus House. Shortly before your note arrived, several boys whom I was having difficulty placing in apprenticeships were able to secure not just suitable but impressive employment."

"How very good to hear," Mycroft said. He had meant his tone to sound even, not flat; but his preoccupation with other matters betrayed him, for as they followed the attendant to Zaharoff's suite, Douglas muttered:

"So, you had nothing whatever to do with it. The timing is sheer coincidence. All promises to me notwithstanding."

"I happen to need your undivided attention on this matter," Mycroft said in his defense.

"And you have it. I told you I was in. What is more in that 'in'? You are being manipulative for sport!"

"Surely you cannot be *too* put out to know that your charges now have the possibility of living past the age of seventeen," Mycroft replied.

Their conversation was halted by a secretary who barred the way to the suite.

"Kindly include the time and date of your arrival," the secretary said, handing Mycroft a ledger and indicating a line just below the signature of the previous visitor.

Douglas dutifully passed Mycroft a pen, while Mycroft managed to fumble the ledger onto the floor.

"My apologies, sir," Douglas murmured to Mycroft, assuming the blame.

Both Douglas and the secretary reached for the ledger, but Mycroft was quicker.

"No bother, I have it!" he exclaimed while leafing through the pages. "Here we are! No, wait, here…"

"Please allow me," the secretary said, nervously reaching for it, but to no avail, for Douglas—in an attempt to be helpful—got in the way.

After a bit more fumbling, Mycroft found his place, signed and dated it, and they were allowed inside.

The brisk efficiency of Vizily Zaharoff's offices, and the casual air that belied its costly furniture and well-regarded but inoffensive art, seemed to Douglas to reflect the man himself. He was tall and angular, with close-cropped white hair, and dark eyes framed by broad, gold-rimmed glasses that obscured rather than enlightened. He was approaching fifty but looked ten years younger, with the rolling gait and brusque familiarity of the sailor he had once been—although, this many years later, he exuded none of the sailor's innate suspicion of worlds beyond his comprehension but instead carried the easy confidence of someone accustomed to being in charge.

When Mycroft and Douglas were introduced, Zaharoff reacted not at all to Douglas's height, nor to his hue, giving nothing away beyond a gracious hello. So rare an occurrence was this that Douglas had to remind himself that his relief (and the possible lowering of his guard) could prove deadly, for Zaharoff was nothing if not a cunning foe.

The three of them sat in a beautifully appointed but comfortable drawing room populated by rare books and punctuated by more fine art, while a manservant poured afternoon tea. Mycroft sighed quietly as his cup was being filled, something that Zaharoff noticed at once.

"My friends, forgive me," he said in a suave, smooth tone accompanied by an apologetic smile. "I do not indulge in alcohol: at least, not before darkness falls! Moderation must perforce accompany daylight, yes? But perhaps you would care for something more… robust?"

Both men assured him that tea would do just fine, and Douglas thought to himself that this man, with his agreeable countenance and mellifluous voice, could have made his mark in any trade he wished, savory or otherwise. How egregious that such charisma had been put to such questionable use.

"Now gentlemen, what can I do for you?" Zaharoff asked pleasantly.

"Mr. Zaharoff," Mycroft began. "I fully realize with whom I am dealing. In Vienna recently, I watched a man sail out of a window, rather than face you with a loss of your capital. Another has cloistered himself in a sanatorium, hoping against hope that your Mr. Schliemann will discover the hidden gold of Troy, so that he might be able to repay your money, and leave Switzerland and his confinement with his head intact."

Douglas was startled that Mycroft would open his volley with such a blatant show of force. But Zaharoff seemed nonplussed.

"Weak individuals," Zaharoff said with a shrug. "To be

pitied. As for Schliemann, he will find the gold. Perhaps you should invest, Mr. Holmes."

"I was asked to do so by Schliemann himself," Mycroft admitted. "But I am not fond of uncovering strata via dynamite—simply blowing everything to kingdom come. It may be perhaps less efficient to preserve artifacts as one goes, but I do believe it is the right idea. Now, Mr. Zaharoff. During the Crimean War, you cornered the market on saltpeter, lead, and sulfur, the constituents to ammunition, and sold to Her Majesty's enemies."

"Naturally. I sell munitions to many nations. Everyone is quite aware when they do business with me that I play no favorites. For me, it is solely a question of supply and demand—"

"This very year," Mycroft interjected, "you are helping to arm the Ashanti Empire against Britain. Granted, you are not a British national, but you own a business here, and property in London."

Zaharoff looked suddenly like a child who'd been told there was to be no Christmas.

"Mr. Holmes," he said, his tone thick with disappointment, "news of your excellent brain precedes you. And, much like Herod Antipas of old, I expected to be dazzled by your miraculous intellect. I even heard talk that you predicted, to the *hour*, the collapse of Austria's economy. Instead, here you are, regurgitating commonplace news."

"Forgive me, sir, if I do not dazzle," Mycroft replied. "But, since you steadily venture into arms sales with countries upon the brink of war, or at opposite sides thereof, surely selling to Japan and China at the same time would not be an unusual move for you. Nothing that would cause one of your employees to be taken by force and charged with high treason."

Mycroft paused for a reply. But when Zaharoff said nothing, he explained:

"I am here to glean but three things: the whereabouts of your employee, Bingwen Shi; an understanding as to why he might be in his current predicament; and a method of extricating him from same. I would appreciate if you would bestow upon me, as a personal favor, said information at your earliest convenience."

Zaharoff rose to his feet.

"I am one of the richest men in the world!" he said indignantly. "Why should I do a favor for you, Mr. Holmes? I too have the means of unearthing whatever I wish to unearth. I know of your wealth, but in comparison to mine, it is a fleabite. The talk of your great brain intrigues me, but unless it entertains or it can be used to line my coffers, it is just another disposable piece of gray matter."

"What makes you so certain I cannot use my 'great brain' for just such purposes, Mr. Zaharoff?" Mycroft countered. "Both to entertain *and* to line?"

"I cannot utilize you *or* your brain, Mr. Holmes, because you are a patriot, and of the worst kind. You are well aware of England's faults, yet you slavishly align yourself with her all the same. Even in this, your reputation precedes you. As for you, Mr. Douglas," he added, "you have seen more of the world than has our young Mr. Holmes. Perhaps you can agree with me that the notion of a 'good' versus a 'bad' country is naïve at best, and foolhardy at worst."

"I agree that patriotism can be a cudgel, Mr. Zaharoff," Douglas said as mildly as he dared. "But I also believe it can be a badge of honor. That is how I view it in my friend—not because I choose to, but because I believe it to be the truth."

"Well then you disappoint me as well, Mr. Douglas. As I have no use for a patriot, or his blindly loyal friend, I am now obliged to bid you both a good day."

Having been thus dismissed, Douglas began to rise… until he realized that Mycroft had not stirred so much as an inch, nor did he intend to. Douglas resumed his seat, though he was not at all hopeful as to where it would lead.

"It seems, from my studies of you—and I *have* studied you, Mr. Zaharoff, do not doubt," Mycroft said, "that your real skill is in knowing precisely when and in what matters to offer and solicit bribes. Firearms laws, export control laws: all sticky wickets. Your maneuvering in that regard is uncanny."

Zaharoff's head darted towards him like a curious bird.

"You were not, however, successful in bribing my former employer, Edward Cardwell," Mycroft went on, "to look the other way whenever you choose to sidestep a legal regulation or two. For if you had been, I would not now be sitting here."

"On this we agree, Mr. Holmes. Your Edward Cardwell is a very stubborn man, with a streak of impracticality. I heard in the wind that the famous 'Cardwell Reforms' were in truth orchestrated by you."

"Then the wind has misled you, Mr. Zaharoff, and I am not susceptible to flattery."

"And you have no proof of the bribes," Zaharoff replied as if suddenly enjoying the repartee. "I know you do not."

"No, I do not," Mycroft admitted. "Everyone who has ever been in the position of revealing that particular skill of yours, at least from first-hand experience, is either just as culpable, and so *will* not; or has been disposed of, and so *cannot*."

"And so. Notwithstanding my need to bow to your Mr. Cardwell and the War Office, you have no proof of wrongdoing," Zaharoff said. "Once more, I bid you a good day."

When Mycroft again remained where he was, Zaharoff looked highly displeased. As the tension in the room increased, Douglas placed his hand on the pocket that held his Smith & Wesson.

"There *is* something that I find terribly queer," Mycroft said, staring up at their host. "That you should choose Bristol as a holiday spot for three years running."

Mycroft's gaze seemed unflustered, his tone more curious than combative. Nevertheless, the innocent-sounding query seemed to catch Zaharoff unawares, for he removed his glasses and, with his eyes at half mast, glared down at his unwelcome guest.

"Do not misunderstand," Mycroft added, his bland-as-milk expression belying the steel in his tone. "Bristol is a fine city, as good as any in England. Still, I am not certain that it suits one of the richest men in the world."

"An easy explanation for that, Mr. Holmes," Zaharoff said, sinking into his chair again as if there'd never even been a hint of ire between them. "I studied at Oxford. As a student, I did not possess the capital that I do now. I spent several happy summers in Bristol with friends; and I find that, as I grow older, sentimentality can trump both luxury and awe-inspiring settings."

"Of all of the adjectives that I might use to describe you," Mycroft said, "'sentimental' would not top the list. Nevertheless, it is strange that, among reams of information about you, some true, most embellished, all from widely circulated, *noted* periodicals the world over, I should come upon an article in one of Bristol's papers, dated two years ago. Instead of lauding your notoriety and financial prowess, this local rag—which caters to the small Ottoman community—seemed fixated on your humble beginnings as an immigrant from Turkey, treating you as a sort of 'native son makes good.' Oh, and this was not regurgitated fare; some quotes came directly from you. It was almost as if its intent had been to make a positive statement not of your money or power, but of your *character*. Naturally, I was curious. Whom were you trying to impress, in *Bristol*, with your faithfulness and uprightness? At Somerset House, I found my answer. The record of your marriage to a Greek girl, only twenty years of age, dated 18 March 1872, that I believe would come as an unhappy surprise to the wife you married in Rotterdam in 1860."

Zaharoff stared at Mycroft as if he wished nothing more than to murder him where he sat. But then, his expression crinkled with what Douglas could only describe as sheer delight.

"Well played, Mr. Holmes, well played!" he said, clapping his hands. "Excellent. Please, address me as my friends do: Zed-Zed, for you have earned the right! To reward you for such thorough work, may I gift you with the newest Winchester, the 1873?"

Zaharoff rose with a flourish, popped open a mahogany cabinet, and drew out the rifle.

This time, Douglas did more than lay a hand; he was retrieving his own weapon when Zaharoff turned to them, holding up the rifle for inspection.

"Glorious!" he crowed. "Walnut stock, twenty-inch-round barrel, chambers a more potent, centerfire cartridge, I praise it to the skies!"

"A fine piece," Mycroft said mildly, while at the same time Douglas slowly replaced his pistol in its holster. "Not a complete surprise, for, as I recall, you do business with the Winchester Repeating Arms Company."

"Yes, I do, Mr. Holmes! From whence did you ferret that out? Another obscure newspaper article, perhaps?"

"From the War Office," Mycroft replied in the same mild tone of voice.

A shadow passed over Zaharoff's face, but it was fleeting.

"I confess they do not cost me as much as they would you," he parried. "All the same, they make a very nice gift. And I can, of course, provide its twin for Mr. Douglas, should he wish it."

"Thank you, no, Mr. Zaharoff. Zed-Zed," Mycroft corrected himself. "What I wish above all is what I came for: information about Bingwen Shi."

"So, at least now we are negotiating like men! In exchange for your discreet silence regarding my forays in Bristol, I shall provide you with Bingwen Shi's whereabouts. And I shall do you one better: as proof of my goodwill, I shall even give you the means to extricate him. As to why he is in that predicament, I cannot reveal, for it would jeopardize my business interests, and that must be where I draw the line."

"Thank you," Mycroft said, rising to his feet. "I will provide your secretary with my address, as well as that of Mr. Shi's fiancée, who must be kept apprised of matters as they unfold."

"You must have a deep regard for Mr. Shi—or perhaps for members of the Lin family?" Zaharoff asked as he led the way out. At the exit, he placed his hand upon Mycroft's shoulder.

"You must understand, Mr. Holmes," he said, leaning in, "that in shifting political winds, what was not remotely dangerous becomes suddenly fraught. Reputations are destroyed in an instant. Thus, I am sometimes compelled to make a severe example of someone with whom I associate."

"And why did you feel compelled to make an example of Bingwen Shi?" Mycroft asked.

"Ah. Once again, you know more than you let on, Mr. Holmes. Let us say that Bingwen Shi did not hold up his end of a bargain with me. He was a disappointment. If you, who are not at all in my line of work, have heard the more scabrous mythologies of my reputation, then it stands to reason that whatever I am doing to guard against perennial mutiny and shoddy maneuverings must be working adequately, yes?"

"Indubitably," Mycroft said. "It is stunning how open to reason people can be, the moment they fear you. Is that not so, Zed-Zed?"

"Oh, it is, Mr. Holmes, it is," Zaharoff replied, seemingly overlooking Mycroft's jab. "I truly look forward to our ongoing association, for I believe you shall be invaluable to me.

"As for you, Mr. Douglas," he added, "I should be remiss if I did not know a thing or two about all my guests. I know that you are an owner of the excellent Regent Tobaccos, as well as the secret benefactor of Nickolus House, named after your deceased son, if I am not mistaken. I know you are an expert in the art of *capoeira*, and I would love nothing more than a demonstration someday. Given all that, your value has yet to be proven. But, as you are Mr. Holmes's dear friend, I must assume it is substantial indeed."

"Thank you, Mr. Zaharoff," Douglas said curtly. "But I cannot fathom what value I could ever have to you."

*Or what value I would ever wish to have*, he thought sourly, for he knew full well that the purpose of Zaharoff's recitation was meant to intimidate. Far from having been lulled into complacency, as he had feared, Douglas could not recall disliking anybody more than he disliked 'Zed-Zed' Zaharoff.

# 30

BY THE TIME MYCROFT AND DOUGLAS WERE BACK outside, the rain had lessened to a trickle and the street was swelling with mid-afternoon foot traffic anxious to get about its business once again. As Mycroft waved for the Queen's chartered carriage to come back round, he thought that he might offer Douglas a lift back to Nickolus House. For Douglas, likely as a money-saving measure, had traveled the two miles from Old Pye Street to Berkeley Square on foot, and Mycroft could tell from the scent in the air and upon the ground, and from the shape of the clouds, that the current respite would be temporary.

The offer was not entirely altruistic, for Mycroft was feeling victorious and in the mood for a good Cognac and a cigar, an indulgence he allowed himself with less and less frequency. Though both could be had back at Greville Place, he dreaded an encounter with Sherlock, due back for a night's rest before proceeding north. The vision of his brother, gleam in his eye and swirl of acrid smoke circling overhead as he recited all things foul—from rampsmen and smashers, to hunters and duffers, and the means and methods of butchery—was simply more than he could bear.

Whereas at Nickolus House, he and Douglas could have a civilized jaw about this more intriguing, and for the moment, less sanguinary case. Douglas's humidor at Nickolus House held a batch of Mycroft's favorite smokes of the moment, El Rey del Mundo, though an H. Upmann would do in a pinch. And Douglas might even be persuaded to open that 1800 Napoleon that Mycroft had helped him to luck into a few months before, and that they had set aside for a special occasion. They could indulge while perusing Parfitt's notes, which Mycroft had not yet had the wherewithal to remove from his pocket…

"The man is a bigamist! Truly, do you intend to remain mum upon that point?"

Mycroft was startled out of his reverie. Douglas, standing beside him, seemed intent on a reply, which made Mycroft feel misunderstood and a tad violated.

"I cannot fathom your priorities, Douglas," Mycroft said in his own defense. "That Zaharoff may be a murderer is no longer your principal concern, whereas bigamy is the sacred line that one must not tread upon?"

"I find no humor in this," Douglas shot back. "Clearly, in the panoply of sins, murder is at the highest tier. However, his murdering ways are as yet unproven, whereas there is a woman in Bristol who deserves to know that she is not the only wife to that man. As does, by the by, his *first* wife."

In the tense silence that followed, Mycroft watched the maneuvering of the carriage past the jumble of rigs, carts, and pedestrians, all dodging the young boys whose job it was to scrape up newly deposited horse dung before the clouds opened again. He wondered if the traffic had grown worse over the years, or if his mood simply rendered it, at times, more infernal.

The carriage at last drew up beside them. Carlton, their impressively mustached driver, lowered the folding steps, his impassive expression remaining thus even when neither of his charges made a move inside.

"You admire him," Douglas said as if he were wiping something unpleasant from his shoe.

"I have no moral judgment of him at all," Mycroft parried. "It was simply a stratagem: to go on the attack, using the same ethically questionable business moves that Zaharoff has defended many times before, thereby lowering his guard—"

"This, I could not fail to notice," Douglas replied. "As I cannot now fail to notice your 'stratagem' of not answering my question."

Other drivers were beginning to weave around their carriage and to ring their bells, and when that failed to rouse them, to curse aloud.

"In fact," Mycroft replied, "if I inform either wife, I lose my ability to negotiate. Bingwen Shi shall be executed, and perhaps you and I shall lose our heads—all for being such short-sighted dullards!"

"I cannot vouch for the rest, but I would wager that we shall be able to keep our heads," Douglas said.

"Oh? You are certain of that, are you?"

"I am. For I know you, Mycroft. You wear your victories upon your sleeve. To this juncture, at least, he is canary to your cat, which means that we are perfectly secure."

Circumstances aside, Mycroft had to admire Douglas's ability to gauge the situation, as all around them the ringing and the cursing grew louder and more vile.

"I am asking you, as a friend, to step inside the carriage," Mycroft said under his breath. "For I have much to discuss with you, and it cannot be broadcast in the middle of the street. Quite apart from the fact that we are about to start a riot."

Douglas turned to the driver. "Kindly go about the square a few times—"

"Carlton, you shall do no such thing," Mycroft protested. "Douglas, I mean to take you as far as Nickolus House—"

"No. Say what you have to say and let us get on with it," Douglas stated as he climbed aboard.

Mycroft followed meekly, while the driver snapped the stairs into place.

As the brougham once again entered the chaotic flow of traffic, Douglas did not deign to even look at Mycroft; instead, he held open the curtain with one finger and stared outside.

Mycroft waited.

"What," Douglas said at last, turning to Mycroft as if reluctant to engage, "did you see in that ledger that piqued your interest?"

"You noticed that, did you?" Mycroft said with a smile that he hoped was ingratiating rather than smug.

"Your acumen in reading and retaining might be awe-inspiring," Douglas replied, "but your skills as an actor are abysmal."

Clearly, Douglas was not about to give him an inch. Mycroft attempted to keep his temper in check, hoping to salvage not merely the conversation but the friendship.

"Let us not begin at the ledger," he counseled, "for it contains elements that perforce must come last—"

"So what comes first?" Douglas challenged. "For Zaharoff kept his offices as inoffensive as possible, so that nothing of his business dealings could be discerned therein."

"He did," Mycroft agreed. "Nonetheless, there were clues here and there as to what motivates him. Such as the illustrated translation of Alexander Pope's *The Iliad*, first edition."

Douglas nodded. "I did see that," he said. "Impressive binding, hard to miss. What of it?"

"Did you also see that small portrait of an obscure subject, the one with the gold tag that read 'Giovanni Aurispa'?"

"I did not."

"From what I recall, Aurispa was a fifteenth-century Italian savant and historian who is credited with bringing a tenth-century manuscript—the earliest known version of Homer's epic poem—to Venice. Both the book and the *Venetus A*, for that is what the manuscript is called, point irrevocably to what I had already surmised upon seeing Count Wolfgang's suite in Vienna: Zaharoff is more than simply 'invested' in Schliemann's archeological digs; he is *obsessed* with finding the elusive golden treasures of Troy. A rather ironic Achilles heel, do you not agree? In any event, I am keen to use it to my advantage. For he does not know how much money I have. He cannot know. Why would he? To this point, I have been no threat to him. And by the time he finds out that I might have a *bit* more than he thinks, I shall have won away a goodly portion of his treasure."

"It is that very thing, Mycroft, that concerns me. You seem to view this as a game."

"Surely there is nothing alarming in that. For do you not also gauge various aspects of mortal life to be a test?"

"I do indeed," Douglas admitted.

"Well, then. A test, a game—what is the difference? Another clue to Zaharoff's business ventures was his offer of the 1873 Winchester itself," Mycroft continued. "Even if one has close dealings with the company, those newest models are quite hard to come by. Which means that Zaharoff must have been instrumental in Winchester's largest sale to date: forty-five thousand of the *earlier* model, the Winchester 1866. Now,

Britain's spy network did manage to alert the War Office just this year as to the sale, for it was substantial; but no one to this point had been able to establish either broker or *buyer* of said weapons."

"You are saying that Zaharoff is the broker."

"I can guarantee it. Usually so open with his double dealings, he has managed to hold this particular transaction close to the chest, which of course piqued my curiosity the moment he mentioned his association with Winchester, for I perused all documents at the War Office pertaining to him, as well as all arms transactions of the past three years, and I saw no such link."

"So you made a guess."

"An educated one. And when I saw his countenance darken, I knew I was correct."

"So now you have guessed the broker," Douglas underscored. "But how can you, from that, make out the purchaser?"

"From what I have read of Zaharoff, there is but one country that is near to his heart. His homeland. I believe that cache of weapons was sold to the Ottoman Empire, for their burgeoning conflict with Russia. That of course would come as a very unwelcome surprise to the Russians. A bit of faulty intelligence, and Russia could underestimate both the cache and the quality of weapons coming against them. Our advance knowledge of the matter could save them thousands of lives."

"*If* you choose to reveal it," Douglas interjected. "If instead it is to England's advantage to remain silent on the matter, those 'thousands' will die… the unfortunate detritus of war. Rather hideous. Out of curiosity, this information about Zaharoff that you unearthed—when did you do so?"

"Earlier today. Why?"

"And in how much time? Two hours? Three?"

"How is that pertinent?"

"In how much time, Mycroft? Give me the satisfaction of knowing, at least."

"An hour five, and I still do not see—"

"Because we mortals are astounded by such things," Douglas declared. "Because it seems that momentous decisions affecting many upon the world stage can turn on just this sort of a detail that you ferret out in moments and then place into your pocket for later use."

"Surely you are exaggerating for effect," Mycroft countered.

"Am I? You decide whether or not to reveal such information depending on how it serves Britain. Or your family. Or me, for that matter."

"What would you have me do instead?" Mycroft asked, feeling his anger rise.

"Tell the truth. I grant that the cost is high. But to act ethically, regardless, does not make one a—what did you call it? A 'short-sighted dullard'? Your newfound friend Zaharoff is a monster, one with myriad tentacles. And one does not negotiate with monsters," he concluded.

Mycroft stared at him impatiently. "He is not my friend. And you know better than to try to twist my arm with a bromide. Now, might we cease to go around in proverbial as well as literal circles? For, as I said, I shall gladly give you a lift wherever you wish to go."

"Again I thank you, but I prefer to walk," Douglas said.

He rapped his knuckles against the trap and requested that the driver halt.

"Douglas, do not be a goose," Mycroft exclaimed. "The lull in the clouds is fleeting; you will catch your death!"

But Douglas would not be mollified. "By the by," he said softly. "There *is* a difference between a test and a game. A test presupposes the existence of a *tester* as well as of a test-*taker*, whereas a game is naught but competition between two human beings, and presupposes nothing but itself."

Mycroft watched Douglas step out of the carriage, dig his hands into his pockets, and, with his head slightly bowed, move away until he became one among the throng and was finally out of sight.

Douglas had gone on foot less than a mile when, as Mycroft had predicted, the lull ended and the rain returned with a vengeance, complete with blasting draughts that laughed the month of May to scorn. Turning up his collar did no good at all, for the wind was a ruffian, and a noisy one at that, peppering its ceaseless complaints with whistles and moans. A rapid walker regardless of the weather (lest anyone object to a black man strolling along at too leisurely a pace), Douglas lowered his head another quarter inch and hugged himself into his sodden overcoat just as a gust of wind funneled past the walls on either side of him and buffeted him sideways. He realized that to attempt to push on all the way to Old Pye Street and Nickolus House was nothing but sheer stubbornness and stupidity on his part.

Perhaps he could take a detour to the Red Lion. The owners had always been kind, and would welcome him; but even that might be too severe a trek. So he turned back and headed in the opposite direction, for the closest respite where he might wait out the frenzied rain was his own Regent Tobaccos. At least Mr. and Mrs. Pennywhistle would not cast him out because of the color of his sodden skin!

As thunder rumbled above, temporarily undoing any other sound but itself, Douglas dashed down Conduit Street and then turned onto Regent Street towards the shop.

He sprinted up the steps and tried the door, but it was locked, and he had not thought to bring his key. Assuming that Mr. P. was in the back with a customer, he rang the bell and called out; and he heard the faint voice of Mr. P. return the call: "Douglas? Is that you? A moment!"

Douglas was reaching again for the knob when he felt something hard land squarely upon the crown of his head.

He spun around to see what it was, or to defend himself if need be, when he felt his legs collapse beneath him… and after that, he felt no more.

# 31

WITHIN MOMENTS OF DOUGLAS'S DEPARTURE, THE STORM that Mycroft had predicted made its appearance. By the time the carriage was approaching St. John's Wood, it had become a veritable draining of the heavenly fountains. Mycroft calculated the first volley and what he knew to be Douglas's usual walking pace. He considered which inns were likely to welcome his friend, along with a handful of others that would not—at least not without a fair-skinned companion by his side. He would most likely have sought shelter at the Red Lion, though the smarter move would have been to retrace his steps and make for Regent Tobaccos, which lay less than a half-mile from Berkeley Square, and so was the closest of the two better options.

Whichever locale he had chosen, Mycroft assured himself that his friend was out of the weather, perhaps nursing a beer at the first locale or having a nice cup of tea at the second, while Mrs. Pennywhistle fussed over him like a brood hen. But, if Douglas were biding his time for the storm to pass, he would have quite the long wait. Newspaper predictions notwithstanding, it was certain to remain stubbornly overhead for the next several days.

*Serves him right!* Mycroft thought. For Douglas had upended their plans. Instead of lingering by a welcoming fire in a homely kitchen, Mycroft was being jostled about in the back of a cold, damp carriage, with barely enough light to read by.

At least Carlton had repaired the bad wheel. One had to be grateful for small blessings.

A half hour before, he had finally taken Parfitt's notes in hand—and then had forgotten all about them, immersed as he was in other miseries. Now, in the drab glow of the carriage lamp, and to put his mind elsewhere, he squinted down at the lad's chicken-scratching to learn about the Via Esmeralda Mining Company.

At an ancient site in Colombia, South America, worked originally by the Aztecs, abundant emerald deposits had been 'rediscovered' in the 1500s by the Spanish, only to lay fallow for hundreds of years, while Colombia endured political and financial crises. In March 1873 came a savior: a syndicate composed of Deutsche Bank, the primary partner; the precious metals conglomerate Jobine, Mathison; and a Colombian civil engineering firm which held the least significant piece of the pie, a paltry four percent. This triune had snatched up mineral rights for a price dramatically below actual value: a little under four million pounds.

The entire endeavor carried with it the odor of political chicanery.

Mycroft thought again of Prussia—or Germany, as Douglas would have it—with more land, more people, and four times Britain's troops—not to mention a single-minded interest in procuring arms and military positioning. An emerald mine could certainly add to the necessary funds.

Then there was Count Wolfgang, a rogue who had deep ties to Prussia… possibly at the expense of his own cousin and the country she ruled.

Mycroft looked up just as his townhouse came into view. He considered redirecting the driver first to the Red Lion and then to Regent Tobaccos, to ferret out Douglas and to insist that he accept a proper passage home, but he discarded the notion as unworkable. For Douglas would not take kindly to that sort of coddling. He was not some poor unfortunate who could not care for himself, and for Mycroft to insinuate otherwise would be to insult him, something that he was not keen to do under the cloud of the present misunderstanding.

Thus resigned, he stepped out of the carriage and was hastening towards his gate, with Carlton hoisting the umbrella beside him, when Zaharoff's monogrammed carriage and pair turned the corner at speed and halted just behind the brougham. From the rig emerged a tall, distinguished-looking messenger underneath a gargantuan umbrella of his own, which bore the same 'VZ' monogram. The liveried messenger handed him an envelope, bowed his farewell, and hastened back to Zaharoff's carriage, while Mycroft ducked inside his own so that he might open it in peace.

Inside the envelope were two notes. The first, on monogrammed stationery, read:

*My dear Mr. Holmes,*

*The method for extricating your subject consists of a personal entreaty. You shall find that the Chinese, being proud, will settle for nothing less. Your emissary must perforce be someone who is intimate with the subject and must bring with him proof of the subject's innocence. I can furnish a letter that underscores that no one in my employ or tasked with serving as my emissary in any arms sales to Japan was of Chinese extraction. The original is on its way to Miss Ai Lin's*

*address at Stafford Terrace, so that she might pass it on to the*
*appropriate envoy, with a copy of the same to your address in*
*St. John's Wood.*

*As for this employee's whereabouts on the date of the suspected*
*treason—the 4th of April, the day of the purported sale in*
*London—I can in no way vouch. There, you are on your own.*

*As to the date of execution, my operatives tell me it shall take*
*place at midnight on the 19th of June, one month from today.*
*Time, therefore, is of the essence.*

*In continued friendship and goodwill ~ ZZ*

A second note, on coarse, unmonogrammed paper, and in a different hand and pen, had upon it an address in the town of Zhouzhuang, in Jiangsu Province. This, and the fact that Zaharoff had been careful not to mention Bingwen Shi by name, seemed a strange but notable caution.

Mycroft checked the date of disappearance again. It agreed with Cardwell's information, and with Ai Lin's: the 4th of April. Perhaps 'Zed-Zed' could not prove Bingwen Shi's whereabouts on that day, but Ai Lin might, provided that she had kept Shi's train ticket. For Shi could not be simultaneously in a sleeper car on its way to London and *in* London, selling arms to Japan!

The thought of Bingwen Shi walking about Glasgow with Ai Lin flooded him with jealousy. Though he knew they would not be strolling hand in hand, nevertheless he pictured them thus; and it could easily have set him to sulking, wiping any other thought from his mind, were it not for a sharp rap upon the carriage door.

On the other side of curtain and the breath-steamed glass stood his brother, gesticulating, seemingly unaware that rain was descending upon him in sheets.

"I distinctly heard your carriage seven and a half minutes ago! What are you about in there?" Sherlock demanded.

Carlton had once again abandoned his cloistered perch and was standing dutifully beside Sherlock, holding up the umbrella, which Sherlock was assiduously ignoring.

Mycroft opened the carriage door, reconciling himself to hearing every tawdry detail of Sherlock's travels and travails when instead his brother exclaimed:

"There has been another murder! Huan and I must be allowed to proceed at once, while the body is fresh!"

# 32

THE FIRE FOUR ELEVEN KILLER HAD MURDERED HIS eleventh victim that very morning, in Kingston upon Thames. The newspapers reported that the victim's name had been Rupert Jurgins, aged forty; that 'the simple man' had been found lying on his back across the threshold of his home; and that his elderly mother had been left 'alone and inconsolable.' The time of death was not reported, nor was news of who first found him, though Sherlock assumed that dubious honor had fallen to his elderly and inconsolable mother.

Thankfully, as Jurgins's abode lay little more than fifteen miles from London, Sherlock and Huan would be able to reach it by late afternoon, provided that they depart as soon as possible.

"This is spectacular news," Sherlock said. "The body is still under scrutiny; perhaps there is *something* I can do to gain admittance."

"On a case of this prominence," Mycroft responded, "and so close to town, Scotland Yard will doubtless make an appearance. If their man, Martin Speckle, is present when you arrive, you may drop my name and hope for the best."

"Drop it? I shall wave it about like a flag!" Sherlock replied.

After receiving his brother's blessing, Sherlock paced the

front hallway, waiting for Huan to come round with the carriage. He was all but despairing of it ever arriving when there it came, sporting a handmade canopy over the sprung seat. Upon closer examination, the canopy had been fashioned from canvas and oiled green silk, and then attached to the body with clips that one might use for sailing vessels.

"What have you done?" Sherlock marveled to Huan.

"I cannot have you sopping wet, Master Sherlock," Huan explained. "And since she will not stop raining on us, the little beggar…"

He wagged a finger at the sky.

Mycroft emerged to see about the delay and frowned, displeased.

"So, instead of resting a while, as you were commanded, you stood in the pouring rain, creating a canopy?" he huffed. "All because my brother does not have the wits God gave him to stay out of the rain?"

Huan squinted at his handiwork, and then shrugged. "Let us hope it remains upright," he said.

"It shall withstand a hurricane!" Sherlock declared, which made Huan smile more broadly than ever.

Sherlock tossed his traveling bag and *vielle* inside the carriage, though he had not yet found a moment to play it. Closing the door, he clambered up into the sprung seat, newly dry, and aiming to remain that way.

It was not that Sherlock minded getting wet. In truth, it hardly fazed him. Still, if anyone had ever made such an effort on his behalf—one who was not family or obligated to him in some way—he could not recall when.

Huan climbed beside him, took the reins, clicked his tongue, and they were off.

Mycroft, who had been dreading his own return home, watched as the carriage disappeared, with Sherlock waving a perfunctory goodbye. He waved back, suddenly feeling as light as a feather. Although he could not, in good conscience, thank heaven for some poor unfortunate's demise, he was not above going back inside to smoke a cigar in peace, at long last, and to reconsider Parfitt's notes in blessed solitude and cosseted by a nice, warm fire.

He chose the drawing room, and an eye-pleasing Turkish rocker that he'd had reupholstered in soft black leather. He had a glass of scotch at his elbow—for when one had his heart set on an 1800 Napoleon, every other Cognac seems suddenly lacking— and had just taken his first puff of an El Rey del Mundo when an errant thought darkened his mind:

*I wonder what has become of Douglas…*

He shook it away, annoyed with himself:

*Really, Holmes, you are worse than a mother hen…* until a second came fast upon its heels:

*I must go and speak to Ai Lin!*

Mycroft sighed and took a sip of his scotch. He had chosen twenty-year-old single malt Macallan specifically for its inoffensive smoothness and unfussy nature. Why, then, did it taste so harsh?

*Ai Lin can wait until morning*, he told himself sternly. Yet, like a persistent gnat, the notion would not let him be.

Since becoming friends with Douglas, he'd kept on hand— both in his library and in the drawer of the small writing desk in the drawing room—timetables for ships for London and Liverpool. It seemed that a steamer bound for Shanghai would be departing from Liverpool in two days' time; and, but for a small and impractical sailing vessel departing three days after that, there would be no other steamer making the trek to Shanghai until June.

*There, that should settle it!* he told himself. *You must go at once and tell her!*

Instead, he sat again, immobilized by doubt. Could it be that he was delaying a visit solely to increase the odds of the Shi family finding no emissary? In that event, Bingwen Shi would not be reprieved and would therefore be executed.

*If that is your plan, it is absurd! Regardless if Shi is alive or dead, Ai Lin is not yours, nor can she ever be.*

No, something else was giving him pause, something he did not yet understand, a sort of foreboding. He took another angry swig of scotch to chase away both angels and demons, then a third and a fourth to inspire in himself some artificial bravery.

*Foreboding be damned!* he thought at last.

He stood a bit unsteadily upon his feet, put out his cigar, and called for the carriage, all the while fretting that the notion of visiting Jennings Rents in a rainstorm, just as the day was ending, would cause poor Carlton to hasten off at a gallop back to Buckingham Palace, never to return.

As he waited for the carriage to come round, Mycroft stared at himself in the hallway mirror. He was glad to see that his pallor had abated; that his eyes looked clear; and that the scar upon his cheek had grown more faint with the years, unless he was simply becoming used to its presence. He ran a comb through his blond hair, wondering what Samson-like powers he thought he might lose if he submitted to a much-delayed cut, and with anxious fingers straightened his tie not once but thrice.

*You are not going courting,* he reminded himself, *but to help to recover her fiancé. Your appearance should be the last thing on your mind!*

He heard the carriage wheels outside the door, collected his hat and overcoat, and drew a deep breath. At least his heartbeat was steady. He took one last look in the mirror, feeling pity for the rather pathetic, yearning young man that he saw reflected there.

# 33

SHERLOCK GAZED DOWN AT THE SHAPE OF RUPERT Jurgins's head. Victim eleven had large, slack lips, rounded eyes, and a heavy brow. Even death could not mask the fact that he had been of limited mental acumen, that he was indeed, as the newspapers had declared, 'simple.'

Who on earth would wish him dead? Who, but his suffering mother, would mourn him, or be punished by his absence?

The police surgeon from London was indeed Martin Speckle, who had grudgingly granted Sherlock two minutes with the body—hardly a proper amount of time, but better than nothing.

As he felt the back of Rupert Jurgins's head and neck, he heard Speckle conversing with the parish officer, whose various jobs included rounding up witnesses and renting premises for viewing, for Kingston upon Thames had no police morgue.

"In truth I was hoping this case would bypass me altogether," Speckle fumed.

"And what of me?" the officer declared. "You would think this takes precedence over all else, but no! Everyone still has his own little task to complete. The ribbons of bureaucracy one must cut through…"

*No splinters*, Sherlock thought as his fingers palpated the back of Jurgins's neck. *Nothing here at all.*

"Do not speak to me about bureaucracy!" Speckle declared. After which the two men vied to top each other with the most egregious examples they could recall.

Near Jurgens's Adam's apple, Sherlock spied a rather large nick, but there were others, from too many close but not terribly well-managed shaves over the years.

Sherlock felt inside his ears and mouth. He picked up the dead man's hands and inspected his fingernails. Though the bones had been twisted somewhat by rheumatism, Rupert was not a nail-biter, nor did he pick at his cuticles. Each nail was well cut and polished.

"Finding nothing, am I right?" Speckle called over to Sherlock in a world-weary tone.

Rupert Jurgins had lived in Kingston upon Thames, in a handsome detached house whose neighbors resided at too great a distance to have been of any discernible use. Mrs. Jurgins, Rupert's mother—despite her debilitating grief—had managed to do the utmost for her son. Black crepe ribbons adorned every window casing. An enormous garland upon a stand, arrayed with gigantic white chrysanthemums, was displayed to the side of the steps leading to the front door. And on either side of the entryway stood two funeral mutes, in black crepe from top hat to boot heel, and holding brooms encircled in same. As they were paid to do, they said nothing and stared at no one but served as silent witnesses that someone beloved had sloughed off his mortal coil.

Within the residence, every mirror had been covered and

every clock halted at 4:01 p.m., the moment that Rupert's mother had come upon his body.

Mrs. Jurgins was no more than sixty years of age, but sorrow had siphoned away all color and moisture from her flesh so that she seemed more like a needlepoint of veins and wrinkles. She was draped in black bombazine stretched over a wide-cage crinoline of the sort that had not been in fashion in thirty years. The cage made her already small waist look the size of a wasp's.

Though Huan had not been permitted entry—he was a mere carriage driver, after all, and a foreigner—Sherlock had bandied about his own prestigious post as Secretary to the Secretary of State for War, so that Mrs. Jurgins would be more amenable to answering a few questions.

"I am aggrieved for your loss, madam," he said with a slight bow.

"Thank you, young man," she replied, her voice constricted by sorrow.

"My name is Mycroft Holmes," he said, pitching his voice slightly lower so that he might sound older. "Secretary to the Secretary of State for War." He pulled out one of the half-dozen old calling cards that he had thought to purloin from Mycroft's desk drawer for just such an occasion. "This terrible man has claimed too many victims," Sherlock said. "My employer, the Honorable Edward Cardwell, has taken a personal interest."

"Again I thank you, Mr. Holmes," she said, placing the card into the reticule tied to her waist. "Perhaps when the others have departed, we might have a talk?"

Sherlock bided his time until the guests were gone, at which point Mrs. Jurgins provided a bit of space for Huan in the kitchen, alongside the servants, for it had begun to rain again, while she and Sherlock sat in the parlor.

"Rupert is not used to being alone," she began. "Although I suppose he isn't…"

Her affection, and her agony for her son, were genuine.

"Mrs. Jurgins, before you gave the killer's note to the police, did you have a look at it?"

She nodded.

"How large was the note?"

"About so large," she said, her thumbs and index fingers joining to form a three-by-five square.

"And do you recall the type of paper?"

"Something coarse," she said. "Unrefined. If I had to venture a guess, I would say hemp."

"And what of the dot over the 'i'?"

"In truth, it seemed more like a little line."

"Are you certain?"

"Oh yes. Before I married, I was a school mistress. I can tell a dot from a line."

"Had the paper been pierced through?"

"I don't know, I… cannot say, I am sorry."

"And Mrs. Jurgins, when you came upon Rupert, did you notice anything unusual? Foaming at the mouth, convulsions?" Sherlock asked.

"No, nothing." She began to cry softly.

"There, there, Mrs. Jurgins," Sherlock mumbled, realizing that his tone was perhaps a bit too atonal to be comforting. "I noticed he had rheumatism."

"Yes, since he was a child."

"And several nicks in his neck and jawline."

Mrs. Jurgins nodded. "His father had taught him to shave. He always insisted on doing it himself."

"His nails, on the other hand, were perfect," Sherlock said.

"That is because he permitted me to do them," she replied, smiling. "He had his father's hands."

Sherlock followed Mrs. Jurgins's gaze to the portrait of a stern-looking older man above the hearth, his fingers clasped together over his belly.

"How long has Mr. Jurgins been deceased?" he asked.

"He died in an accident, Mr. Holmes. He was the supervisor of a colliery that exploded back in December 1866, killing 384 men and boys. The Oaks Explosion, perhaps you have heard of it?"

"I am sorry to say that I have not."

"Well, you were young then. Younger, I mean to say."

"Yes. Forgive me if this sounds impertinent, Mrs. Jurgins, but how have you managed to preserve your lifestyle these seven years since your husband passed?"

"Ah. My husband's brother Rupert, for whom Rupert was named. He sends us a monthly stipend, quite generous. He works for Jobine, Mathison and Company," she said proudly. "They deal in minerals. My brother-in-law Mr. Jurgins is a geologist, you see. But please do not ask what sort of work he performs, for it is much too technical for me."

Sherlock could tell by her untroubled expression when she spoke of financial matters that she was not being coy; she truly had little notion what her brother's husband did for a living.

"Do you perchance have a list of people with whom Mr. Jurgins works?"

"Dear me, no, Mr. Holmes!"

"No matter. Now, you said you found Rupert upon his back, across the threshold of your front door, on or about four p.m.?"

"At one minute after, which is when I stopped the clocks. But he always opened the door at four on the button!" she replied.

"Rupert liked to open the door and take in the fresh air at precisely four p.m., regardless of the weather. He had done it for years, was quite punctual about it. He had trouble reading words, but he well knew how to tell the time. I did not allow him to leave the premises on his own, and so I assume that the simple act of standing upon the threshold was akin to, well, standing upon the precipice of freedom! He was such a happy soul, but always at that moment in particular. That is how Cotton escaped."

"Cotton?" Sherlock asked.

Mrs. Jurgins nodded. "Rupert was particularly kind to animals, especially any that had been ill-used, for he well knew what it was to be tormented. Cotton followed him everywhere. And now she is gone!"

"Ah. A pity," Sherlock said distractedly, for his mind was still on Rupert's daily visits to the threshold, and what they could have meant to his stalker and killer.

"Did you happen to hear Cotton bark?" he asked.

"I should hope not!" Mrs. Jurgins replied. "For Cotton is a cat. White As Cotton, Rupert named her himself. I was looking through the upstairs window and saw her dash away."

"When?"

"Right before I heard the bang upon the threshold, when Rupert fell." Mrs. Jurgins blinked back tears and continued: "I expected her to be back by now, but perhaps all the strangers and the commotion frightened her. I did hear a peculiar sound the moment she ran off."

"A bird, perhaps?" Sherlock asked.

"If so, it was no bird that *I* ever heard," she replied. "It was a sort of a... a whistle."

"Mrs. Jurgins, did Cotton appear to be startled by something? Or was she perhaps *pursuing* something?"

"Well I am sure I cannot say——"

"It may be important," Sherlock insisted. "Might you picture her in your mind's eye?"

Mrs. Jurgins concentrated mightily.

"Yes! She was pursuing something!" she said triumphantly.

"Mrs. Jurgins," Sherlock said, "would you have any objections if my driver and I attempted to find Cotton?"

"Oh, I should be gratified," she said. "For White As Cotton is the only living thing of Rupert's that I have left!"

# 34

CONTRARY TO MYCROFT'S SURMISING, CARLTON THE driver did not run away upon realizing that their destination would once again be Jennings Rents. And although his eyes grew wide and his eyebrows knitted into fleeting disapproval, his mustaches did not quiver; rather, he seemed determined to show fortitude in the implementation of his duty. And when they arrived at the designated locale, he held the umbrella with a steady hand and a noble bearing—though Mycroft could tell he would not so much as inhale until he was safely back in the carriage.

Certainly, bad weather did not help Jennings Rents to look any more agreeable. Although the mist, as heavy as a marsh, did manage to mute the harsher sounds of local squabbling and bickering, it also heightened the smells of mold, offal, and putrefaction to a nearly intolerable degree.

Mycroft considered placing a kerchief across his nose and mouth but thought better of it. His fine trap and attire already marked him as a well-to-do and entirely too-fortunate stranger. No sense in compounding the offense with loutish behavior.

Near the entrance to Ai Lin's makeshift hospital, Mycroft noticed two large men loitering underneath umbrellas. One bounced upon his heels and glanced about warily while the other felt for his pocket watch and toyed with the chain but did not look at it.

*He cannot*, Mycroft thought. *For it is too tempting to thieves, of which there are many more than he can fight off.*

He assumed they were Ai Lin's bodyguards, hired by her fiancé's family and waiting to escort her home. This was confirmed when he was near enough to see that they were, indeed, Oriental. Though gratified at their diligence in protecting her, he was equally glad that he had arrived at her door before they spirited her away.

"It is a quarter past the hour," he murmured to one of them as he passed. And although the bodyguard did not acknowledge him with so much as a nod but continued to stare straight ahead, Mycroft knew he had heard, for his fingers holding the chain grew slack, and the jiggling ceased.

He knocked upon the door and, when there was no answer, he opened it and called out:

"Miss Lin? Are you about?"

When she did not reply, Mycroft placed his damp hat and topcoat on a hook and went down the dim hall, wondering at the quiet. With an annoying sense of unease, he pulled aside the thick curtain that separated the reception area from the makeshift infirmary, and there he saw her.

She was wearing a sage-colored, close-bodied gown with the skirt draped *à la polonaise.* Her black hair was pulled into a high chignon held in place with jade pins in the shape of grasshoppers. Unlike the time before, there was no one else in the sickroom, save a patient lying on a cot. Ai Lin was kneeling before it. At the sound of Mycroft's entrance, she turned to look, thereby moving aside slightly, and Mycroft very nearly lost his bearings.

She had been ministering to an old man. His skin looked black, as if he'd been burned alive. His eyes wcrc the color of blood. He did not look human.

"What in the *world*!" Mycroft gasped aloud—only to be greeted with a strict "Shhh!" from Ai Lin, one long, sleek finger pressed against her lips.

She motioned for Mycroft to remain where he was; then she turned back to tend to her patient. Mycroft watched, disturbed, as she smoothed back his hair and placed a wet compress upon his forehead. Those red eyes stared up at her beseechingly and then fluttered closed. Within a few moments he was snoring lightly.

"You should not be in here," she whispered severely as she moved away from the cot and hurried Mycroft out of the sickroom. "Smallpox."

"And what of you, then?" Mycroft cried in a hushed voice. "You should be nowhere near him! And that looked nothing like smallpox!" he added by way of protest as she pulled the curtain closed and ushered him into the small kitchen.

"I grant you have not likely seen it in this stage; and in fact, it is fairly rare—"

"There are no pustules!" he protested again more feebly.

"No, there are not. But you noticed how his lesions are very nearly flush with the skin?" she inquired, manifesting a great deal more enthusiasm about the subject of epidemics than they tended to warrant.

"Do sit down, Mr. Holmes," she added, "for you appear to be out of breath."

Mycroft pulled out a wooden stool near the kitchen table and did as instructed.

"Yes, I... I noticed them," he said, staring up at her, "the lesions, I mean, naturally I did, but I..."

"He has a malignant, hemorrhagic form of the disease," she explained. "Caught too late, I fear. There is nothing I can offer now but to allow him to die with dignity, and that is what I intend to do."

"Miss Lin, need I remind you that smallpox is infectious?" Mycroft declared, thereby retaining his compunction, with her, to state the obvious.

"It is *contagious*," she replied patiently, correcting him. "But I was inoculated some few years back, and so am protected well enough."

"But... can you not wear a mask at the very least? And gloves?"

Ai Lin shook her head. "A man like that, having endured such a hard life from cradle to grave, deserves more than to see his last human face shrouded in a mask."

*I cannot imagine beholding a lovelier face than yours*, Mycroft thought. *If you were the last thing I saw, I would die in peace.*

"I must leave him for the night, for the Shi family does not permit me to remain here too much after dark, but I shall be back by eight tomorrow morning. He is stable for the moment, and I believe he shall wait for me. Tea, Mr. Holmes?" she asked, wielding an empty kettle.

"I would happily do the honors," he said, rising. "And so allow you to rest."

"Oh dear," she laughed, brushing a stray hair off her forehead, "is it as bad as all that?"

"No, no, I did not intend, that is to say, I..." he replied, stumbling over his words again.

Knowing he could not salvage the moment, he ceased to protest but sat back down.

"Besides, when it comes to tea, I have my methods," she said. "And I fear I am rather a stickler about them."

As she opened the cupboards and extracted her ingredients, she added, her back to him: "I hope you will forgive my turning round to look at you the other day. I know that it was improper. As is my announcing it now, I suppose…"

"No need to apologize, Miss Lin, in truth I was much comforted by the gesture. But now I bring news."

"Yes, I… imagine you do," she said. This time, she turned and gazed directly at Mycroft. "Please know that I cannot thank you enough for your kindness."

"It was a promise that I made to your father—" Mycroft began, but she interrupted.

"Yes, that too is a kindness, but it is not the one to which I refer."

"I am sure I do not know what you mean, Miss Lin," he replied. For indeed, he was so flustered that he had no notion.

"Oh, come," she teased, her tourmaline-colored eyes shining with good humor. "For who but you would dispatch a clean supply of water to a contaminated tenement house, one that is in the process of being pulled down board by board *and* cleared of its tenants? Who but you would pay to repair a water spout in order to care for fifty people whom no one else cares for?"

"*You* would," Mycroft said softly, suddenly recalling which good deed she was referring to.

"Quite right, Mr. Holmes, I do care, there is no question," she said as she took a seat across from him, the preparations for tea temporarily forgotten. "But as I am in limbo, neither fully my father's child nor fully married, I do not have the resources at hand. Naturally, I inquired as to who the Good Samaritan might be, and the landlord informed me that the work had been paid for 'in full' by one Mr. J. Snow."

"Well," Mycroft replied. "Other people besides me must know of your admiration for Dr. Snow, and certainly many people would deduce that a deposit of clean water to Jennings Rents in his name would be fitting and proper."

"'Other people, many people'… and yet, never have I met a one who is anything like you. But, forgive me; I can see from your expression that I have once again overstepped my bounds. It is never my intent to embarrass you, although I do appear to do so with some frequency."

She rose again, removing a pinch of this and that from tins she had taken from the cupboards. He could smell turmeric and hawthorn leaf, and he realized that—irony notwithstanding—Ai Lin was still attempting to repair his ailing heart. He was tempted to tell her about his surgery, and how it had been a success, at least for the moment. But he could not think of one earthly reason why he would, and he felt himself suddenly aching for something that would never be.

"Miss Lin," he said abruptly. "I may have stumbled upon a plan to bring your fiancé home."

# 35

NO MATTER HOW ASSIDUOUSLY HUAN TRIED TO KEEP Sherlock ensconced underneath a large umbrella, he was on the hunt for a fluffy white feline and would not allow an inconsequential issue like water falling from the sky to deter him. And although he had never experienced it before, he found that, rain and incipient darkness notwithstanding, tracking a cat over wet, muddy ground was not difficult.

The ground was rife with human and animal prints. Even so, here and there were light but distinct impressions of the cat's travels.

Once in a while, in the boggier sections, they would lose sight of the prints, for the cat's trajectory was never straight; rather, it looped and meandered. But if they paid attention, they could pick it up again within a few yards.

After a half hour's diligent search, they had found her, a white ball lying beside a silver birch. Even from a distance it was clear that she was deceased, for she was sopping wet and not moving so much as a hair.

Sherlock approached. The cat was rigid to the touch, her eyes wide open, her tiny jaw fixed and slightly open.

He took the umbrella out of Huan's hands.

"Sorry, old man," he said to him as he stared up at the branches, searching.

"Do not say 'sorry' to me!" Huan protested with a grin. "For I have been aiming to keep you dry for the past half hour. What is it you seek now?" he added, covering his own brow with his palm and staring up in the same general direction as Sherlock.

"A bird," he replied. "A strange bird. Perhaps with a wounded wing. For I believe that is what the cat was chasing."

"If so, she must have eaten it," Huan said. "For her stomach is big and hard, you see?"

Sherlock looked down again. In truth, he was not well acquainted with cats. He had not grown up with them. It seemed that everywhere he turned of late, there was a distinct and deeply disquieting chasm in the depth and breadth of his knowledge.

He handed the umbrella back to Huan, and as Huan kept him covered, he crouched down beside the cat and turned her so that her belly was facing upward.

"Kittens?" he wondered dubiously.

Huan shook his head. "She is too old."

He looked at Huan quizzically. "Truly? How does one discern the age of a cat?"

"You can feel how bony she is," Huan replied, palpating her ribs. "Her teeth, they are worn," he said, pushing wider her tiny mouth. "Her fur, thin."

"Well. If she is not expecting," Sherlock replied, "then I shall require your penknife."

"You must take care," Huan warned as he placed it in Sherlock's hand.

"She is dead, Huan."

"I am speaking of your fingers, Master Sherlock, for the knife is sharp, and it grows dark."

Sherlock sat down upon a nearby rock and then set to work. Cutting through fur and tissue, even of such a small creature, was more laborious than it looked. Clearly, he was not an experienced surgeon, but he was a persistent one, especially since the only tool at his disposal was Huan's penknife.

As the darkness grew, Huan commenced to light one match after the other so that Sherlock might complete his onerous task without slicing into his own skin.

At last, he reached the miniscule invader.

"No! Do not touch it!" Huan cried out.

"Why?"

"The color!" Huan declared.

"What of it?"

Huan lit another match and brought it as close as he dared without setting the cat on fire.

"You see there? It is too bright," he said. "Bright colors are to attract, or to warn other animals: 'Bad taste! Poison!' That is why I say to you do not touch."

"Huan, that thing, whatever it is," Sherlock countered, pointing at it, "is no larger than an inch in diameter. Surely, there is nothing that it can do to me…"

Just as he was reaching inside the stomach cavity to retrieve it, the cat slid away from him.

"Huan! Truly, this is outrageous!" Sherlock exclaimed—for Huan had pulled the dead cat by the tail out of Sherlock's reach.

"Master Sherlock," Huan replied—holding Cotton's body behind his back—"whatever the cat ate, that is what killed the cat, yes? We are in agreement there, yes?"

"Huan…" Sherlock warned; but Huan would not be deterred.

"Now. It is my job to care for you," Huan replied firmly. "I cannot let you near this animal again until you swear to me that you will not handle it with your naked hands."

Since attempting to wrest the cat from Huan's grasp would be futile, Sherlock let out a martyr-like sigh.

"I swear," he agreed.

Whereupon Huan gingerly returned the cat to the same spot where it had been. He then snapped two twigs off the tree and held them up.

"What I *could* use," Sherlock replied testily, "is a good set of tweezers. But, as I failed to pack a shaving kit, and as you do not grow any sort of a beard, I suppose your sticks will have to do."

Sherlock took them and, with the utmost care and dexterity, lifted out the object in question.

"Hullo!" he exclaimed. "What might you be, then?"

Huan lit another match, and they both stared in wonder.

It was still perfectly intact, as if it had crawled inside of the cat's belly and fallen asleep.

Between the two sticks was a tiny golden frog.

# 36

AS AI LIN HUNG THE KETTLE OVER THE FIRE, MYCROFT, in a flood of words, repeated all that he had been told: that Bingwen Shi was being held in the town of Zhouzhuang, in Jiangsu Province; that someone related to him would have to make the trek in person so as to plead his case; and that said emissary would have to bring proof that Shi had not been hired by Vizily Zaharoff in the capacity of arms dealer, merchant, or conduit.

"But where would we find such proof?" she asked.

"Zaharoff himself shall furnish a letter," he told her, "in which he declares that Bingwen Shi was not employed by him nor scheduled to sell arms on his behalf on the 4th of April. It shall be delivered to Stafford Terrace within the next few hours."

"To Stafford Terrace? Not to his family?"

"Yes, I wondered about that too," Mycroft replied. "I assume it is because Zaharoff understands what I myself discovered: that their English is limited, and it is best if you explain to them what they need to know."

Oddly, though they had been speaking a while, Ai Lin had not turned to face him again but had remained where she was, busying herself with preparations for the tea. When he had first mentioned freeing Bingwen Shi and bringing him home, he thought that perhaps her shoulders had slumped, just a little. But when at last she removed the kettle from the fire, filled the teapot and finally turned towards him, he could read nothing upon her face beyond a grateful smile.

"You are a worker of miracles," she declared, her voice quavering. "Truly, is that all it takes to ensure his freedom?"

"It is no small matter for a family member to board a steamer so as to arrive in time to plead his case!" Mycroft declared. "Any delay, inclement weather, difficulties on arrival, all could cause such a plan to founder."

*Founder?* Mycroft nearly bit off his tongue at this insensitive choice of words. But if Ai Lin noticed, she pretended otherwise.

"I have all confidence that it shall be done," she declared, placing cups on a tray and bringing it to the table. "Bingwen Shi shall be spared, and I am glad of it."

"As am I," Mycroft said, meaning it. For as much as he would have desired a future with Ai Lin, it could not be. And certainly not at the cost of a man's life.

Ai Lin took a sip of tea. Mycroft did the same, thinking that he had never tasted anything so wonderful—all because she had made it for him, with her very own hands.

"And so this is where my freedom ends!" she exclaimed.

Mycroft looked at her, startled.

"Forgive me, Mr. Holmes," she said. "A well-brought-up Hakka woman does not speak of such things as love and marriage, and certainly not to a man. And I do not mean to burden you with my double-mindedness. You have done as my father requested, and it is in all ways admirable and extraordinary, which is what I have learned to expect from you…"

"What I hope is that you have kept train tickets," Mycroft

said, embarrassed. "Perhaps a hotel receipt, anything that can prove that he could not at the same time have been in London, arranging an arms purchase."

"I have both his train ticket and mine, along with the hotel receipt with his signature. Bingwen suggested that I keep them as a memento, but I believe he was concerned that someone in his family might find them in his possession and unearth our terrible misdeed."

"There is a ship leaving for Shanghai from Liverpool the day after tomorrow," Mycroft said. "As the voyage will take between twenty to thirty days, your emissary would have to be aboard. If there is no room, I can call upon my resources to secure a first-class passage."

"Again, I thank you," Ai Lin said. "But there is no need. The *Latitude* and the *Royal Richard* are docked at the Victoria. My father is there now, overseeing the unloading of goods, for he is determined to have it executed tonight. For the very noble cause of rescuing my fiancé from certain death, he shall certainly provide one or the other."

She took another sip of her tea and then added: "And though I grant you that the cost is quite dear, a steamer burdened by neither cargo nor passengers can increase its storage of coal. Without the constraint of stopping to refuel so frequently, we can hope to arrive sooner."

"'We'?" Mycroft repeated, assuming he had misheard.

"I meant myself and the crew."

"*You?*" he exclaimed. "Absurd!"

He was on his feet before he could stop himself, looking down at her.

"Why, naturally!" she replied, slightly startled as she gazed up at him. "Who else should go, but I?"

"Miss Lin, truly, this is beyond the pale. Surely Mr. Shi has a male relative who can be persuaded to go to his rescue!"

Ai Lin bit her bottom lip, and then said: "Please sit down, Mr. Holmes, for I so enjoy your company. And your rising puts me in mind that we cannot remain here forever as we are, talking and sipping tea."

Mycroft did as she asked, though he could hardly breathe.

"As I confided to you and to your Mr. Douglas, what we bring to the Shi are our ships and our connections abroad. For this reason, it was thought a fortuitous match. And because Bingwen already had dealings with that man, Vizily Zaharoff, it stands to reason that Bingwen hoped our ships could profit Mr. Zaharoff by transporting armaments, that they could make a lucrative deal. The moment that I put an end to that incipient partnership, Mr. Zaharoff had no further use for him and so most likely did not protest his abduction—"

Mycroft did not dare to reveal what he knew: that it was Zaharoff himself who had alerted the government of China.

"—so you see," Ai Lin concluded, "it may well be my fault that he was condemned to death."

"It is in no manner your fault!" Mycroft exclaimed. "But, even if what you say is true, I still do not understand why you, of all people, should make the trek to Zhouzhuang!"

"You have met the Shi, Mr. Holmes. I believe you understand that they are not accustomed to hostile environments—"

"Oh, and you are!" he replied with such a tone of righteous indignation that she laughed.

"Mr. Holmes! Truly—" she began, but he found the temerity to interrupt.

"Your father's ships, efficient as they might be to move cargo, have not even the most basic facilities for passengers!"

"The Lin family did not always enjoy such means as we have at present," she reminded him gently. "I am, after all, no more than the daughter of a seaman, and quite accustomed to travel by ship, my father's in particular. And, as it so happens, I am well acquainted with several dialects of the Jiangsu Province. Not all, by any stretch, or even most; but enough that I should get by. Whereas the Shi family speak only Mandarin and their own dialect."

"But they would never agree to place you in that sort of danger!" Mycroft protested.

"Under normal circumstances. But they are so ashamed of their son's plight that if they hear of a way to prevent this tragedy, they will do it. They will do whatever I ask. They will contribute the two bodyguards outside, along with another dozen, should I need them. Who else can assure Bingwen's release better than I, his abandoned fiancée?"

Though her tone was leavened with humor, her eyes brimmed with tears.

"But there you are!" Mycroft said, for he was not willing to cede the argument. "You are merely a fiancée, not a wife, and as such you are not the 'relative' that they seek."

"Yes," she said, nodding somberly. "But even prisoners condemned to death may marry. Before making my formal plea, I shall therefore request that he and I do so at once."

Mycroft swallowed so loudly that he was certain that it could be heard all through Jennings Rents.

"Please believe me when I tell you," he said, his voice raw, "that if I'd had so much as an inkling that you would take it upon yourself, I never would have darkened your doorstep, never would have said a word… and let the devil take the hindmost."

"Mr. Holmes. You are my dearest friend," she said, her

own voice breaking. "I shall not pretend, with you, that it is not miserably hard—"

They heard the front door open.

"The bodyguards, come to take me to Stafford Terrace," she announced, rising abruptly. "I must go, for I cannot give the Shi any reason to doubt my sense of duty, or my fitness to accomplish this task."

Mycroft rose to his feet again. As he did so, she leaned towards him and brushed her lips against his.

"There," she said, pulling away and blushing slightly. "My first kiss is one that I stole from you. Let it be our very own secret, my dear Mr. Holmes, for it cannot be otherwise. But you and I will know it, and for me, at least, it must suffice for a lifetime."

# 37

A DAZED AND BEWILDERED MYCROFT WATCHED AI LIN being escorted away by her fiancé's bodyguards. As their carriage disappeared, he removed his handkerchief, thanking Providence that it was clean, and lightly dabbed it across his lips. Then he folded it carefully and returned it to his pocket. Absurd, he realized. But it could very well be the only unadulterated memory of Ai Lin that he would ever possess.

Within moments he found himself back inside his borrowed carriage, on his way to Regent Tobaccos. Whatever transpired from here on out, he had to speak to Douglas, though he had little notion what he would say.

*The woman I love is in love with me. She kissed me…*

No. He would not break her confidence.

He lost himself once more to his thoughts, so that when he happened to glance out of the window again, the carriage had already made the turn onto Regent Street. He quickly rapped his knuckles upon the trap.

"Here we are!" he called to the driver, in a sing-song tone so false that it shamed him.

The carriage halted. Waiting neither for stairs nor umbrella, Mycroft leapt out of the vestibule and hastened to the front door of Douglas's tobacco shop, where he rang the bell repeatedly, like a madman.

He heard footsteps. The front door opened, and a moment later he was staring down upon the startled visage of Mr. Pennywhistle, who seemed to have grown even shorter and stouter in the weeks since he had seen him last.

"Mr. Holmes! How very nice!" Mr. P. said, squinting up at him, for his eyes were weak. "The missus and I were about to close shop, but come in do, for I can have a lovely fire going in the shake of a lamb's tail. May I take your coat?"

"No, Mr. P., I am on the hunt for Douglas. Is he here?"

"Cyrus? No, I fear he is not. Has not been around for days! Have you gone by Nickolus House?"

"Not yet, but I shall do so now…"

"You are certain you would not care to imbibe a little something first, along with a hearty smoke? The newest Punch have just come in, quite fresh, and such a pleasant aroma, good for what ails you—"

"No, no, thank you, Mr. P.," Mycroft said as he scribbled a note upon a calling card and then turned and waved for the carriage to come back round to fetch him.

"Well. Next time, perhaps," Mr. P. said, taking the card. "And Mr. Holmes? Should you see Cyrus first, tell him a telegram arrived for him! Better yet, might you deliver it to Nickolus House? For it is marked 'personal and urgent!' Now, where did I put it…?"

Before Mycroft could protest, Mr. Pennywhistle had already disappeared inside to fetch it. Mycroft waited impatiently and listened to him rummage about… until he heard his own voice in his head saying to Douglas:

"*You might begin by sending telegrams to your contacts at various ports of call with instructions to immediately send back such information as they are willing to share about Zaharoff or Shi.*"

A telegram marked 'personal and urgent' could be precisely what he had been waiting for. Instead, here he was, in a muddle, his thought processes clouded, his mind on something else entirely.

Was he becoming ill again? What in the world could be wrong with him?

*Nothing but Ai Lin*, he thought.

"Here it be!" Mr. P. announced brightly, waving the missive like a fan as he trotted back to the door.

Mycroft recognized the sender's name, a man with whom Douglas had often conducted business, whose line of spirits was shipped internationally, and which made him an invaluable font of information. Port cities tended to be the canary in the coal mine; the first subtle stirrings of trouble were nearly always felt there, passing from ship to ship and from deckhand to deckhand, before moving inland.

He pocketed it with thanks and was already halfway down the front steps when Mr. P. added: "Do let Cyrus know that it's been so long since we have lain eyes upon him that we are even imagining his voice at the door!"

"Whatever do you mean?" Mycroft asked.

"I mean I… I thought I heard him calling to me, and the missus heard too, from the kitchen, but when I come to the door, no one's there."

"When?"

"When?" Mr. Pennywhistle looked puzzled. "Why, when I thought I heard him, and so came I to the door—"

"No, I meant, was it today?"

"Ah yes, today! Indeed!"

"At what hour?" Mycroft asked, trying to keep the irritation from his voice.

"Ah! Earlier, I should say! Several hours, in fact, though to be frank I did not consult my timepiece, for on dark days like this, I cannot make out the hands."

Mycroft felt a flutter in his chest, followed by a sudden tightening. He said his goodbyes to Mr. P. But by the time he had ducked inside of the carriage and was seated, he was reevaluating both his nerves and his haste.

*The anxiety you feel is about her, not him! He is a grown man! Surely he can be allowed leeway to do as he pleases!*

Besides, Douglas was a savvy sort; except under circumstances of the greatest provocation, he would not be traipsing about unaccompanied, and certainly not in a rainstorm at night. To say nothing of the fact that he had acted the child, stomping off simply because they had disagreed on a matter of protocol, or if not that precisely, then little more!

Thus assured, Mycroft decided upon a compromise. He opened the trap and instructed Carlton to take him, but with leisure, to the Red Lion at Crown Passage, and from there to Nickolus House on Old Pye—for Douglas was at one or the other and would be easily located.

The moment that the carriage was underway, he reached into his pocket for the telegram, and then carefully unpeeled the envelope. On the slim chance that it *was* of a personal nature, and meant for Douglas's eyes alone, it could be resealed, none the wiser.

Telegrams were, by necessity, blunt, for they cost by the word. But this one proved also cryptic. The sender seemed troubled by what he had discovered. Thankfully, having toiled in the War Office, Mycroft was well versed in cryptic.

POST MERGER BS NEW OWNER =
DHL SHIPS TO CARRY VZ GOODS

Since Douglas had specifically requested information on Zaharoff or Bingwen Shi, the acronyms were simple: 'VZ' was Vizily Zaharoff, and 'BS' Bingwen Shi, which meant that 'DHL' had to be Deshi Hai Lin, Ai Lin's father. And so the 'merger' most likely referred to the marriage between Bingwen Shi and Ai Lin… after which—or *post*-marriage—something of note was to transpire.

From there, the missive took on peculiar shadings. For why would marriage necessarily indicate new ownership of the vessels? The patriarch, Deshi Hai Lin, had never intimated that he was in the market to sell, nor had Ai Lin. And, even if something untoward were to occur, the ownership would pass to Ai Lin's brother, Dai en-Lai Lin, and not to a son-in-law!

*Only according to English law*, Mycroft reminded himself. For Douglas had, over the years, schooled him on Confucian wisdom, which dictated that ownership could indeed pass to a son-in-law, if the two married in China. In that case, Bingwen could own a third, and rule his wife's third, for women had no say. Her brother Dai en-Lai would hold the remaining third—a minority vote in any decision, and he still young in years and with scant knowledge of how the business worked.

Mycroft recalled Deshi Hai Lin's words: "I thought that he could be like a son to me; for, unlike my boy now at university, he was keen to learn my business."

*Exceedingly keen*, Mycroft thought bitterly.

In spite of Bingwen Shi's promises not to engage with Zaharoff, what if the opposite transpired? What if he were plotting to do some permanent damage to his father-in-law so as to take possession of the business? And, if that was his plan, once they had married, what could Ai Lin possibly do with such a monstrous *fait accompli*? Especially if her father's death was made to look like an accident? The weight of family, and of society, would be against her. It was entirely feasible that the best thing that ever happened to Deshi Hai Lin, to his family and to his daughter, was the kidnapping and eventual execution of his future son-in-law.

*I must go and find Ai Lin*, Mycroft thought in a panic. *I must show her the telegram. I must beg her not to leave! Beg her not to risk her life to save this man!*

"Carlton?" he called out. "We must go to Stafford Terrace!"

"After Nickolus House, sir?" Carlton replied through the trap.

"No, now. And quickly!"

# 38

THOUGH THE ROAD WAS STILL SLICK WITH RAIN, THE sky had ceased its onslaught and the carriage made good time. There were few people still on the streets, for it was growing late, which meant that they had clear passage to park directly in front of Ai Lin's lodgings, a part of the terrace built on Kensington's Phillimore Estates. Mycroft hastened up the steps and politely but firmly knocked upon the door.

After a moment, the door opened a crack.

"Yes?" she said. She was the chaperone who oversaw the ladies therein; a gray old thing with yellow horse teeth and stringy black hair who peered out at him with unvarnished suspicion.

"I am enquiring about Miss Ai Lin," Mycroft announced as he removed his hat.

"Are you indeed?" she declared, pursing her lips so that they resembled a rotten fig. "As you are neither her relative nor her betrothed, you have no business here, and so cannot be asking impertinent questions as to where a young lady may or may not be at this hour of night!"

"Madam, if I might have but a moment of your time…"

Mycroft pushed open the door wide enough that she could have a better look at him, and at the Queen's costly carriage parked directly behind. And indeed, as she glanced from one to the other, her expression softened a bit.

"A gentleman like you could do better," she murmured.

"I am… a friend of her father's," Mycroft replied.

"Ah. In the ship business, are you? Queer indeed, for you do not look the sort. Regardless, I must say that I am most vexed. For though the girl paid me through month's end, and double, it is no excuse for hurrying off without a word of adieu!"

"She is gone, then?" Mycroft asked. "Would you know what time she departed?"

"Some two hours back. A note was delivered here, in a monogrammed carriage belonging to a real roiderbanks, quite uppity, he was. She took the note and left right after."

"I wish you a pleasant evening."

Mycroft started to go when the old woman darted out a hand and laid it upon his bicep.

"If you must know," she whispered as she leaned her scarecrow body out of the door, "I was already hard-pressed to take that sort of girl under my wing."

"What sort of a girl, madam?"

"Why, an Oriental!" she declared. "Yes indeed, for I was not keen to hear the grumblings of the others. But she had already been refused by three other respectable places, and I only did so out of Christian charity."

Mycroft swallowed bile and started to walk off. Indeed, he quite knew that he should do naught else. Still, his errant feet planted themselves, and his errant torso twisted back towards the woman and the door.

"Christian charity teaches one to be charitable, madam, a virtue which seems to be quite outside your purview."

Thus unburdened, he climbed inside the carriage, with instructions for Carlton to head, in all haste, for the Victoria Dock, for that was where two of Deshi Hai Lin's steamers were berthed.

The Victoria Dock, a little less than twenty years old, had been constructed on the top of the old Plaistow marshes. It boasted a main dock, and on the west side a basin that allowed access to the Thames. Unfortunately there was no means of guessing where a ship might be docked, for they sat in no conceivable order, and Mycroft had no talent for spotting them by sight, as did Douglas. Naturally, if a ship were being unloaded, logic dictated that it would be as close to a warehouse as possible. But the Victoria had been designed specifically to accommodate large steamers, of the sort that Deshi Hai Lin owned. All around the berths were looming, pythonic structures: warehouses, sheds, storage buildings of various kinds, even granaries. The Victoria was, in every conceivable way, bewildering to one who had never set eyes on it before.

Braving the dark, slick walkways, Mycroft hurried from path to path and from berth to berth, asking the very occasional passerby if he had heard of steamers the *Latitude* or the *Royal Richard*. But this was not the sort of a place where strangers were catered to; or perhaps they took him for some sort of a regulator or bureaucrat. Having no success of it, and growing ever more desperate, he quickened his pace… and on a slithery walkway made a misstep, one foot sinking into a deep puddle. In quick succession, his knee hit the ground, as did the palm of his hand. From that sad vantage point, he watched his left shoe float off and then sink into the muddy flow.

Damning his own clumsiness, Mycroft got to his feet once more and pressed his scraped and bleeding palm against his jacket, for he would not use his handkerchief for the job. And though his trousers had cushioned his knee well enough, the fabric had torn so that now it flapped freely as he limped along.

*Douglas would laugh to see to what I have been reduced*, he thought bitterly, before realizing that Douglas would do no such thing.

"Sir? Sir!" a phlegmy voice said behind him.

He turned and saw an old man sizing him up. He had a peaky, grizzled face, and his trousers, shirt, and coat were all too short, as if he had put on the garments while still a lad and then grown up inside of them. The term 'old salt' could have been invented especially for him, for he seemed sculpted of it.

"Rumor is, yer seek the *Latitude* and the *Royal Richard*?"

"What do you know about them?" Mycroft asked more brusquely than he intended. But his foot was wet and cold and his knee was beginning to throb and he was feeling in all ways out of sorts.

"I would tell 'ee sir, but me mouth is parched so that I can barely strain to speak…"

The old salt wrapped one gnarled hand about his throat and emitted a pitiful little cough to make his point.

Mycroft dug into his pocket, but the smallest coin he could find was a half sovereign. Reluctantly, he held it aloft, close enough that the old goat could see it. And indeed, as the man drew in his breath and opened his eyes wider than they had probably opened in a good long while, Mycroft added:

"But it will not be yours unless I have particulars worth having."

"Yes sir, yes guv'n'r, for I ain't one wot prevaricates!" the salt declared, suddenly able not merely to speak, but to do so with rapidity, if not the utmost clarity.

"I meself 'ad an 'and in tidyin' 'er up, yer see, for when I am ashore, I tidy up wot 'as been befouled!"

"What were you unloading?"

"Now I ain't one to judge, sir, but some of it looked like weapons, all brand-new!"

"Where were they going?"

"Why, they wan't goin' nowhere, sir—word was, they was loaded and then unloaded! Like someone changed their mind! So they'd just been done wif unloadin' the hold, an'—now I ain't privy as to what transpired yer see—but all the sudden, sir, the deck'ands is all a flutter, they undo her anchor shackles... but 'in waters so contrary'? say I. Wait fer fair mornin', say I! But nay, they do not listen to good common sense, neither will they tarry, not for love nor gold!"

"What are you saying, old man?" Mycroft demanded.

"The *Latitude*, sir! For the pilot leadin' her out 'as returned, yer see! There he be! And if yer look further out upon the water, *there*," the old man pointed, redirecting Mycroft's eyes to the spot, "that be 'er wake; she be underway, full steam ahead!"

And indeed, Mycroft noticed a lone ship belching out coal smoke as she made for the Thames.

"I must stop her!" Mycroft cried, and the old salt let out a phlegmy cackle and slapped a knee.

"Stop a steamer in 'er tracks? Y'ell never do that, sir. For already she is beyond the horizon. All ye can do from here is to wave goodbye."

Mycroft looked out helplessly. The old codger was correct: there was nothing he could do, for there was no manner of communicating with a ship once she had set sail. He remembered Ai Lin's words, that the weight of extra coal would be offset by the absence of passengers, so that stops along the route would be unnecessary.

He had to speak to Deshi Hai Lin. He had to tell the patriarch what he suspected about Bingwen Shi. Perhaps he was still somewhere on Victoria Dock. Mycroft snatched up the old salt by his frayed lapels, all but lifting him off the ground.

"Take me to Deshi Hai Lin. Now!"

"No need to get 'andsy, guv'n'r!" the old salt huffed, prying Mycroft's hands away. "The Chinaman you seek, 'im what owns the ship? 'e sailed off!"

"*He* sailed off?" Mycroft repeated. "Was a female aboard?"

"'is daughter, yer mean? The pretty one? They say she is off to be married!" He grinned through blackened teeth. "And I've more than earned that 'alf sov!" he declared, stooping to pluck up the coin that had fallen out of Mycroft's fingers. "I'll 'ave meself a benjo tonight!"

As the old man gleefully bounded away, Mycroft stared out at the churning black water. He could no longer see the *Latitude*, nor her wake. *An hour five* it had taken him to peruse Zaharoff's files: that was what he had said to Douglas. Sixty-five minutes to doggedly pursue one train of thought while blithely neglecting others, for his mind had already been made up.

Yes, Zaharoff was wealthy enough to purchase his own ships, but he could not do so without arousing tedious international oversight. Better to utilize four steamers that already had predetermined routes, routes that he wanted, and whose ownership was above suspicion. Not to mention that Deshi Hai Lin utilized coal-powered ships for cargo. As Douglas had pointed out, more expensive but much more efficient.

*It has always been about the ships.*

The ships were Occam's Razor, the obvious prize.

Blinded once again by the haze of love, and of his own prowess, he had badly underestimated his enemy, and now it was too late.

Or was it?

# 39

THE MOMENT HE CAME TO HIMSELF, A SMALL FLOOD OF realizations occurred to him. The first was his name. He knew it was his, but the urge to say it aloud was so strong that he had to grit his teeth against the temptation. When that proved too great, he compromised, forming the letters furtively, as a child might sneak a forbidden sweet:

*Cyrus Douglas.*

Then a phrase, like a penny sparkler in the dark:

*Cogito, ergo sum.*

The language was not native to him, of that he was certain; yet he understood the meaning. *I think, therefore I am.* It reminded him that he was not some disembodied spirit but corporeal. And though his 'cogitation' was feeble, the small victory of awakening from a dreamless sleep to realize that he could still think, and therefore *was*… almost made him weep aloud.

Then there was the state, or more accurately, the *location* of his body: down upon his knees, back arched, his arms wrenched behind him, wrists shackled to ankles by a chain that emitted a dull clank each time he moved. It was not, judging from the weight, particularly thick; but it would do.

Whoever had bound him had disrobed him, save for his

trousers. He was barefoot and bare-chested, but to what end? To better feel the chill? To freeze to death before awakening? If someone had wished him dead, why not simply kill him and be done with it?

Finally, there was the matter of the blindfold wound tightly about his head. He had not only been hog-tied and trussed like a condemned man before a firing squad but had also been rendered incapable of seeing so much as a shadow.

Douglas brushed his fingertips against the floorboard behind him, feeling wood so old that it buckled. His smallest movement made it creak and groan.

He listened for other sounds: footsteps, breath, embers or coal emitting their last crackling gasps in a hearth somewhere. But there was nothing beyond a light pitter-patter of rain. Was anyone likely to sit quietly in the gelid air, waiting for him to awaken? Unlikely.

*Wherever I am*, he thought, *I am alone.*

The ceiling was so low that he could smell it, blackened by years of wafting soot and candle fat—though no candle had been lit for him, he could ascertain that much.

A low ceiling, then. And how many windows? He listened for the rattle of raindrops against the glass.

*One.*

An ancient buckling floor, a low ceiling, one window. He was likely in a garret. Good. An easy leap from casement to rooftop to street, provided he could undo the shackles: a lofty proviso indeed.

Whatever made him figure that, even unbound, leaping about would be so easy? Once freed from this foggy delirium, whatever person he turned out to be, surely modesty was not his greatest virtue!

He attempted to shift positions, to see what his shackled body was capable of. But before he could discern if it was flexible, indeed if it could move at all, the numbness in his limbs gave way to the spider-like prickling of paresthesia, followed by a sensation of fire.

*Slow the breath*, he commanded himself. *Close your mouth. Shallow and steady.*

The burning ache told him he'd been tied up for several hours. The unnatural pose—bent back in the crippling cold—was one he could have held without much bother at age twenty. But at forty-three, it was excruciating.

*Forty-three*, he repeated. *Cyrus Douglas, aged forty-three. Born in Trinidad…*

He was giddy with progressive revelations until the thought concluded:

*…blindfolded, and bound half-naked in a garret.*

About the chain or the nakedness—or the garret for that matter—he could, for the moment, do nothing. There was but one unfortunate state of affairs that was his to alter.

Douglas carefully leaned to the side and lowered his face to the ground. Then he began to rub his cheek and temple repeatedly against the moisture-warped floorboard, his head pounding from the motion as if he'd consumed a bottle of whiskey. Yet, he knew he would keep it up until his cramping arms and stiff neck cried out for relief.

At last, the burning in his limbs abated… only to be replaced by a sudden chill that made him catch his breath. Then a shiver began, uncontrollable, from the nape of his neck downward, the chain clanking like a dissonant gong against the floorboards as he quaked and shook in protest to the stinging air.

*Shallow breaths. Easy. Easy, I say.*

Within moments, his body did as he'd commanded. He seemed a master at circumnavigating pain. If only his mental powers were as keen!

*If only I were Mycroft Holmes!* he thought. The name ricocheted through him like an errant shot. Mycroft! Yes. A name nearly as familiar as his own.

*Steady, Douglas! What year is this?*

*1873. The Year of the Rooster,* came the obedient reply.

He remembered sitting in the mess hall of a ship, talking to a Chinese man with a scar upon his neck. After that, he was walking, drenched to the bone.

But what had led to this present predicament?

It had been afternoon and raining. He had had words with his friend Mycroft Holmes, and he had opted to walk home.

Instead, he had found himself going down Regent Street and up a set of stairs towards a sign—

### REGENT TOBACCOS

*Importateur de Cigares de la Havane,*
*de Manille, et du Continent*

—when something had struck him upon the head.

He had very nearly rubbed the blindfold up past his cheekbone when he heard a different sound, one that shut down all but the strain of listening. The voice of that same young man—Mycroft Holmes—calling his name. Were his ears playing tricks? Or was it the detritus of concussion? Once again, he was forced to command his heart to slow its pace. With one last rub of his cheek against the floorboards, the blindfold finally lifted.

If he had hoped for a revelation, it was a disappointment, for there was no light in the room at all. He waited for his eyes to adjust, until he could see at the very least shadows and shapes. Then, he looked about.

Though he was, as predicted, quite alone, what he did manage to discern was not encouraging. The room itself was indeed low-ceilinged. It was also empty of any furniture, and some of the floorboards were black with rot. There was but one garret window set into the roof that appeared to be no more than one-foot square, much too small to be of any service, other than to let him know that it was night. If he could figure out a way to get undone from his chains, he supposed he could open it and scream for help, though there were no guarantees that whoever appeared would be friend and not foe. When he recalled his earlier plan to leap from it to the rooftop, he nearly laughed aloud.

There was also a door. Among a series of pitiful options, it was his only hope.

He crawled to it much as an earthworm might, one inch and one wiggle at a time, trying to ignore the splinters that pierced his bare skin as he went. Upon reaching it, he felt the wood of the door with the side of his arm: a sturdy wood, probably oak.

Beside the door, on the wall and attached to a swivel, was an enormous iron crossbar latch that swung up and then into a pair of giant bearings on the other side, thus barring the way for any intruder attempting ingress. It was a medieval-looking contraption, as if someone were expecting an attack by battering ram.

Odd that a thing meant to keep one safely inside should be his best hope of getting out.

Utilizing the strength of his shoulder, along with the top of his head—not nearly so strong but conveniently placed—he managed after several failed attempts to heave the large crossbar upward.

It turned on its swivel, went up and—after balancing straight for a moment—fell into its bearings with a mighty clank. After that he waited, anxious that the sound should draw attention. But when he heard no one approaching, he moved into the second phase of his plan.

Unfortunately, that plan called for him to perform a headstand. Not only that, but to balance himself on the very portion of his head which had suffered the concussive blow.

*I cannot,* he began, and as soon as the thought came, he felt what little strength he had ebbing away. He could not allow that to occur, or he really was done for.

*The God you say you believe in,* he adjured himself firmly, *is the God of the long odds.*

Douglas slithered an inch at a time towards the crossbar until he was lying right underneath its bearings, where perhaps a foot of crossbar jutted past. With tremendous effort, and using his long, flexible body to his advantage, Douglas sidled up against the wall, balanced his chained body upon his throbbing head into the most awkward headstand he had ever executed, and then tried to 'catch' the jutting edge of crossbar with the chain wrapped around his wrists and ankles.

That accomplished, he hung there, suspended like a skinned goat at market, while he waited for his skull to stop throbbing.

He had been hoping that, by tugging in opposition to the chains that held him, he could break them. But the ground was so close that it impeded momentum.

He would have to lift the bar, with himself upon it.

Still hanging upside down, he began pushing his way up the wall with his bound feet. Utilizing the chains, he lifted the bar off of its bearings bit by excruciating bit. When he thought he had climbed far enough, he simply let go.

The heavy bar fell back into its bearings, his body falling with it and missing the floor by inches. It was like being stretched upon a cross. The pain was agonizing. And the chain remained intact.

Even so, he still believed in his plan as his only route of escape. For the bar was solid iron, heavier and stronger than the chains that held him fast. Combined with the pressure his falling body could exert, all twelve stone eight pounds of him, it *should* snap open the chains, provided his bones did not snap open first.

Inch by inch he climbed the wall again, and once again, having reached the top, he let go.

A second later, he found himself sprawled out upon the floor. The chains had given way. Best of all, the main ring had ceded, releasing not only wrists from ankles, but ankles from each other.

Wobbly and in great pain, Douglas stood upright. He pushed the heavy bar out of its casement, wondering if he could somehow pry it from its swivel—for if he could, he might use it to batter open the door. Barely able to see for the darkness, he felt its three large bolts with his fingertips.

He was puzzling how he could remove them with no tools, when he absent-mindedly touched the door handle… and felt it lowering in his hand.

The door was unlocked.

That startled him more than finding himself blindfolded and chained in a garret. He waited a moment to still his breath, then he opened it as quietly as he could and stared out into a narrow, dark hallway.

He heard Mycroft's voice a second time dully, faintly, calling his name.

"Mycroft!" he called back, but his own voice sounded hoarse and weak.

He tried again.

"*Mycroft!*" he called out with all of his might as he lumbered his way down the pitch-black corridor.

Suddenly, a shadow was coming towards him at a goodly clip. Crying out had been a mistake, for he had no energy left to fight.

A moment later, he was enveloped in familiar arms. Mycroft removed his own coat and wrapped it about his shoulders, then—keeping a steadying arm about him—slowly walked him to freedom.

# 40

DOUGLAS AND MYCROFT SAT IN THE BACK OF THE carriage, with Douglas all but buried in blankets, on their way to the London Hospital in Whitechapel. For although Douglas had longed for nothing more than his own warm bed, Mycroft had pointed out the awkwardness of explaining to staff and boys alike why Mr. Smythe's personal secretary (and suspected tattle-tale) Cyrus Douglas would need to come half-broken to convalesce at Nickolus House, of all unlikely places. With his head still smarting and his teeth still chattering, Douglas gave up on his rather feeble protestations and allowed himself to be transported wherever Mycroft wished.

"You said that the bolt was inside," Mycroft said. "But, in order to leave you alone in there, with the door bolted, that inside bolt had to be put into position from the *outside*. How?"

"The crossbar, it was on a hinge," Douglas explained. "With a point of balance in the middle, a sort of fulcrum. To have it lock from the inside, you had but to place the bar at that point of balance, walk out without jostling it, and then slam the door behind you—and the bolt would fall into its bearings."

"Clever," Mycroft said.

"By half. Even in the dark, that medieval-looking crossbar was an intimidating sight. And though I have no proof, the room had the feel of a torture chamber."

"Well now that it has been discovered, I doubt it shall be used for that purpose again."

"How long did you search for me?"

"It took a while, I'll admit," Mycroft said. "From the docks I went home to get into dry clothing, seething all the while at how Zaharoff had bested me. And more and more, your being gone at this particular juncture seemed less coincidence and more by design. Once I made up my mind to search for you, it took three hours. With Zaharoff's minions no doubt reporting each moment back to him for his amusement."

Mycroft's voice all but dripped with venom. Douglas pitied anyone who could reduce him to such a state, for he was not one to turn the other cheek.

"So you believe that Zaharoff planned all of this from the first? That seems a bit *too* diabolical," Douglas said.

"No, I think he just made the best out of a bad situation," Mycroft replied. "Zaharoff never planned to have me nosing about, looking into Bingwen Shi's kidnapping. That was a surprise to him. Given that, he had to let me know that he is not the canary to my cat, as you had it, but I to his. That nothing I care for is beyond his reach. Including you."

"Then why did he not simply kill me and be done with it?"

"To begin with, he sees himself as a businessman, Douglas, not a madman. He does not kill willy-nilly. And, as you pose no threat to him, it would be a risk to no good end. Secondly, he must realize that if he kills you, he shall never be rid of me."

"Yes, I can imagine that he would be none too happy to have you as his albatross. But how did you track me?"

"Track?" Mycroft repeated, feigning offense. "I am no Afghan hound. I leave that to my brother. No, once I reasoned that he would not kill you, I knew he had you abducted. As it so happens, I had just read about him. I therefore recalled all the buildings that he owned in the vicinity. Regent Tobaccos was point zero, as it were, and I began searching for you in concentric, ever widening circles. I called out your name, figuring that sooner or later you would be clever enough to respond. Thank Providence that it had finally stopped raining, else I would not have heard you at all. I assume that Zaharoff was also curious about your prowess in *capoeira*—"

"Yes. Unusual to be left chained but shirtless and barefooted," Douglas said, smiling.

"He hoped you would put on a good show."

"I tried my best," Douglas muttered.

"And your old bullet fragments held steady!" Mycroft exclaimed.

"That they did," Douglas said, nodding.

There was still so much that he wished to know and to discuss. There was Ai Lin, and Bingwen Shi. And Mycroft still had that infernal compunction to skirt morality, to embrace—what was it that he had said once?—ah, yes. *Necessary Inhumanity*. But instead of continuing the conversation, he found himself lowering his eyelids and sinking into the inestimable luxury of a safe sleep.

Mycroft was sitting in Edward Cardwell's library just as the grandfather clock in the hall chimed midnight. He had requested, and been provided, a glass of Cognac as he waited for his former employer to be rousted from bed. The Camus brand, though prestigious, was not his favorite. Nevertheless, he was gratified that it was not tea. Mycroft made a silent and solitary toast to his friend Douglas, recovering at the London Hospital, and took a sip.

Mycroft had insisted upon paying for a private room with a nice view of the grounds, along with round-the-clock nursing care. But he knew that Douglas would make scant use of it and might even, the moment he was better, rally enough to pour his own liquids and to make his own bed—perhaps even give the personnel a hand with any other small tasks they might be too busy to execute.

"Mr. Holmes?" Cardwell said as he walked in.

"Forgive this intrusion, sir," Mycroft replied, rising to his feet.

"No bother, no bother, for I was not yet abed," he replied, though creases in his left cheek and a tuft of hair knotted by a sleeping cap, hastily removed, gave the lie to his words.

"Scotch," he muttered to his butler, who had followed him inside. Then, suppressing a groan, he fell into the seat opposite.

Mycroft removed a document from his inner pocket and passed it over.

"What's this?"

"Zaharoff's declaration that Bingwen Shi had naught to do with arms sales to Japan," Mycroft said, sitting down again. "That Shi never spoke to any Japanese officials about arms, and that no one in Japan can contradict that claim or say otherwise."

Cardwell reached for a set of spectacles on a small table beside his chair and peered at the paper.

"The original is on its way to China as we speak," Mycroft added.

"Is it legitimate?" Cardwell asked.

"Quite, in the sense that Zaharoff wrote it. But I would need the War Office to mark it as perjury, for that is the quickest way to nullify it."

"Though it is *not* perjury."

"No, sir."

"Then you might want to explain, and carefully, from the beginning…" Cardwell growled. He put down his scotch in one swallow, and as the butler poured another, Mycroft began.

"Bingwen Shi's family is aristocratic but in need of funds; while the Lins are very well off but lack social cachet. So they made a good match. And, once the nuptials were arranged, Shi went to Zaharoff with a deal to utilize his father-in-law's ships. When Zaharoff agreed, Shi went to his father-in-law, who consented to the partnership.

"So Zaharoff began arranging for his weapons to be transported on the Lin ships, vaunting their speed and their reputation for efficiency and timeliness. But when Lin's daughter got wind of it, she put her foot down. And so her father—without telling her that a deal had already been struck—abruptly called off the partnership.

"By that time," Mycroft concluded, "Zaharoff had made promises abroad. When Deshi Hai Lin severed the relationship, Zaharoff lost face and money, and that would not do. He had to make an example of the weakest link in the chain."

"Bingwen Shi."

"Yes, sir," Mycroft replied.

"I take it that Shi knew what his future held: that he would be beheaded?" Cardwell asked. "That he knew it was just a matter of time before Zaharoff would have to make an example of him?"

"Yes, sir, he knew. And he panicked."

"As would we all," Cardwell said, motioning to his butler to refill the glass.

"Shi was desperate," Mycroft continued. "So he went to

Zaharoff with an alternate plan. If he and Ai Lin could marry in China, and something untoward were to happen to his father-in-law, he would inherit the ships."

"You are saying that he planned to murder Deshi Hai Lin?"

"I am saying that he was willing to do so. And possibly his future wife. But to do so in Britain, our laws of inheritance being what they are, would not serve. So he and Zaharoff set a scheme into motion: Zaharoff let the Chinese government know that they had a traitor on their hands, and Shi was duly abducted and spirited off to China for trial."

"But this letter proves that Zaharoff always had the means to free him," Cardwell said.

"Yes, sir. But he could not do so directly; it would raise suspicions. He needed someone like me, sir. Someone who thought he was forcing Zaharoff's hand. A dupe, in other words."

"You are no dupe, Holmes."

"Not usually, no. But certainly in this case, I was. Then there was a fortuitous trip to Scotland that proved Shi was not in London on the 4th of April," Mycroft explained. "Now, a trip to Glasgow by train would not—strictly speaking—be necessary. It is not difficult to prove that one is not in London on a certain date, if one is aware of the date in advance."

"Nevertheless, it was convenient," Cardwell opined. "For it legitimized his relationship with the girl, with Ai Lin. He might even be able to hold it against her, if she ever thought to break off the engagement."

"Yes, sir," Mycroft said, swallowing. "What he *did* hold against her was her strong-willed but compassionate nature. If he could have her believe that she was his only salvation, she could be counted upon to sail to China to rescue him. And of course her father would never let her go without him. So you see, sir, what must be done in order to save them both."

Mycroft paused and took a sip of his Cognac, and Cardwell grew pale.

"Holmes, you do know what you are asking. If we declare that this note from Zaharoff is counterfeit—"

"—I do. It gives Zaharoff and Bingwen Shi no time to recalibrate. The execution will be carried out as planned."

"It is not just an 'execution,' but a terrible way to die," Cardwell said, shaking his head. "I do not see how we can justify—"

"Mr. Cardwell," Mycroft interrupted. His tone was even, though there was steel in it. "Deshi Hai Lin and his daughter are naturalized British citizens, whereas Bingwen Shi is a Chinese national who conspired against his own countrymen. Just because he did not personally do the deal, he was still instrumental in attempting to transport arms to Japan. As I said from the first, 'If Shi was in fact treasonous to his homeland, *should* he be saved?' In my humble opinion, sir, the answer is no."

Cardwell finished his glass, took a full one from the butler's tray and drank half before putting it down again.

"It appears that we have just condemned a man to death," he said.

"No, sir, we have not. He condemned himself."

"What about Zaharoff?" Cardwell said quietly, after a moment. "How shall he be punished?"

"With Zaharoff, I cannot hope for a victory, but I *can* work for a *détente*. Stop him from doing harm to Deshi Hai Lin or to his daughter, or from attempting ever again to procure any ship that flies the British flag."

Cardwell reached for a half-smoked cigar upon the nearby ashtray, and Mycroft noticed that his hands were shaking.

"Allow me," Mycroft said, lighting it for him, his own hands as steady as a stone.

# 41

IN SPITE OF HUAN'S SILK AND CANVAS AWNING, IT WAS A wet, nearly four-hour slog back to London. Visibility was nil, slowing their progress significantly, and even the best of shelters could not prevent the wind from blowing the rain sideways. Since Huan's small victory with the cat, he had continued to press his way, insisting for example that Sherlock not place the golden frog inside his jacket pocket.

And, even though Sherlock had taken every precaution to lay not a finger upon the little creature—he had even wrapped it in his handkerchief!—Huan seemed suddenly immune to reason.

Huan's solution, in fact, was an abomination; he had suggested entombing the beast at the bottom of the flower vase on the inside of the carriage door, where any rut in the road could knock it out and onto the floor.

Sherlock managed a compromise: a very nice mahogany and copper box with red silk padding, wherein both of his finds— frog and thorn—fitted quite well.

"It protects a very dear carriage clock, Master Sherlock," Huan fretted when he saw the clock lying unprotected upon the seat, where Sherlock had left it.

"This might be a very dear frog, Huan," Sherlock replied.

The two finally arrived at St. John's Wood just after midnight. Sherlock was so anxious to be about his work that he all but dashed to Mycroft's front door without so much as a nod of farewell.

"Good night, Master Sherlock!" Huan called out behind him.

Sherlock turned and saw Huan still perched on the sprung seat, fog so thick around him that it appeared to be erasing him even as he sat, and waving so enthusiastically that he might as well have been on a tropical beach at midday, instead of wet to the bone on an unseasonably cold London night.

"Sleep well, my friend," Sherlock managed to say, waving back.

Carriage-clock box safely in hand, Sherlock knocked upon Mycroft's door; and when it opened, he breezed past the sleepy-faced housemaid with a, "No, thank you," to whatever it was that she was offering, be it towels or sustenance. For the first time, he did not sprint upstairs to the guest bedroom to mull over his yarn-and-pin creation but went directly into Mycroft's well-stocked library, where he had never before set foot; for Mycroft was so fussy about his books that it would be hardly worth the bother, were Sherlock not desperate to peruse a reference or two.

There was no fire in the hearth: a shame, for he was still quite sodden. He shooed away the yawning page boy with bloodshot eyes whom the housemaid had no doubt roused to come to his aid. Blessedly alone, he lit a couple of lamps, hoping against hope that identifying his specimen would be as simple as opening Linnaeus's *Systema Naturae*, and turning to 'Frogs.'

He sat at Mycroft's desk, the clock box beside him, and perused the pages listed in the table of contents. But none of the fourteen species mentioned therein resembled the little golden one that he had extracted from the belly of the cat.

Ever less hopeful, he turned to 'Accipitres,' under which the author had enumerated 'Corvus,' crows and ravens. But none of the twelve species listed were in any way unusual. And another volume on botany had too many cacti with thorns identical to the one he had found.

He was rifling through this chapter and that, hoping to come upon something else that might provide a useful link, when he heard an appalled voice at the door:

"*Sherlock....?* In my *library?*"

His brother stood at the threshold fully dressed and wearing a haunted look, as if he had misplaced something of great import.

"Mycroft!" Sherlock greeted him with as much affability as he dared. "Well timed, for I could use a hand—"

"No. Do not request my aid," Mycroft replied, "for I can be of no use to anyone tonight... But what you are so abusing?" He drew an alarmed breath. "Not My *Systema Naturae*, tenth edition!"

Whereupon, he marched over and snatched both volumes out of Sherlock's hands, and fixed him with a glare. "And is that my *carriage clock?*"

"Not at all!" Sherlock protested. "The clock is safely in the carriage. This is merely the box," he explained, holding it up.

"The clock *requires* the box!" Mycroft exclaimed. "The box shelters the clock!"

"The clock is unmolested, brother. And even if it weren't, you are able to tell time perfectly well by, I don't know, wetting your finger and lifting it up into the air or something. As to why I am here," he continued with a broad smile: "I have found a golden frog in the belly of a cat!"

Mycroft stared at him, aghast. "You have truly gone around the bend. How long has it been since you have slept?"

It took Mycroft a good half hour to catch up with all that Sherlock was telling him, for he wasted the first few moments simply attempting to calm himself down. But even then, he found that he was struggling with his younger brother's story. His thoughts kept returning to Ai Lin, to Zaharoff, and to the allegation from the War Office, signed by Cardwell, of a counterfeit. It would arrive first thing in the morning to Zaharoff's offices in Berkeley Square; and then by telegram to the British Legations in Peking, Wuhan, Taipei, Shanghai, and Xiamen.

In some three weeks' time, Ai Lin and her father would disembark the *Latitude*, only to be told, after their long and arduous journey, that the document they carried as proof was useless, and that Bingwen Shi would be executed for treason.

Mycroft's heart bled for her, but it could not be helped.

As for Sherlock's tale, it sounded mad, stuffed as it was with strange birds, dead felines, cactus thorns, blowguns, and golden frogs. He wondered, not for the first time, if lunacy— of the sort that their mother occasionally suffered—might be hereditary. New theories pointed to that very possibility. Sherlock, fine-boned, thin, and highly strung like her, had all the markers of incipient madness; whereas Mycroft himself could well be a passive, or asymptomatic carrier, one who did not experience psychological imbalances, yet could pass them on to his progeny.

*Seeing as how I shall never marry, there is no danger of that!* he thought.

In any event, one problem at a time. He had refused to become Sherlock's sounding board until his brother had dried himself off and changed his clothing. In the peaceful interlude that followed, and grateful for the distraction, Mycroft had examined the frog under a magnifying glass. He had been careful to utilize tweezers, as he was in agreement with Huan that a creature so colorful should not be touched until one could ascertain what it was.

From his schoolboy studies of biology, Mycroft recalled that coloration to prevent attack was called *aposematism*, and that its function was primarily visual, indicating to predators that the colored prey was noxious.

"'Conspicuousness evolves in tandem with noxiousness,'" he recited aloud, as if addressing the dead amphibian under his lens. He recalled that the colors that most effectively repelled predators were black, white, red, and yellow, which meant that gold certainly fitted the bill. Other odd behaviors, sounds, and even odors were often a part of these creatures' modes of deterrence. Sherlock had mentioned that Mrs. Jurgins had heard a whistling sound at the moment that the cat had run off. Sherlock had assumed that it had come from a bird. Most likely, it had been emitted from the frog itself, as a warning to the cat to stay away.

"Clearly ineffectual," he muttered to the frog.

Other than coloration and size—it was an inch in diameter—Mycroft could deduce nothing of worth. Oh, it had tiny adhesive discs upon its toes, most likely to aid it in climbing. And its left hind leg was scarred on the bottom: two identical scars, as a matter of fact, a millimeter apart. But the possible causes were too diverse for a solid guess.

At any rate, he did not recall reading about this particular frog, certainly not in *his* library, whose panoply of books he knew by heart. The same could be said of the strange thorn, undoubtedly from a cactus, that Sherlock had pulled from Elise Wickham's neck.

He agreed with his brother that the two items were somehow related, in that both were foreign in the extreme, in that both had manifested far out of their natural habitat… and in proximity to the killer's appearance.

Sherlock waltzed back in, at long last dry and wrapped in a clean robe. He was also as wide awake as if it had been nine in the morning.

He took a seat across from Mycroft and extracted his shag and papers from the robe's pocket.

"Anything?" he asked.

"Nothing untoward," Mycroft replied. "Did you notice the scars on its left hind leg?"

"Naturally. Ideas?"

"None."

"Well then, here's something you *might* be able to help with," Sherlock said—managing to sound, as he often did, insulting while requesting a favor. "Have you ever heard of an enterprise called Jobine, Mathison?"

"Why would you ask me that, out of the blue?" Mycroft replied, surprised.

"Because Mrs. Jurgins's dead son was namesake to his brother-in-law, who is employed there."

"As it so happens, Jobine, Mathison specialize in precious metals, nothing remotely nefarious about them."

"Then why do you look as if you are withholding something? No use denying it, you are entirely too fragile this evening to pretend otherwise."

Mycroft sighed. "I may be keeping an eye on Deutsche Bank for… a variety of reasons."

"Surely not because they are German!" Sherlock teased.

"Stop it. In March of this year, Jobine, Mathison partnered with Deutsche Bank to purchase the Via Esmeralda Mining Company."

"Now *there's* a familiar name."

Sherlock struck a match to his ghastly cigarette and then blew out an obscene amount of smoke. "I believe that Percy Butcher's relatives might have an investment therein, as does Lady Anne…"

"What do you know about Lady Anne's investments?"

"We may've exchanged a few words in passing," Sherlock admitted with a shrug.

"Sherlock! You were *strictly* prohibited—!"

"And yet, here we are! And my doing so may have placed us that much closer to the answer. I suppose you have information about their other investors at your War Office?"

"It is not 'my' War Office, and no. That would be the Board of Trade—"

"What about the Oaks Colliery?"

"Truly, you have traveled all over the map!" Mycroft declared. "First, Jobine, Mathison, then Via Esmeralda, now the Oaks Colliery?"

Sherlock eyed him plaintively. "What has taken place tonight, brother? For it is more than exhaustion, or vacillating health."

"My health is not remotely vacillating!" Mycroft shot back. "And, unless you wish to revisit your breaking the *single, solitary* rule that I imposed upon you, other than being forced to go about in a very fancy carriage, I suggest that you leave it alone. Again: why did you bring up Oaks?"

"Because Mrs. Jurgins's husband, a supervisor at the colliery, was killed there. At first my ears pricked up, for our murderer is of course obsessed with fire. But then she listed the dead as numbering 384…"

Mycroft stared at him.

"What did I say?" Sherlock asked, staring back at him.

"There were indeed 384 victims," Mycroft said slowly.

"Upon the first day. Then, the following day, rescuers arrived. The colliery blew again, a residual explosion that killed twenty-seven men who were attempting to free the dead bodies from the rubble."

"411 men dead?" Sherlock gasped.

Mycroft could feel himself slump further into the chair. He was so very tired.

"Well. There is nothing that can be done about it tonight. Tomorrow first thing," he said, "I shall pay a visit to Chichester Parkinson-Fortescue, president of the Board of Trade, to beg for a list of investors in Via Esmeralda and the Oaks Colliery, and see if there is a link."

"What about me?" Sherlock asked, as if in fear that Mycroft would snatch it out of his hand at the last moment.

"Our bargain holds. I expect you to knock about the British Museum's natural history collection to investigate the crow and frog and what have you. For *if* we are able to stop this man in his tracks, we shall have to understand his methods. Now. When you are done with that cigarette, kindly extinguish it, and do not so much as cast an eye upon my books again."

Just as he was shutting the door behind him, praying that the smell of that cheap shag would not permeate the carpets, Mycroft heard Sherlock call out his name in a strangled voice. He opened the door again, and there was his brother, on his feet and facing him.

"I... I cannot feel my hands," he murmured as the cigarette dropped from between his fingers.

# 42

KNOWING THAT SHERLOCK WOULD NOT WONDER AT THE extravagance but would take it as his due, Mycroft hired not one but two physicians. After the medical sages had observed him for several hours, and after the numbness had neither abated nor spread but remained confined to his hands, they confirmed only what he and Sherlock already suspected. The little frog, still unknown and unnamed, had most likely released some sort of poisonous brew that in turn had made its predator—the cat—toxic to anyone who touched her.

Huan, who had handled the feline by the tail, had suffered no ill effects; whereas Sherlock, who had cut into the cat's belly and opened up the flesh with his fingers before noticing the frog therein, had been compromised. Neither physician had ever seen anything like it, and both seemed incurious to pursue it. The only call of duty they heard, in Mycroft's estimation, was home and bed, with the rather terse suggestion that he send word again in the morning, should Sherlock's condition take a turn for the worse.

When morning finally came, Sherlock's fingers were demoted from fully numb to merely tingling, but he was still quite incapable of even dressing himself properly, much less of carefully leafing through the pages of a brittle old book.

"Perhaps Huan can help me," he suggested, for he dearly wished to go to the British Museum and did not relish being left behind.

"He cannot read, Sherlock. It would take forever."

"Perhaps Douglas?"

"No."

"Where *is* Douglas?"

"Busy."

Mycroft was just as glad to go alone. For, while sleep would not come, his mind had strayed back to Heinrich Schliemann. Though he very much despised Schliemann's methods of archaeology, his instincts told him that the excavator was on the cusp of a weighty find. Since there was no way of halting his momentum, why should Zaharoff, or Count Wolfgang, for that matter, gain from this potential discovery of the century? Especially since Zaharoff was likely to funnel a portion to the Ottoman Empire, and Count Wolfgang to Prussia! Britain should have no lack. In a battle of the wallets, Mycroft was determined to emerge victorious. For his country's sake, he would match Zaharoff and Wolfgang arm for arm!

The first stop of the day, therefore, was to his bank, C. Hoare & Co., nicknamed The Golden Bottle. Mycroft instructed his banker, Mr. Dalrymple, to invest as much as he dared in the venture.

The next stop was to the Board of Trade. The president, Chichester Parkinson-Fortescue, had left London for the day, but he had done Mycroft the courtesy of assigning his secretary to the task. As it so happened, the secretary was possessive of his files, and Mycroft was forced to cool his heels for over an hour while the bespectacled, balding little man juggled ledgers, one for the Oaks Colliery, the other for Via Esmeralda Mining Company.

Mycroft watched him turn to this page and that with what he could only describe as methodical lethargy. It was infuriating.

"There are hundreds of small investors in Via Esmeralda, Mr. Holmes," the secretary opined at last, squinting up from his labors.

"I can well imagine," Mycroft replied, praying for patience. "For it is, after all, an emerald mine, in one of the countries that is richest in emeralds. But, as I said an hour ago, if some of those investors are found to have also invested in the colliery that exploded in 1866, *that* is the link that I seek."

"Of course. There are fewer investors in the colliery. Twenty-one in all."

"Yes!" Mycroft said with forced bonhomie. "And of those twenty-one, how many have also invested in Via Esmeralda?"

"I am sure I do not know, Mr. Holmes…"

"Might you check?" Mycroft asked.

"I suppose…" he said with a frown, as if Mycroft had asked for the moon.

The little man looked from one ledger to the other, from one to the other again, and then again—until Mycroft was dizzy from watching. At last, the little man said, "I believe it is twelve. Twelve people have invested in both!"

"Wonderful!" Mycroft cried. "And may I have those twelve names?"

"They are written in these two ledgers, do you see?" He indicated the books in his hand, both opened to pages that Mycroft could not see at all. "Now," he said. "I must double-check to make sure they are correct. That these twelve individuals each had dealings with the colliery—and then invested in Via Esmeralda. That is what you need, is it not?"

"Yes," Mycroft said. "Yes, that is exactly what I need. Perhaps I can assist you with—"

But the little man lifted his chin for silence.

"Here, then, is number one. Ah, and *there* is number two… No, wait, incorrect spelling. Off by one letter. *There* is number two!"

He scanned the columns with his index finger, wetting the tip of it with his tongue as he did so. "That one, I believe, is number three. Yes, for it is a match, d'you see? Christian name, middle initial, surname, done! Now then, we seek number four…"

"So might you call out the names as you go?" Mycroft interrupted, leaning over the desk between them, his voice perhaps more boisterous than warranted.

"Well I believe I might be able to give you them all, if you will but have a moment's patience!" the little man scolded.

He removed his spectacles, blew upon the glass, cleaned them with his sleeve, and then put them back on.

"Now, where was I? Ah, yes. I was seeking number four, was I not? Four, four, four…"

Mycroft found himself sliding across the desk and snatching the books out of the little man's hands. He knew that there would be hell to pay at some point, but no matter.

He was going after a killer. The rest would have to wait.


Huan skidded the carriage to a stop in front of the museum steps. Mycroft took them two by two. Inside, after a few false starts, he found an illustrated journal so old that the edges crumbled in his hands, but it had the information he sought.

Though nearly all crows were adept with tools, it informed him, the most adept were two island dwellers. The New

Caledonian crow was black and sleek and looked very much like Britain's domestic. But the other, the '*Alalā*, was found solely in the western and southeastern parts of the Hawaiian islands. Its wings were more rounded, its bill thicker. It had brownish-black plumage, with bristly feathers at the throat, which could account for the old man's description of its looking 'buffeted about.'

"'Omnivorous, extremely resourceful, and intelligent, it emits a guttural caw,'" he read, which also fit what Sherlock had said.

That done, he moved on to frogs. So many frogs, more than six thousand species. Mycroft rushed through the *amphibia animalia* of Western Europe, Russia, and North America; but what he was really after, and was hard-pressed to come upon, was information on the frogs of South America, and Colombia in particular.

Just as he was bemoaning the paucity of resources, in a stack of unmarked journals he came upon one that featured amphibian species in the northwestern jungles of Colombia.

He roused a museum assistant, napping on a nearby chair.

"Might this be purchased?" he asked.

The man gave him a bedeviled look, and wiped a hint of spittle from the corner of his mouth. "Sir, we do not sell—"

"Half a crown."

Within moments, he was back in his carriage, the journal opened upon his knee, hastening to pick up Sherlock.

# 43

OF THE TWELVE NAMES UPON THE LIST, ONLY ONE HAD not yet lost a member of her family. She was a former investor in the Oaks Colliery by the name of Dorothea Greer. Thankfully, she resided not far from St. John's Wood, and turned out to be neither old nor infirm, neither hard of hearing nor stubborn. Instead, impressed by Mycroft's credentials—rather, by his former credentials—she stood upon the threshold of her tidy, semi-detached house and with frightened eyes enumerated all of the people whom she loved and would be deeply wounded to lose, until finally she came upon one who fit the killer's parameters.

Isolated, yet accessible. Ideally, living alone, and a creature of habit.

"Should we alert the authorities?" she asked, her forehead creased with worry.

"Best not," Mycroft said. "For we cannot risk scaring him away."

"Might I come with you, then?" she implored. "For my cousin Gwyneth is dear to me. We spent summers at the seaside together—"

"No," Sherlock interjected. "All should stay as it is. Mrs. Greer, do you know of anyone who might wish to hurt you?"

"Not a soul!" she assured them.

"And were you yourself an investor in Oaks Colliery?" Mycroft asked.

"Mycroft, we must go," Sherlock urged, for his brother seemed to be wanting too many extraneous details.

"One moment," he replied. "Mrs. Greer, I assure you that you are not speaking out of school…"

"Yes, I understand. No, I was not. The original investor of Oaks was my late father. But my husband and I used the profits from Oaks to buy into Esmeralda."

"Profits from an explosion?" Mycroft asked, surprised.

"Well yes, not from the first, of course, but from the second. When those poor rescuers died, the company was shamed into paying back double to all the investors, so that we would not make a fuss, I suppose. They established the Oaks Colliery Relief Fund, and people sent in cash donations. The Queen herself contributed."

"What of the dead rescuers? Did you get to know any of their immediate family?" Mycroft asked—and Sherlock suddenly comprehended his line of query.

"Yes, of course. We commiserated with them. They too were recompensed. One man, as I recall, lost his only son."

"Do you remember his name?" Sherlock asked.

"No. For in '66 I was still too young to pay much attention. But one detail did impress me greatly: on holidays from work, he traveled. He had gone all over the world!"

Sherlock's small golden frog turned out to be *Phyllobates terribilis*, also known as the golden poison frog, the golden arrow frog, and the golden dart frog, which pleased Sherlock no end. It was found in only one place in the world, a small area of Colombia. The source of its poison was its skin, which was coated with an alkaloid toxin known as batrachotoxin, a self-defense mechanism emitted at the first hint of danger. It carried, on its very small body, a large enough dose to kill ten men.

"Huan saved your life," Mycroft said, as he and Sherlock sat in the jostling carriage, on their way to Dorothea Greer's cousin's home in Prittlewell, Essex.

"Symptoms?" Sherlock asked. For he could not yet hold the journal in his hands and was therefore dependent on Mycroft's recall.

"Nothing overt, which is what makes it so difficult to diagnose. No foaming at the mouth, no tremors. It attacks the sodium channels of nerve cells. Kills instantly. Stops the heart."

Sherlock sat back in his seat and drew a breath. "And how much toxin is required to take down a human being?" he asked.

"The equivalent of two grains of rice," Mycroft declared, and Sherlock smiled.

"So it would fit on the tip of a dart. Or on a thorn."

"In order to keep it poisonous," Mycroft explained, "the killer had to procure its native food, and keep it in a highly humid climate."

"London can do for the second," Sherlock said, smiling.

"The little beast also emits a whistle when alarmed, which is what your Mrs. Jurgins no doubt heard."

Sherlock nodded. "The killer must have had it somewhere upon his person. It got away, and the cat pursued it."

Mycroft sat for a moment, dumbfounded. "Here is a man who walks about with a crow, a frog, and a blowgun, and no one notices?"

"Ah, so you are at last willing to accept my blowgun theory!" Sherlock exclaimed.

"I had never heard of one that could shoot so far. But it seems the Chocó Emberá Indians of Colombia use blowgun darts to hunt game, and can strike with a great deal of accuracy up to one hundred yards."

Sherlock's smile grew wider. Mycroft slipped on a pair of opera gloves, opened up the carriage-clock box, and took out the little frog. He had read how native hunters prepared their darts. In one method, they impaled the frog onto a plank of wood and then held it near a flame. As its skin blistered from the heat, bubbles would fill with poison. The hunters would then touch the tips of their darts to the toxic bubbles to take down their quarry.

"None of its marks match that," Sherlock said, eyeing their little subject.

"No. But in another method, a wild frog is captured and then confined inside a hollow cane. When poison is needed, the hunter passes a bamboo tooth, called a *siurukida*, into the frog's mouth, down its gullet, and out one leg. Unsurprisingly, the poor frog becomes distressed and begins to sweat out its frothy poison… though it does survive the indignity. One 'withdrawal' can kill up to ten grown men, as I said, and retain its potency for a full year."

"That would also account for those two identical scars on its left hind leg," Sherlock declared. "And a hollow cane? That could also work as a blowpipe, could it not? Constructed properly?"

Mycroft nodded. "In Vienna, I spied a fine walking stick, one that the owner seemed quite anxious to use upon Douglas. Ivory horsehead handle, with a pneumatic gun hidden inside—"

"Well, there we are, then!" Sherlock replied. "In the same way, a hollow walking stick could mask a blowpipe capable of shooting a great distance. Perhaps a separate compartment for the frog? And of course no one would question why a man would be walking about with a cane!"

Mycroft stared out of the window. It was a fine day: still gray, but mild as a kitten, and not yet noon. Summer would be arriving soon. And here they were, speaking of murder and death, and if that weren't enough, riding towards it, to meet it face to face. The entire venture seemed to energize Sherlock, as much as it enervated him.

"What if the crow never attacked the parakeet?" he heard Sherlock say, in one of endless speculations. "What if it had just plucked the thorn from Penny Montgomery's neck, was flying with it in its beak, and pierced the caged bird by accident? Would that not account for the small drops of blood, and its sudden demise?"

"I suppose."

Mycroft stared down at the list of twelve names that he had copied from the ledgers, though he knew them by heart. Cantwell Squire, the only investor who had also become a victim. Jenna Squire, his niece, who was said to love her uncle, and therefore most likely suffered at his passing. George Jury, Will Jury's great-uncle and godfather. The Swinton family, whose fourteen-year-old boy was taken from them. Angela Rider, who lost her brother Phillip, the chaplain. William Greyson, who lost his elderly father George. Percy Butcher's uncle, Samuel Butcher, who lived abroad, and who had no heirs but Percy. Roland Sykes, who lost his young daughter Abigail. Harold Navarro Rogers, who lost his beloved Aunt Penny. Lady Anne, who lost her daughter Elise. And Rupert Jurgins, who lost his namesake nephew.

And then of course there was Dorothea Greer, whose loved one might still be saved.

"I believe," Sherlock was saying, "that the '*Alalā* crow was able to extract all the thorns but two: Elise Wickham's, which I recovered, and Abigail Sykes's. With the latter, the mother never left her side, and the crow had no opportunity to pull it out. Then Abigail spun round and broke the table, thus masking the means of her demise. Do you believe that is how it played out?"

"We may never know," Mycroft said softly.

"It does seem quite a bit of luck for the killer," Sherlock murmured.

"Yes, it does. But then, I suppose that, every once in a while, fortune smiles even upon murderers."

# 44

*Leigh-on-Sea, Essex*
*Sunday, 25 May 1873, 7 a.m.*

IT WAS TOO EARLY FOR THE TRAIN THAT LED TO TOWN, and he had already walked for so many miles that he could barely count them. She was to be his final one, number twelve. And perhaps the thought of ending her, and then ending it, was making him careless; or perhaps he had imbibed too much of his own success and was now drunk with it. Whatever the reason, he had never accepted a lift before, had never revealed himself to a stranger. And, after said stranger brought him near her cottage, what then?

Killing him hardly seemed sportsmanlike.

Then again, he had weathered seven long years of planning, of research, of study; countless hours of practice, burning through all of the money that they had foisted upon him after the death of his son, as if anything could make up for such a loss as that. And then, for some of them to take what they had been given, that blood money, and invest it in another hazardous venture, another hell-on-earth for people who had no choice in the matter… Would they never learn?

Probably not. Which was why he would have to teach them.

"Mighty fine cane you've got there!"

His driver was the sort of a man who made one dizzy just to look at him, the sort made out of spare parts: low forehead, large nose, small eyes, fleshy mouth, thin cheeks, prominent jaw, bulbous neck. The man wished to engage in conversation, he could tell; but the crow was stirring in her box; he could feel her shuddering. And though she knew not to make a fuss, occasionally she disobeyed. Most of the time it made no difference, for they were alone, or on a noisy train, or among a crowd where her low, strange caw would not be noticed. But here, sitting upon a cart next to this stranger? What if he asked about her? What if he grew suspicious? Then he *would* be forced to kill him. What else could he do?

But nothing happened. He was let off at the intersection of two streets that lay at right angles to each other, and he went on his way with a wave.

*Just as well. Save the killing for one who deserves it.*

This last one, Gwyneth Greer.

Her modest, Tudor-style cottage sat on the northern side of the Thames estuary, trees on the sides and the back, the sort of house that had been passed down from one generation to the next with few alterations. She was a thirty-year-old spinster and recluse, from what he had learned. A younger version of Penny Montgomery. He would barely need to track her. If she chanced to look out of her window, all she would see would be a man of middle years, walking along the gravelly sand at low tide, leaning upon a rather fancy cane and carrying a box that most likely held his lunch. If all went well, his form would be the last image imprinted upon her brain, and she on his.

He spied her through the gauzy curtains of the sitting room. He marked her as a nervous type, a pacer and a biter of fingernails. She had on a simple gray dress, her yellow hair pinned up in an equally simple bun. He thought that she would wait until later in the morning, when it grew warmer, and he would thus be forced to wait with her; but no. Gwyneth Greer opened the windows, no doubt believing that the crisp air would do her good, pulled back the curtains, and then sat beside one opened window and picked up a book.

She could not have made it more convenient if she had asked him where to sit.

He opened the copper latch on the lunch box. The bird flew out and up into the nearest tree, on the lookout for his signal.

He pulled the note from his pocket and set it aside. The bird had misbehaved and pecked through two other copies before he could persuade her to make her slashes small and clean, the way he wanted. Well, she was growing older, and fussier. Thinking she knew best.

He unscrewed the cane and pulled out the blowgun, with its perfect aperture. Such a beautiful instrument. Then he opened his tobacco pouch, carefully extracted the piece of barkcloth that held the splinter and dropped it into the aperture.

He placed the larger end of the blowgun into his mouth; wrapped his lips around, rather than inside, it, as he had been taught so long ago; and puffed out his cheeks. For the hunt had less to do with power than with concentrated propulsion. A quarter of a second was all it took—less than the time it took to say *Poof!*—and it was over.

But instead of shooting, he hesitated, let his cheeks go slack. He closed his eyes for a moment. He was so weary. He would never have permitted himself to do such a thing with his first, with Rosalie White. But that one was an artist, and she had brought out the artist in him.

"Whereas you feel like work," he said under his breath.

"Then why do it?"

The voice was so close that it startled him. He hastily took his shot, but it was wild; he missed his mark. He turned to see a man but barely a man, more a boy with the loose, gangly limbs of a scarecrow, and the shrewd, inquisitive face of an eagle.

He turned away, determined to ignore the strange young man, to walk unhurriedly but definitively in the opposite direction, when there stood a Chinaman, a grinning moon! He pivoted again, only to find another, a blond one this time, looking like the Angel Gabriel in a bespoke suit!

"Three against one; hardly fair, is it?" he opined.

They drew towards him slowly, carefully, as if concerned that he might explode all at once, like a colliery. He could tell that they knew who he was: or, at least, that they knew what he had done.

No, it could not end like this, not so close to the finish line! Or perhaps, yes. After all, it was time.

He raised up the blowgun. The Chinaman lunged for it but it made no difference, for she had seen the signal, and she had obeyed. He had not noticed where the splinter landed, but she had. It had embedded itself in the curtains. She swooped over and pulled it out then came flying at them, her fierce yellow eyes staring them down in turn, ready for battle.

As they ducked away from her, he held out his shoulder as a perch.

"What I did, I did for my son!" he declared.

Then he stretched out his neck as if for a guillotine. She landed where he told her, flapping her wings as she did so. Then, with one clean move, she turned and pierced his jugular, and he fell.

# EPILOGUE

*Sunday, 21 June, 1873*

*My dear Mr. Holmes,*

    *I thought of writing to you for so long, it seems, though in truth it is little more than one month since I saw you last. As you may have already heard from other sources, I have been in Zhouzhuang for four days now. And, though Bingwen Shi and I were permitted to take our vows, and though my father and I made our pleas, it was denied. Then, because I had become his wife, they thought it best that I share in his agony and humiliation, and so I was made to witness his execution.*

    *I wish to burden you with none of it, for you did the very best that you could for us both. And if there is an angel anywhere upon this earth, I know where he resides. You gave me hope that I could save him. For this alone, were I not already indebted to you, I would be doubly so.*

    *Bingwen Shi is now beyond all suffering. My goal is to make proper arrangements for the care and maintenance of his remains and shrine, after which my father and I shall embark upon our return journey to London.*

    *I fear you will find me much altered, and not just by sorrow.*

*I should have listened to your wise and caring advice. It seems my inoculation of several years back was not enough. After I boarded the ship, I developed smallpox. And though I am grateful that the disease finally released its hold upon me, it did not go quietly, leaving its imprints upon my cheeks and neck.*

*Do not feel pity for me, Mr. Holmes. Now as a widow and a vessel that has been marred upon the potter's wheel, I shall be allowed to pursue my vocation, at least so far as I am able.*

*I send my deepest regards to you, my benefactor and friend.*

*A.L.*

# ACKNOWLEDGMENTS

THE AUTHORS ARE DEEPLY GRATEFUL TO OUR MANAGER and friend Deborah Morales, forever willing to go to the mat for us—to be mensch, bulldog, or whatever the occasion calls for— so that we can have the privilege of working on the best projects while surrounded by the best people. Those best people here at Titan include our editor, the supremely talented Miranda Jewess, who has helped to raise our game with each subsequent book, and whose patience, good humor (or, as she would say, *humour*), and knowledge of Victorian soul food knows no bounds. The other talented and indefatigable members of the Titan team, who make our lives easier and smooth out the rough spots, are the ever-diligent Sam Matthews, Paul Gill, Laura Price, Chris McLane, Lydia Gittins, Polly Grice, Hannah Scudamore, and Katharine Carroll. And finally, a tip of our collective hat to George Sandison, who took over the helm, and did so with diligence, steadiness, and the utmost professionalism.

# KAREEM ABDUL-JABBAR

AT 7'2" TALL, KAREEM ABDUL-JABBAR IS A HUGE Holmesian in every way. An English and History graduate of UCLA, he first read the Doyle stories early in his basketball career, and adapted Holmes's powers of observation to the game in order to gain an edge over his opponents. His first novel featuring Mycroft Holmes was published in 2015; it received multiple starred reviews and was lauded as a story that "rivals Conan Doyle himself" by the *New York Times* and a "triumphant adult fiction debut" by *Publishers Weekly*. This was followed by *Mycroft and Sherlock* in 2018, in which Mycroft's irrepressible younger brother played a starring role.

Abdul-Jabbar played basketball for the Milwaukee Bucks (1969–1975) and the Los Angeles Lakers (1975–1989), scoring 38,387 points to become the National Basketball Association's all-time leading scorer. He was inducted into the Basketball Hall of Fame in 1995. Since retiring, he has been an actor, producer, coach, and a *New York Times* best-selling author with writings focused on history. His previous books include *Giant Steps*, *Kareem*, *Black Profiles in Courage*, *A Season on the Reservation*, *Brothers in Arms*, *On the Shoulders of Giants: My Journey Through the Harlem Renaissance*, and the children's books *Streetball Crew: Sasquatch in the*

*Paint, Stealing the Game*, and *What Color is My World?*—which won the NAACP Award for "Best Children's Book." His most recent books are *Coach Wooden & Me: Our 50 Year Friendship* and *Becoming Kareem: Growing Up On & Off the Court*. In 2012 he was selected as a U.S. Cultural Ambassador by former Secretary of State Hillary Rodham Clinton. In 2016, former President Barack Obama awarded him The Presidential Medal of Freedom, the USA's highest civilian honor. Currently he is chairman of the Skyhook Foundation, and a regular contributing columnist for the *Hollywood Reporter* and the *Guardian*.

# ANNA WATERHOUSE

A PROFESSIONAL SCREENWRITER AND SCRIPT consultant, Anna Waterhouse has worked alongside such legends as Robert Towne, Tom Cruise, and producer Paula Wagner. She has consulted for premium cable miniseries and basic cable series, and co-produced a feature-length documentary for HBO. She was supervising producer and co-writer (with Kareem Abdul-Jabbar) of the critically acclaimed feature-length documentary *On the Shoulders of Giants* (Netflix and Showtime), which won Best Documentary NAACP Image award and two Telly awards. She is currently writing and co-producing a limited TV series alongside multiple-Oscar winners Robert Towne and Mike Medavoy. She has written several how-to screenwriting seminars for *Writer's Digest* and has taught screenwriting at both Chapman University in Orange, California, and at the University of Southern California; and is hard at work on her novel, *Orphans*.